DEAR CONSPIRATOR

The conspiracy in this story has deep roots, and the young hero is launched into it hot upon his discharge from the Army while he is trying to adjust himself to a world which is strange to him, and in which, so far, he has little more than a precarious footing. There is never a dull moment from the commencement until the curtain rings down after a truly strange sequence of events.

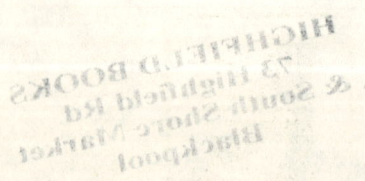

GEORGE GOODCHILD

◆

DEAR CONSPIRATOR

Complete and Unabridged

LINFORD
Leicester

First published in Great Britain

First Linford Edition
published 1996

British Library CIP Data

Goodchild, George
    Dear conspirator.—Large print ed.—
Linford mystery library
I. Title II. Series
823.914 [F]

ISBN 0–7089–7857–6

06656161

Published by
F. A. Thorpe (Publishing) Ltd.
Anstey, Leicestershire

Set by Words & Graphics Ltd.
Anstey, Leicestershire
Printed and bound in Great Britain by
T. J. Press (Padstow) Ltd., Padstow, Cornwall

This book is printed on acid-free paper

1

NEVILLE BRANDON reclined in the long and comfortable chair under the huge mulberry tree at Fouracres and allowed his mind to take a short journey into the past. It was a pleasant enough occupation since at any given moment he was perfectly free to switch back from all too-frequent hells of torment in Normandy and Holland to the comparatively blissful present, which comprised a comfortable house on the South Devon coast, with incomparable views of sea and moorland, the war over and his wounds mended, and, last but not least, a devoted elder sister who ran the house with matchless efficiency, despite an almost complete lack of domestic help.

Two years previously his father, Colonel Brandon, had been killed in

Burma — a sad fact not yet completely accepted by Neville, for somehow the garden seemed full of the Colonel, who had spent so many happy years there after his early retirement from the Indian Army. It required only a stretch of Neville's imagination to see that tall figure tinkering with the two hives of bees, or busy with a trowel prodding the rockery. A push on the door of memory would have revealed another form there — the Colonel's 'lady' who had passed from this mortal coil when her two children were but toddlers. How good those days had been, with the world at peace, and the war that was to have ended wars fought and won. Neville, like so many of his generation, had never believed it could happen again — that six years of his own life would be sacrificed at the altar of human madness. Yet it had come, dragging him from an Oxford College into the whirlpool of horrible and incredible mass murder.

Now here again was peace, and

victory. Before him was the wide world of which he knew so little — an impoverished world in which he must soon play a part.

"Europe's a madhouse," said Uncle Peter. "I know what I'd do if I were in your shoes."

"What?" asked Neville.

"Emigrate. You and Teresa have the house, the furniture and a few thousand quid. There's Canada, Australia, New Zealand, wanting healthy young people."

"Isn't England wanting us too?"

"There's no opportunity here. We're over-populated. We can't even feed ourselves, and are going to be less able to do so in the future. All you'll get here is more austerity, higher taxes and, finally, another war, probably just when you've got children of your own of an age to be used as cannon fodder. And next time there won't be a winner."

"There hasn't been one this time."

"That's true. You think it over."

Neville was thinking it over, now as his glance roved over the garden and beyond to the little church on the green hill in the graveyard of which his two parents lay. But Uncle Peter's philosophy seemed the philosophy of despair. It did not seem to Neville that the circumstances warranted it. It was true there had been two world wars in Uncle Peter's adult life, but by some miracle Uncle Peter had managed to keep on the right side of the battle area, and to have done quite well for himself, notwithstanding high taxation, for it was common knowledge that Uncle Peter owned blocks of flats in London.

"No," he muttered. "It's you, Uncle Peter, who ought to emigrate."

The sound of a car engine caused him to sit up and turn his head towards the house. It was half hidden by the low-hanging branches of the great mulberry tree, but he got an incomplete view of the rear part of a motor car which had pulled up at the front door.

"Nev — ille!"

It was Teresa's voice, and now he saw her standing outside the casement window of the study, shouting through her cupped hands. He tumbled out of the comfortable seat and made his presence obvious.

"Who is it?"

"Come and see, lazy bones."

He advanced and met Teresa half-way. She had the family straight nose and brown eyes, and was two years older than Neville. At the moment she appeared to be flustered.

"A friend of yours," she said. "Took me by surprise. I had that filthy old apron on and must have looked like the most broken-down char. Our daily help, by the way, hasn't shown up. Anyway, I've shown him into the lounge. Come on!"

"But who is it?"

"He looks rather nice. Says he was in your regiment. His name is John Wallace."

"Wallace!" exclaimed Neville delightedly. "Is he in uniform?"

"No."

"Demobbed, I expect. John's a great chap. He was adjutant all the time I was with the battalion. Come and be properly introduced. I say — have we any sherry?"

"Yes."

"Good."

But Teresa had no intention of being introduced in her present garb, and at the door of the lounge she bolted upstairs. Neville entered the pleasant room to find six feet two inches of familiar bone and muscle staring at the family portraits.

"John, you old scoundrel!"

"Nev! I bet you never expected me."

"You're right," said Neville as he wrung Wallace's hand. "Are you in civvy street, or what?"

"No. I was persuaded to stay on. Having no job to go to and no one who cares a damn, I fell for it. At the moment I'm on leave — on my way to Cornwall. What's the best news?"

"I suppose the best news is that all

those loose bits of shrapnel have been removed from my interior, and that I'm feeling fit for anything."

"Any ideas?"

"Nothing definite. I think I told you my father was killed in action, while I was in Italy?"

"Yes. That's he, I presume?"

Wallace indicated a clever water-colour sketch of the Colonel in full uniform, which was hanging over the mantelpiece, and Neville nodded.

"That left only me and Teresa," he said. "Teresa's my sister. You met her just now, much to her embarrassment, because she does all the filthy work in this ménage while I laze and ponder the mysteries of life. She'll be here in a minute. Do help yourself to cigarettes, and tell me about yourself."

Wallace lighted a cigarette and stared through the window at the lovely garden.

"What a spot!" he said. "Rather different to what I'm used to. You just ought to see the view from my office window in Hamburg. Just miles and miles of rubble, and they tell me that Berlin is worse. I think that if I had had a place like this to go back to I should have thought twice about signing up for further service, even though they chucked me a crown on my shoulder."

"Congratulations! You always wanted that."

"Did I?"

"You know you did. What about Hacket and Robson?"

"Demobbed six weeks ago. Oh, I've one bit of news that came in just as I was leaving. They've solved the Larkin mystery."

"You mean he's been found?"

At that moment the door opened and Teresa entered with a tray in her hand on which were glasses and a decanter. Neville blinked at his sister's changed appearance. In the short interval she had changed into a very becoming frock, had put her mass of auburn hair straight and had had recourse to limited cosmetics.

"This is my sister," said Neville. "Teresa, meet Major John Wallace, straight from re-educating the Germans."

Wallace rose for a moment and shook Teresa's slim, cool hand.

"Don't believe him," he said. "I've scarcely had time to educate myself."

"Are you still in the army?" asked Teresa.

"Very much so."

"Have you really come from Germany?"

"Yes — Hamburg."

"Are conditions there as bad as some people say?"

"They're horrible. You can have no conception of it. People are apt to say, 'Well, the Germans brought this on themselves, I'm not going to weep tears over them', but when you come face to face with starving women and children, whose only home is a hole in the ground . . . "

Teresa winced and Neville pushed a glass of sherry into her hand and then passed one to Wallace.

"Spare us the horrors," he said. "When Teresa came in you were telling me about Larkin. What happened to him?"

"He was shot by the Germans after being wounded and taken care of by a Dutch family. Apparently he tried to get through the lines dressing himself in peasant's clothing, but it didn't work. He was shot dead by a sentry. The farmer who gave him shelter was himself wounded and removed to hospital. He had buried Larkin's uniform, identity disc and sundry personal articles, and at the first opportunity he came back to his battered property and dug up the stuff which finally reached the C.O. The farmer himself came to give evidence later. He saw the body and found out where it was buried. He had erected a small wooden cross there."

"Poor old Larkin," mused Neville. "What a wild character he was. Forgive us talking shop, Teresa, but I think you once met Larkin. I brought him home on one leave. Big red-haired chap."

"Oh, I remember. You called him Phil."

"That's right. He was a good soldier, but absolutely unpredictable in his behaviour. Seemed to have no relatives or friends who cared."

"He had you," said Wallace. "You were about the only chap who could tolerate him. I simply couldn't stand him."

"He had a lot of good points," said Neville. "If he hadn't been such a soak he'd have been promoted over our heads. He didn't know what fear was."

"That's true, but he was nearly always tight when at his bravest. Still, 'De mortuis, etc.'"

Neville was reflective for a few moments. His mind was going back over the years to a particular occasion just before the Battalion was due to go overseas. It was astonishing how vividly the details of that occasion came up in his mind.

"I've just remembered something," he said. "It happened before I knew you, John. Phil and I were on short embarkation leave and I think we were both a bit sozzled. Phil had a will form and he asked me to witness his signature. He already had one signature, and he wanted a second. I signed it. The comic thing was that he was broke, and I asked him to whom he was going to leave his colossal fortune, and that seemed to annoy him a little, but he pointed out that if he got bumped off there would probably be some back pay due to him, and why the hell shouldn't some deserving creature have it, along with the few other personal effects which he possessed. Heaven knows what he did with the will."

"It's quite clear that you intend to live the past all over again," said Teresa. "So with your permission I propose to forsake this party and attend to the lunch. You'll stay to lunch, Major?"

"I wouldn't dream of it," replied Wallace. "I happen to know the size of the civilian meat ration; besides, I really do want to push on. I have to pick up a chap in Plymouth and our destination is Penzance. My tyres are so bad that I want to leave myself plenty of time. Thanks all the same, but I mean it."

"You're sure?" asked Teresa.

"Absolutely."

"Well, excuse me now. See you before you leave."

"Look here, old man," protested Neville, when his sister had gone. "We can't meet and part like this. How long will you stay in Penzance?"

"A week."

"Then this will be a nice place to break your return journey. Will you put in the night here on your return journey? We've got bags of room, and there's so much to talk about."

"Are you sure I shan't — ?"

"Not another word. Will it be this day week?"

"Yes."

"We'll expect you. Get here as early as you can. If you start early you could get here by lunch time."

"You don't know my bouncing Lizzy. Genuine 1931 model. Tyres about the same period. But I'll try."

"Good for you. We may as well finish what is left in that bottle."

The glasses were refilled.

"Reverting to Phil Larkin," said Neville. "There was a sequel to the business of the will. I couldn't tell you while Teresa was present. We got back to our hotel in the small hours. It wasn't a very respectable place, but it was the best we could get. You know what London was like in those days. A woman was hanging about in the lounge and Phil, who was more than half-seas over, fell for her. I tried to get him away, but it was no use, and finally I went to bed and left him with her. I went to his room the next morning and found the door locked. Later I found a chambermaid and told her I wanted to

14

get my friend down to breakfast. She opened the door and revealed that his bed had not been slept in."

"The woman?"

"Yes. He came to the hotel later and told me he had gone home with her. I told him what I thought of him. He just grinned and asked me not to call the heiress to his estate rude names. I was amazed, but pretended to disbelieve him, whereupon he dragged out the will which I had witnessed, and showed me the top part of it. Originally his sister had been named as the sole beneficiary, but it had been scratched out and the name of his late bed-partner written in. The alteration was initialled. I called him all the damned fools I could lay my tongue to, and advised him to tear the thing up, but he was evidently determined to go through with it. He had had a good time, he said, and it wasn't as mercenary as I thought. As a matter of fact, all the money he had was a pound. He had given her that and promised to make the will in her favour. "Of course she thinks I'm pulling a fast one on her," he said. "Well, if I do stop something fast and hard, she'll have reason to change her mind. Quite a nice kid. Nice name too — Berenice!"

Wallace made sounds of incredulity with his tongue. Yet he was not really astonished, for he had always held the opinion that the late Captain Larkin was capable of any lunacy — and any villainy. It had seemed to him regrettable that Neville with his transparent honesty and decency should have befriended the brute.

"So you've made no plans about the future?" he asked.

"No. I dallied with the notion of going back to Oxford and working for my degree, but I don't think it would pan out. It would take me a couple of terms to readjust myself to that routine. I've tried it out in a mild sort of way and it was a ghastly failure. If I take up a text-book I find that my mind simply won't concentrate. None of it seems to make any sense and in twenty minutes I'm dreaming. That's what war does to a fellow."

"Don't I know! We're all in the same boat — I mean those of us who were caught very young."

"There's Teresa too. She was engaged to a chap who was killed in the first few months. There's one thing she'd like to have — a small dairy farm. She was in the Land Army for three years. Question is — shall we sell up and buy a place with a few acres where we can keep a small herd? It's not a bad life for those who love the country, but prices for any kind of farm are sky-high. All the same, I rather think it may come to that."

"You're lucky to have a bit of capital, but it would be a wrench to give up this place, wouldn't it?"

"Yes. But it will have to come anyway. I should love to show you round, but we'll defer that until your return."

Wallace looked at the clock on the mantelpiece.

"Is that thing right?" he asked.

"Within a minute."

"Then I ought to be shoving on. Grand seeing you again. I shall look forward to spending a night with you. Well — here goes!"

Neville called his sister as they reached the hall.

"John's leaving," he said. "But he's going to put in a night here on his return."

"Oh, that will be delightful," said Teresa. "What day will that be?"

"To-day week," replied Wallace.

"We will kill the fatted calf — to be more exact a lazy old hen who refuses to deliver any more goods."

Wallace laughed as he shook hands, and a few moments later his battered old car went clanking down the drive.

"Good old John!" sighed Neville. "One of the nicest chaps breathing. We've had some grand times as well as bad ones. He never forgave me for my friendship with Phil Larkin. It was something he could never understand."

"Was Larkin so atrocious?"

"He could be a swine, and yet there were times when I found him most entertaining. About three years older than me and amazingly well-informed. He had been everywhere — the queerest places — even jail. He would gamble on anything up to the last penny he possessed. I've seen him wager his next month's pay on a raindrop running down a window pane against a similar raindrop."

"He sounds like a mental case to me," sniffed Teresa.

"A border-line case perhaps. Men like him are difficult to analyse. He was kicked out of his home before he was twenty with a hundred pounds in his pocket and with strict injunctions to make good or to go to the devil. I should like to think that he didn't fulfil the latter part of his irate parents' directions."

2

DURING the ensuing days Neville and Teresa discussed the future with some seriousness, with emphasis on the family idea. They looked into the matter of finance and Teresa did some tremendous sums.

"We could do it comfortably," she said. "You see, Neville, the chief advantage with a dairy farm is the ready market. You don't have to wait a whole season before you get some money back. The milk-board collects the milk and you get a monthly cheque. The thing to aim at is to be self-contained in the matter of feeding stuffs. That's where you come in. I could manage the dairy side with the help of one girl and you could look after the arable — "

"The what?"

"The feeding stuffs for the cattle.

We'll grow our own and not be at the mercy of the market. You can't run a farm without a man — and here you are."

"But, my dear child, has it occurred to you that I know absolutely nothing about the game? I don't know one end of a cow from the other."

"You don't need to. All you have to do is get yourself a job on a neighbouring farm. Any farmer will snap up a good-looking hefty chap like you — and pay you some money. You can learn to drive a tractor — pick up all tips you can, and then when we've got the farm we want, you just hand in your notice."

"I thought there was a snag in it."

"But there isn't. Neville, it would be wonderful. You'd love it. In any case we can't go on living here with no income. Of course, if you feel sentimental about the old place, you needn't sell it. We could get a mortgage on it, and let it furnished. There's enough furniture to allow us sufficient to furnish a small farmhouse and still leave enough for our tenant. Let's do it. I don't think we can go far wrong."

"It's what you've always wanted, isn't it?"

"Yes. But I never dreamed I would get you down to considering it seriously. You're not just teasing me, are you?"

"No. It's time I faced up to things. You run into town in a day or two and see what the agents have in the shape of small farms. But I'm rather afraid the prices are going to frighten you."

"I'll use my sex appeal on the present owners," said Teresa. "Brother, I could kiss you."

Neville smiled at her wild enthusiasm, and, as he expected, Teresa announced her intention of running into town the next day. He reminded her that Wallace was due to arrive some time that day, but Teresa had that all figured out.

"I'll be back before noon," she said. "We are having cold lunch, and I'm saving that old hen for this evening.

I don't see how Wallace can get here before lunch on that old wreck of a car. If he should come, his room is all ready. Oh yes, there's a new bottle of sherry in the cupboard. But don't drink it all before I get home."

Shortly after she left, a telegram came over the telephone. It was from Wallace, and he said he hoped to arrive about four o'clock. Neville wrote a message for Teresa and then took a walk over the cliff by various field-paths. It was early summer, and Neville became interested in the crops of the various fields, for, in view of the recent conversation, he felt himself to be half a farmer already. And he had to admit that the land looked fresh and lovely after the recent rain. He wished that Teresa were with him to tell him what some of the more unusual crops were, for he had no more idea than the man in the moon.

The upward sweep of the land brought him out of the cultivated area to the wind-blown uplands, above the little church, and from there there was nothing between him and the blue Devon sea. He walked closer and closer to the cliff edge and opened up the wonderful seascape — so familiar to him and yet unspoiled by familiarity. Yes, Uncle · Peter could ramp on about those amazing countries of great opportunity across the seas, but was there another so clean and green as this, so packed with history — the history of free men and great endeavour?

When eventually he got back home, Teresa was there, bright-eyed, and with a sheaf of papers secured from various agents. She was in the mood to go into the matter forthwith, but Neville considered that a drink was far more urgent.

"You saw my note?" he asked.

"About Wallace? Oh yes, I'm rather glad he isn't coming to lunch, because it will definitely be scrappy. Shall we open the sherry?"

"Of course."

Wallace arrived at four o'clock. He looked as if he had spent every minute of his holiday lying in the sun, for his face was the colour of a new penny.

"Had a good time?" asked Neville.

"Wonderful. But my tyres let me down. I had to go on a tyre-hunt. Picked up a couple of re-treads at a fantastic price."

While they were unpacking the car the postman arrived with a single letter addressed to 'Captain Neville Brandon'.

"No such person," said Neville, and thrust the letter into his pocket.

When he had shown Wallace to his room, and left him there to tidy-up, he went to the seat on the terrace and opened the letter. Teresa came and found him stroking his jaw reflectively.

"Unknit those threatening brows," she said. "Is it a summons or something?"

"It's a summons of a sort. Something I never expected. Read it."

Teresa took the typewritten letter, and drew in her breath with a hiss of surprise.

"You didn't tell me that you had agreed to be Larkin's executor," she said.

"I didn't. There must be a mistake."

"How can there be? The writer, Mr. Winslow, says quite clearly that as you are named as sole executor, and as now it has been officially admitted that Captain Philip Larkin met his death on November the 21st, he would be glad to see you regarding the administration of Captain Larkin's estate."

"All the same, not a word was said to me about being an executor. Larkin must have written that bit in afterwards. I know absolutely nothing about legal matters."

"Oh, it's simple enough," said Teresa. "You've always got the solicitor at your elbow, and since your friend Larkin had — according to you — no assets but his back pay and a few oddments — why, what's the matter?"

Neville had stopped her with a short ejaculation, and before he could say anything Wallace joined them. Neville took the letter from Teresa's hand and gave it to Wallace.

"Read that," he said.

Wallace read the letter rather slowly.

"That settles the question of the will," he mused. "But you said nothing about being his executor."

"I didn't know."

"You mean to tell me he had the damned cheek to appoint you as his executor without so much as 'by your leave'?"

"That seems to be the case. But just now I realised why he may have wanted me to do this job. I happen to have seen Berenice — "

"Who is Berenice?" asked Teresa.

"A lady for whom Larkin had a soft spot. He named her in his will as sole beneficiary."

"A lady without an address?" asked Teresa suspiciously.

"Oh no, she had an address, but I

expect Phil thought it might be easier for someone who knew Berenice to deal with the matter. All the same, I think he might have asked me."

"You can always decline," said Wallace.

"Decline! But what would happen then?"

"I haven't an idea."

"I have," put in Teresa. "The Public Trustee might deal with the matter. I think I should write to Messrs. Winslow & Winslow of Lincoln's Inn Fields, and point out that it isn't very convenient for you — "

Neville stopped her with a shake of his head.

"I can't do that," he said.

"Why not?"

"Because he's dead and I should like to carry out his last wish."

"But it wasn't his last wish. The will was dated years ago. The letter gives the date." She peered at the letter. "Yes. August 1942."

"It makes no difference," said Neville.

"He wanted me to make sure that that girl got what little he had to leave her — "

"What about your expenses?" asked Teresa.

"I suppose I am entitled to charge my actual out-of-pocket expenses."

"But you have no idea what they may amount to, and your friend may have left only a few quid," said Teresa. "Was he engaged to this girl?"

"No. She was a stranger."

Neville was immediately sorry he had divulged that fact, for Teresa blinked her eyes in astonishment. Quickly she sensed the real situation.

"A pick-up girl?"

"Yes."

"Well, men certainly are queer animals," mused Teresa. "I can't for the life of me see why you should consider yourself bound by a few words written without your knowledge on a will form on some occasion when Larkin was probably drunk and you too. Major Wallace, tell him he's quite idiotic. I'll go and get some tea."

She bounced out of the room, leaving no doubt behind her as to her annoyance. Wallace's gaze followed her and then came back to Neville.

"She's right, you know," he said, lighting a cigarette.

"You only say that because you always disliked Larkin. Now imagine it had been me, and you had received this communication — "

"I'll imagine nothing of the sort, because I'm quite certain you would never have had the bad manners to have appointed me as your executor without asking me if I were willing to act, and you would certainly have more sense than to sign away your estate to a mere tart."

Neville remained unmoved. There was a lot of the sentimentalist about him, and where his heart was touched logic and even common sense were unavailing.

"The sooner I get it over, the better,"

he said. "Are you quite set on going back to London to-morrow?"

"Yes. I've got all sorts of appointments there."

"Could you take me?"

"Of course. That possibility hadn't occurred to me. It will be grand to have you as a passenger. You certainly are a hustler."

"Thanks, John. Now I think I'll put a call through to Messrs. Winslow & Winslow and tell them I'm coming. At what time do you think we can get to town?"

"Three o'clock. I've got an appointment at four."

"So it will be safe if I make an appointment for that time?"

"Barring unforeseen accidents — yes."

Neville made the appointment and then took Wallace out into the garden. Within a minute Wallace was entranced, for in four acres were enclosed everything that a lover of gardens could desire. It was yet early summer, and the long herbaceous borders were not at their best, but many of the flowering shrubs were in full bloom, and the several large rockeries were a sight for the eyes. The garden ornaments, both in stone and bronze, were of excellent design and beautifully placed. Some had been sent home from China and India during the Colonel's travels, but now they looked as if they had been in their present positions since the beginning of time. A fascinating little streamlet ran through the garden from north to south, and this was spanned in sundry places by little decorative bridges.

"Marvellous!" said Wallace. "But who keeps all this going?"

"We had a full-time gardener until a fortnight ago. Now he's left us, and heaven knows where we'll find another. As a matter of fact, we really can't afford a full-time gardener. The dear old boy's investments all went wrong during the war, and there's precious little left of what was a comfortable fortune. Sooner or later we shall have to move out, and it is just that little problem which is now occupying our minds."

"By jove, you're going to miss all this."

"Yes — terribly, but this sort of thing is happening to thousands of people every day. There's my favourite lounging spot — that lovely old mulberry tree. It has a ton of fruit every year, and nobody seems to like mulberries but me."

"I do," said Wallace.

"Then it's a pity you are about a month too early."

3

M R. HORACE WINSLOW was quite ready for his visitor when Neville presented himself at the office of the firm punctually at four o'clock. He was a ponderous man with heavy horn-rimmed spectacles and a most expansive jaw.

"Ah, Captain Brandon," he said. "Pray be seated. It was good of you to come with such promptitude. May I ask — are you still in the army?"

"Oh no. I was invalided out some months before Germany collapsed. I am now plain Mister, and rather glad to be so."

"Yes, of course. I understand the deceased was in your battalion?"

"Yes, we served together for several years."

"So you knew him well?"

"In some respects very well, but in

others scarcely at all."

"I knew him only as the son of Henry Larkin of Barrowtor, Dartmoor. I have never even seen him in person. Did you know his father?"

"No. He never spoke of his family. I mean, not in detail. I got the impression he had quarrelled with his family."

"That's true. When the will reached me I was surprised, for I had no idea he was in England. I did my best to get in touch with him, but I failed to do so."

"I can understand that," said Neville. "Soon after the will was posted to you we went overseas."

Mr. Winslow delved into a portfolio and produced the will.

"Wretched thing," he said. "I wanted to ask him to let me draw up something a little more professional, but it wasn't to be."

"Do you mean the will isn't in order?"

"Oh no, it seems to be quite in order. But with so much money involved one would naturally wish to have a more respectable document."

Neville took this to be Mr. Winslow's idea of a joke — a joke not in the best taste, but Mr. Winslow hadn't the expression of a man who even imagined he had made a joke.

"This woman," he said, "Berenice Waters — have you met her?"

"Only once."

"I notice her address is given as 27 Glass Street, Bloomsbury. Not a very nice address if my memory serves me."

"Not a very nice woman either," said Neville. "It was all the result of a night out and a lot of drinks. Larkin simply ran into the woman at the hotel where he and I were staying. I am quite sure he had never seen her before in his life. He spent the night with her, and the next morning he told me what he had done. I had already witnessed his signature on the will and there was nothing I could do about it."

Mr. Winslow removed his heavy

spectacles and wiped the lenses with his handkerchief, while he blinked at Neville like an owl caught in the light of a torch.

"Shocking," he said. "I wish we could get out of it, but I'm afraid we can't."

"But why is it so shocking?" asked Neville. "He used to say there was no one who cared a damn what became of him. What little he had he left to this woman . . . "

"Little!" ejaculated Winslow. "A year ago his father died after making a will in his son's favour. Probate has been granted in the sum of ninety-two thousand pounds. If that woman is alive, and was alive any time after the death of young Larkin, all that money must go to her — or her next of kin."

"Good Lord!" ejaculated Neville. "But didn't Larkin ever know of this?"

"No. I advertised for him at home and abroad. Then a few months ago

I heard from his Commanding Officer. He informed me that Larkin had been posted missing, but was quite possibly a prisoner of war. I got in touch with the Red Cross, but they were unable to trace him in the German lists. Then I heard that he was officially posted as dead. A week or two later I received all relevant documents and was informed that certain personal effects have been sent to the house. That is the present position. The estate of the father has been realised with the exception of the house and its furniture. The probate office accepted valuation for those — very fair valuations in my opinion. It occurred to me that the son might wish to occupy the old house, but the question now is what Miss Waters's wishes are in that respect."

"You have made no attempt to get in touch with her?" asked Neville.

"Oh no. You are the appointed executor. But I presume you wish me to act as solicitor?"

"Most certainly. You see, Mr. Winslow,

I had not the slightest idea that my friend had named me as executor."

Mr. Winslow looked shocked at this information.

"Do you mean you would rather be rid of that office?"

"No. But I scarcely imagined it would be as complicated as this."

"It isn't really complicated — presuming Miss Waters is alive. It's just regrettable that the estate should pass into the hands of a woman of the streets, especially when there is a surviving daughter of the family."

"It was Larkin's original intention to leave his sister what little he possessed," said Neville. "But he obliterated her name and substituted Miss Waters. I suppose he imagined his sister was provided for."

Winslow shook his head sadly.

"She became as unpopular with her strange parent as her brother was, but that happened long after he had gone. I don't know just what she did to arouse her father's anger, but she went off on her own soon after the war started. Well, it's no use crying over spilt milk. There are certain formalities. You will need to open an executor's account at the bank, and later I will transfer the balance from my own executor's account into it. We will insert the usual advertisement in the Press re any outstanding debts. It's too late to go to the bank to-day. Shall we say ten-thirty to-morrow morning?"

"That would suit me."

Mr. Winslow made a note on his writing pad and then asked where Neville was staying.

"I haven't got a room yet," replied Neville. "I had only just time to keep the appointment, but a friend who drove me up from Devon has offered to put me up if I have any trouble. I'll give you a ring later. I think you said the personal effects had gone to the house."

"Yes. I have no idea what they consist of. I should have told you that I decided to continue the services of the lodge-keeper. He didn't get a penny under the will, and it would have been foolish to have left the house unprotected, in view of its valuable contents."

"Where is it situated exactly?"

"Two miles from Holne — on the Ashburton Road. That can't be very far from your own home."

"It isn't. It's less than twenty miles by road. I know Holne quite well. What did you say the name of the house was?"

"Barrowtor."

Neville wrote these particulars in his notebook, and then asked the name of the lodge-keeper.

"Tom Barding. He lives alone in the lodge just inside the entrance gates. If you take the road from Ashburton — the one that passes Holne Chase — you will come to the white gate of Barrowtor House about two miles before you reach Holne village. It's rather a fine place, with some fishing on the Teign, but very isolated. I'll write to Barding and authorise him to hand you the keys."

"Thank you," said Neville. "I'll have a shot at locating our lucky adventuress this evening. Tell you the result tomorrow morning."

"I wish you every success," said Winslow, and then sighed. "Ninety thousand pounds! Well, I've heard of heavy prices paid for a night's debauchery, but never a price as high as that. What a fool the fellow was! And yet he met his death like a hero."

Neville left the office a few minutes later, astonished and impressed by what he had learnt. For the next two hours he searched for a room in a hotel, and was amazed to discover there was absolutely nothing to be had. At half-past six he telephoned Wallace and told him of his bad luck.

"Good!" said Wallace. "I can give you a shake-down. It's my mother's flat, but she is out of town. I'll be free after nine o'clock. Will you blow along then?"

Neville promised to do this, and before he queued up for a meal he left his suitcase in the cloak-room of a tube station.

4

IN a large and untidy room on the first floor of No. 27 Glass Street, two men and a woman were engaged in a fierce game of poker. The room was full of tobacco smoke, for all three players smoked endlessly, and filled their glasses at short intervals from bottles on a side table. They were tense-looking creatures, deeply marked with dissipation, and their language in exciting moments was filthy. The bigger of the two men was as swarthy as a Spaniard, and the hand in which he held his cards was covered with black hair. His age might have been anything between thirty and forty. His male companion was small and weedy, with strange pale and almost lidless eyes. The cigarette never moved from the corners of his thin-lipped mouth. Its only change of position was from one side to the other, and the woman called him Sid.

The woman was not unusual in any way. One could have found hundreds of her type hanging round the vestibules of the large London restaurants any time between eight and midnight — looking for prey. On her fingers were several rings of fair quality and with them was a wedding ring. There were indications that in the past she had been beautiful, but all that natural beauty was now plentifully overlaid with cosmetics and she reeked of heavy perfume.

"You deal, Flo," said Sid, with a snarl, "and for heaven's sake give me something better than pairs."

Flo laughed in a deep, throaty voice and dealt the five cards with a dexterity acquired by long years of practice. Despite the miserable surroundings, there was no lack of money. The shilling and half-crowns began to pile up in the kitty. Sid with a seraphic smile, indicated with a rap on the table that he wanted no new cards.

The swarthy man shot him a suspicious glance.

"One for me, Flo," he said.

Flo dealt him a single card.

"I'm sticking too," she said.

Then the game really started. The flow of money into the kitty looked as if it would never end. Flo had her cards pushed up together and never looked at them again. Every time the bid came to her she raised it to the limit. They were now betting in pounds and the two men showed signs of nerves, but poker-faced Flo never batted an eyelid. She began to whistle.

"Cut that out!" snapped Sid. "Why the hell don't you give up. You got nothing."

"You'd be surprised," said Flo. "Waiting for you, Gus."

The swarthy man looked at his cards again and raised to the limit again, but in a manner which looked as if it hurt.

"Waiting for you, Sid darling," said Flo sweetly.

"I'll see you," blurted Sid.

"Cost you four pounds ten."

"I know — I know."

Sid found the money and added it to the kitty just as the door bell rang loudly.

"Who the hell's that?" asked Gus.

"Never mind," said Flo. "Let 'em damn well wait."

"Better get it over," growled Gus. "I'm through. What have you got."

"Money in first," said Flo.

Gus put a five-pound note in the kitty and then Flo put down her hand.

"Four aces and a Jack," she said.

"Blast!" ejaculated Gus. "Only a full house. Shovel up that cash — you cunning bitch."

Flo laughed in her fruity way and swept the kitty into her cavernous handbag. The bell rang again — even longer than before.

"I'll go," she said.

While she was absent the two men helped themselves to more drinks, Sid moaning at his consistent bad luck.

"What have you got to worry about?" asked Gus. "It's all in the family."

"You have another think," growled Sid. "What Flo wins she keeps. Never was such a woman for money. What's she up to out there?"

"S-sh!" hissed Gus.

The sound of conversation now came to them, but the gist of it was not clear. Then Flo came back, closing the door softly after her.

"It's a young man — rather nice," she said. "His name is Brandon and he's enquiring after Berry."

"Eh!" ejaculated Gus.

"He gave her name all right — Miss Berenice Waters. He knew she lived here in 1942."

"What did you tell him?" asked Gus.

"I said she didn't live here now, and asked him what his business was, as I knew her in the past."

"What did he say?"

"Not very much. He acted as if what he had to say was very personal. He said it was rather important. He asked me if I could tell him where Berry was, and I said there was someone in here who might know."

"You know damned well — "

"Yes, yes. But why not hear what he has to say?"

"I would," said Sid. "Can't do any harm."

"All right," said Gus, after a moment's reflection. "Show him in. Sid, get rid of the cards."

A few moments later Neville entered the room. He nodded at the two men, and gave a glance at Flo.

"Oh," said Flo. "This is my husband — Sidney Toller, and this is an old friend — Gus Tamling."

"Pleased to meet you, Mr. Brandon," said Gus with an engaging smile. "You were enquiring after a young woman named Berenice Waters?"

"Yes. I'm anxious to trace her. The last address I had was this one."

"That's true. She used to live here — in this flat. May I ask what is your business?"

"I'm afraid I can only discuss that with Miss Waters. If you can put me in touch with her, I shall be obliged. It is something which will turn out to her advantage."

"In that case you can tell me, because I happen to be the lady's husband. I married her in 1943. Her present name is Tamling."

"Can you provide proof of that?"

"Yes. I am lodging here, and I think I can lay my hands on the marriage certificate. Excuse me a few moments."

He left the room, and Flo offered Neville a cigarette.

"It's true," she said. "I was at the wedding. Unfortunately it wasn't very successful, and Gus isn't very keen to talk about it. Will you have a drink?"

"Thanks — no," said Neville, who found the atmosphere of the place unbearable.

Gus was back in a few moments with the marriage certificate. The ceremony had been performed at a registrar's office and the certificate was dated 24th May, 1943.

"Okay?" asked Gus.

"Yes. Is your wife not living with you?"

"No," growled Gus. "The marriage went wrong. I won't say it was all her fault. I'm a bit short-tempered and so is she. About a year ago we had a hell of a bust-up and she ran out on me. A few months ago I was told by a man I know that he had seen her in Manchester. I went up to Manchester and stayed there for a fortnight in the hope that I might see her, but Manchester's a big city and I had no luck. Truth is, I'm missing her a lot, and would like to let bygones be bygones and make a new start. But I don't quite understand all this. Has she come into some dough or something?"

"Yes."

"Well, that's good news. Berry could always use money. But I didn't know she had any relatives who had any to give away."

"It wasn't a relative. It was a mere acquaintance — a man named Larkin — Philip Larkin. I happen to be his executor."

"So that's it. He's dead of course?" Flo laughed amusedly.

"You don't have an executor until you're dead," she pointed out. "Lucky Berry! Is it much?"

"It's a very considerable sum."

The desire of all three to know just how much the lucky Berenice had inherited was very marked, but Neville saw no reason for satisfying their curiosity.

"Since you don't appear to be able to help me regarding her whereabouts, my best plan would be to advertise for her," said Neville.

"Good idea," agreed Gus. "I was thinking of doing that myself."

"Did she read any particular newspaper?" asked Neville.

"Chiefly the picture papers," said Gus. "Oh yes, she used always to have two weekly movie papers. Did a bit of film work at times. Always had a notion that one day she'd get a real part."

"I'll bear that in mind," said Neville. "Do you know where she was born?"

"Yes — Reading," said Flo.

"Was she living here when she left you?" Neville asked Gus.

"No. I came here after she walked out on me. She lived here with Flo until I married her, and then she and I found a small bungalow out at Kew. When she didn't come back I let the bungalow furnished and came here to live — to economise and for company."

"Better give me the address of the bungalow," said Neville. "It will help to make clear the woman we want."

"It's called Moonstone, Rylands Avenue."

Neville wrote down these particulars and then indicated that he did not wish to trouble them further.

"No trouble," said Gus. "I'd like to see Berry get her legacy. How much did you say it was?"

"The Will hasn't been proved yet, but it should be a nice round sum."

"But what's a nice round sum?" asked Gus. "A thousand pounds or something like that?"

"A good deal more. But now I must go."

"Oh, one moment," said Gus. "Suppose I should hear from her, where is she to find you?"

Neville produced an old visiting card, and on the reverse side he wrote the address of the solicitors.

"Either of these two addresses will do; if she should be in London it will be better for her to go to the solicitors, who will communicate with me. I expect to return to Devon to-morrow evening."

"Okay!" said Gus. "Glad to have met you, Mr. Brandon. I wish I could think of some way of telling my wife the good news myself. Might make all the difference to my domestic future. There are one or two old friends of hers I might look up."

"Sure!" said Flo. "There's that film-chap who was always promising her a nice part and never came up to the scratch. Dirty little tyke I thought him, but still, he might have seen her."

Ultimately the door closed on Neville, and the three looked at each other.

"Can you beat that?" said Flo. "A thousand bloomin' quid — "

"More than that," rasped Sid. "He said, 'a good deal more'. If you ask me, I reckon there's a cartload. There was a look in his eye."

"You're right," said Gus. "I wonder if it's on the level."

"What you mean?"

"What friend of Berry would leave her a sack of money? Who was this Mr. Larkin? You ought to know, Flo. You were her friend years before I met her."

"She never mentioned him to me," retorted Flo. "But why shouldn't a girl have a few rich friends without shouting the odds? No need to be jealous."

"I'm not jealous. He's dead anyway. To think of all that money going begging — "

"Won't go begging for long," said Sid. "Once Berry sees that advertisement she'll come out of her shell all right, and maybe she'll remember her old friends."

An hour later Neville was reclining in a chair in Wallace's comfortable little flat, indulging in a drink and a cigarette, after relating his experiences.

"And that's as far as I've got," he said. "Of course I want to get this matter settled, but it goes against the grain to pay all that money to people like that. I wish old Winslow could find some flaw in the wretched will, but he assured me that that was out of the question. I should like to know just what those people do for a living. Whatever it is, it seems to pay dividends. The woman was loaded with rings, and on the sideboard there was drink galore. The two men were exceptionally nasty specimens. Sid was the loose-lipped sneak-thief type who would sell his own mother for a song. Gus was even worse if I read him correctly. Powerful sort of thug, with shifty eyes and hairy hands. Black oiled hair and a show of colour in his raiment. He admitted having a short temper, and I can well believe it. Coming out of the clean countryside, that meeting was like turning over an old boulder and bringing to light the nasty crawling things that live away from the rays of the sun. I think I hate the big cities, John."

"That isn't quite fair on the poor devils who somehow have to make an honest living in them."

"No. That's true."

"And are you really going back to-morrow?"

"Yes. I've got to see a bank manager in the morning to open an executor's account, draw a cheque-book and supply copies of my signature, et cetera, after which I shall be a full-blown executor qualified to distribute vast sums of money. A few advertisements for the pick-up girl who looks like picking up ninety thousand pounds, and back to lovely, peaceful Devon, where my adorable sister is aching to debate the subject of small dairy farms, which I am told offer a bare living for eighteen hours of work daily for seven days a week."

"You ought to consider yourself lucky, you know," said Wallace. "I'd like to change places with you. Life with the occupation forces is hell. I haven't got used to seeing children starve before my eyes, and I hope I never shall. But have another drink."

"Why not?" asked Neville, and passed his glass across the table. "You've let me do all the talking. What about your own affairs? When are you due back?"

"I've got another fortnight. They tagged some back leave on to my basic ration."

"When does your mother return?"

"To-morrow evening. I expect we

shall do a few shows, and tootle down to the coast for some sea air. But my mother has to go to Bristol next Saturday for an indefinite period. My young sister is to have her first baby, and as her husband is, like me, in the B.A.O.R., prospective grannie is going to look after their house, and prepare the way for the homecoming of mother and offspring. I shall probably run her down in the car and see my sister at the same time."

"In that case why not put in a few days with me and Teresa? It would be first-class fun. You and I could go fishing, play a few rounds of golf, and talk sweet nothings."

Wallace hesitated.

"It would be another eighty or ninety miles each way," he said. "I doubt if my petrol could be stretched out to that extent."

"Don't worry about petrol. We've scarcely used our car for months, and have quite an accumulation of the stuff. Think it over."

"I will. It certainly is an attractive proposition. But what about your executorship?"

"That's not going to involve much work. The major part is done. That woman may hide from her husband, but I imagine that the moment she sees my advertisement she'll lose no time in staking her claim."

The next morning Neville kept his appointment with Winslow and told him the result of his visit to Glass Street. Winslow looked disgusted as he listened to Neville's description of the place and the persons it harboured.

"If old man Larkin only knew, he would do something more than turn in his grave," he mused. "All his life he was a skin-flint, and that fact makes the present situation particularly ironical. Well, we shall have to advertise for her. We'll go into that when we have visited the bank."

During the legal formalities which took place at the bank it was divulged that Philip Larkin also kept his Army account there, and this was convenient to all parties. The account was inspected, and was found to be £150 in credit.

"The last cheque appears to have been drawn three days before Larkin was reported missing," said Winslow. "But the full month's pay has been credited. There will be an adjustment."

"I presume you have no securities of any sort in the name of the son?" asked Winslow.

"No."

Finally Neville and Winslow came away and returned to the Solicitor's office. Here they drew up an appealing advertisement, and made a list of newspapers in which it was to appear.

"We'll do the rest," said Winslow. "I'll let you know if there is any response. When you have examined the personal effects, perhaps you will make a list with valuation. Oh, and you had better take my set of keys. The caretaker has certain keys, but this is a complete set. I expect that ghastly woman will sell Barrowtor and everything in it. I can't quite imagine her and her husband settling down there. Well, I think that is all we can do at the moment. You will, of course, put in a bill for your own expenses."

Neville caught the next available train back to Devon and reached home late in the evening, tired and hungry, for the train had lacked a restaurant car, and he had had nothing to eat since breakfast. Teresa greeted him with undisguised pleasure, for she disliked being alone.

"I bet you're famished," she said. "I found out there was no chance of food on that train, so I forked up a meal."

"You're an angel. Lead me to it."

"It'll be all ready by the time you remove all that train grime from your person."

"Ten minutes then."

During the meal Teresa wanted to know all that had happened, and she looked incredulous when Neville told her the facts.

"What a perfectly insane state of

affairs," she said. "Can't anyone do anything about it?"

"You mean to prevent the woman getting what is due to her?"

"Due! — my foot. She's done nothing to deserve it. Are you standing up for her?"

"No — as a conscientious executor, I am simply carrying out the wishes of a dead man. Pass the bread."

"Ninety thousand pounds! And all for sleeping with an idiot."

"Who told you that?"

"I'm not a child. I hope she doesn't get it."

"I'm afraid she will. I'm going to run over to the house on Dartmoor to-morrow and take over Larkin's effects. After that I shall be free to attend to my own affairs until we locate the lady."

"Oh, what a pity. I hoped you would come with me to have a look at what — on paper — appears to be a perfectly lovely little farm."

"Can't it wait?"

"I've made an appointment — over the telephone."

"Well, you have a first look, and then if it's promising I'll come another day. You won't want the car, I hope?"

"I will. It's eight miles from here."

"What time is the appointment?"

"Three o'clock in the afternoon."

"Then I'll be back to lunch."

"That'll be fine. Neville, you are serious about this, aren't you?"

"Yes. Oh, one more thing — I invited John Wallace down for the week-end. He has to go to Bristol and so I thought it a good opportunity to show him a bit of the countryside. Can you do with him?"

"Easily. He's rather nice. He even folded the blankets before he left. I didn't know such men existed these days."

"I must get him to give me a lesson or two on bed-making," said Neville.

5

NEVILLE took the fast sporting drop-head coupé the following morning and made his way across the lovely country towards Dartmoor. The overcast sky cleared within a few minutes of starting and Neville stopped and let down the hood. He stood for a few moments drinking in the incomparable view across the Devon hills to the sea, now flooded with rich warm sunshine. Westward the land rose in long undulations to end in the familiar but ever-intriguing horizon of tor and windswept uplands that was Dartmoor.

This was no day for hurrying, with the hedge-rows sparkling with flowers and the odour of dog-roses, honeysuckle, and newmown hay on the soft air. Deliberately he avoided the main roads and kept to the lanes and unfrequented by-ways, where chickens, pigs and ducks were the main representatives of animal life. What humans he saw were in the fields, engaged in the various tasks of the land. Now all the trees were heavy with leaf and lively with birds. Came a watersplash and a glimpse of an old-world cottage in a lovely setting which vanished all too swiftly as the car came out of the water and faced a hill of frightful steepness and surface. But the car was equal to anything, and within a few minutes it was five hundred feet above the watersplash and making across heathland to a thickly-wooded area. From here there was a descent into Ashburton, on the main road which skirts the moor. Immediately on leaving the town Neville took a sharp turn to his right, and in a very short time reached a well-loved beauty spot. It was the narrow bridge at Holne Chase which spanned the swift-running Teign. He stopped the car on the hump of the ancient bridge and sighed with extreme pleasure at the vista that was laid open to him. Straight as an arrow the river came at him, held on its course by the granite banks, and swirling and splashing round the great boulders in the river bed. The trees on either bank joined hands overhead to form a green and leafy tunnel into which the sunlight filtered, as if through stained-glass windows in a cathedral. Entranced as ever, he switched off the throbbing car engine, and listened to the incomparable music of the ebullient stream as it laughed its way down to the distant sea. Then, in a flash, a little picture came up in his mind — the occasion when he had first gazed on this self-same lovely view. He and Teresa, and his mother and father, in a car of very early design — in the same spot, with a picnic hamper in the back — on their way on a sunny morning in spring — twenty years ago. Now only he and Teresa were left! How carefree and jolly life had been then! How rich the promise! But nothing had changed here.

Nature had taken no steps to allure herself to human madness. Somewhere above the music of the water he thought he could hear the pipe of Pan.

With a little sigh he started the engine and moved off the bridge and swung the car round to the right. A minute or two later he was climbing a steep hill enclosed on either side by heavy timber, and then, just ahead of him, he saw a woman with a suitcase in her hand, making rather heavy going. Hesitating for a moment, he allowed the car to slow down, and stopped it quite close to her. She turned her head, and he now saw that she was young and beautiful, and breathing hard from her exertions.

"Good morning!" he said. "Can I give you a lift? I'm going just short of Holne."

For a moment he thought she was going to decline the offer, but then the lips parted in a smile.

"Thank you," she said. "It is rather steep."

"That's an under-statement. Put the suitcase in the back. But you will find the front seat more comfortable for yourself. The back seat is merely occasional, to quote the makers of this car. Just slam the door hard. You won't hurt it."

The girl followed his instructions and was soon seated beside him.

"Oh, this is lovely," she said.

"It must be an improvement on Shanks' pony, with a suitcase thrown in."

"I'm afraid I cheated there," she said. "The case is empty."

"All the same, you must have felt like throwing it away."

"I did. I've carried the beastly thing all the way from Ashburton. Did you say you were going to Holne Village?"

"Two miles short of the village."

"That will suit me. My destination is also short of the village. I'll tell you just before we get there."

Neville nodded, and the efficient car killed the steep gradient like the thoroughbred it was. The interior driving mirror was not in its correct position, and he could see his companion's face from time to time. There was much in it which interested him — a strange mixture of what appeared to be conflicting emotions. He wanted to see it in complete repose, but it was like the surface of disturbed water, baffling him by its swift changes from what appeared to be sorrow to unmistakable eagerness — if not anxiety. Once their gazes met in the mirror and she displayed embarrassment, and then smiled again as if by an effort.

"Are you a native of these parts?" he asked.

"Yes. I was born here, but have been away for some time. It's rather nice coming back again and realising how beautiful it all is. The horrible war seems to have missed it completely."

"Nature wasn't at war — only humanity."

"That's true. Oh, I can smell wild violets. They grow in profusion here.

Look, you can see them — just above the ditch."

Neville switched his gaze to the ditch and saw the deep blue patches. Then he noticed that his companion's eyes were very nearly the same colour as the violets.

"I'm Devon-born too," he said. "And nearly as nostalgic as you."

"Perhaps you've been away too?"

"Four years."

"Fighting?"

"Yes."

There was silence for a while, and the car ambled through the delectable lanes. Then the girl spoke again.

"My turning is only about half a mile from here," she said.

"Mine can't be far away. Perhaps you can help me. I'm trying to find a house named Barrowtor."

He saw her give a little start, and then her head came round.

"Why, that's where I'm going," she said.

"Oh, no."

"Yes, really. My name is Isobel Larkin."

"Great Scott! What a coincidence!"

"Isn't it? Are you a friend of my father?"

The question caused Neville to think hard. Did it mean she had no idea that her father was dead? She was waiting for his reply, looking at him fixedly.

"It was your brother who was my friend," he said.

"My brother! But he went away years and years ago. I heard from him twice — from Canada — and then no more. You — you don't mean that he's back at Barrowtor?"

Neville felt most uncomfortable. He had never bargained on anything like this happening. Clearly she had no idea that both her father and brother were dead. It was with the utmost difficulty that he met her anxious gaze, and then slowly he brought the car to a standstill. Now the girl seemed to sense that something was wrong. He saw the lips quiver.

"Tell me," she said, in a low, vibrant voice. "Oh, please — please. I'm used to bad news. Is it my — my father?"

He nodded gravely — feeling as if he were murdering something.

"And — and my brother?"

"Philip died for his country — not very long ago."

She put her hands over her eyes, and he heard a convulsive sob. After a few moments she fumbled in her handbag and produced a small handkerchief.

"I'm sorry," she said, drying her eyes. "Poor father! Poor Phil! Three years is a long time, but I didn't think — You were Phil's friend?"

"Yes. I met him in the Army in 1942. We were together through several campaigns. But he seldom spoke about his family. Only once did he mention you."

"He left home under a cloud. My father was a harsh man, in some respects, and Phil was wild. I'm wild too. I ran away from home, and my father never forgave me. I — I was coming back to-day to get some things that belong to me. I — I hoped to — to make things right with my father. But that — that's impossible now. Why — why are you going to Barrowtor?"

"Your brother appointed me executor in his will."

"Did he inherit the estate?"

"Yes."

"Was he married?"

"No."

"Then who inherits everything?"

Again Neville found himself in a dilemma. This indeed was his unlucky day. It was bad enough having to break the news of two deaths, without having to relate the exact circumstances in which a pick-up girl acquired a valuable estate.

"It's someone he met and got to like," he demurred.

"A — a woman?"

"Yes."

"I see."

"I doubt if you do. Your brother would never have willed away the family

74

fortune to a complete stranger if he had known what he was doing; at the time when he made the will he believed he possessed nothing but his Army pay. He never dreamed that your father would leave you unprovided for and would leave everything to him. He died without knowing there was a fortune of over ninety thousand awaiting him in England. I came here to-day to go through Phil's effects which were sent here by his Commanding Officer."

"Then the house hasn't been sold?"

"Nothing has been disturbed there, because your father's executor thought your brother might like to keep the old home and the furniture. The lodge-keeper is still employed."

"And the woman — is she going to live at Barrowtor?"

"I don't know. So far I haven't found her, but I expect she will be located in a few days."

Isobel was dry-eyed now, and staring into space.

"Shall we go on?" asked Neville.

"Yes. I can still pick up the sketches which I wanted. They are really mine, so I hope you won't object?"

"Of course not. You are perfectly justified in removing anything which is your personal property — personal clothing, and presents of all kinds. Ah, this is the turning, I suppose?"

Isobel nodded and Neville turned the car into a very rough road which wound through the contours like a corkscrew. After about a mile of this, Isobel indicated that they were very close to Barrowtor, and a few moments later Neville saw an entrance gate, with a very attractive lodge standing in its own little garden. Neville drove the car just inside the gate, and then stopped it.

"I'd better knock up the lodge-keeper," he said. "Now what was his name?"

"Tom Barding," said Isobel. "He'll be surprised to see me."

Neville knocked on the door of the lodge, but got no reply. He tried several times with no better result.

"He's probably up at the house," said Isobel. "Oh, but I suppose you want the keys?"

"No. I have a complete set of keys."

"Then we had better go to the house. You'll see it when we turn round that bend."

A few moments later the house came to view. It appeared to be very large, and was of Georgian type, with pillars at the entrance and a flat roof above the two stories. All the blinds were down at the upper windows and the shutters of the downstairs windows were closed. There was an atmosphere of cruel neglect about the whole place. The rather handsome façade seemed to be screaming for a coat of white paint, and the nearby gardens were choked with weeds, through which early summer flowers were fighting their way. Away to the left there were numerous outbuildings, all in bad state of repair, and beyond these there were some fine glass-houses. Isobel seemed a little overwhelmed as Neville brought the car to a halt inside the pretentious plaster columns and before a huge front door.

"Well, here we are!" he said. "I'd better give Barding a toot to let him know we're here."

He pushed the honker button and there was a wail of sound. But there was no kind of response from inside the house. A second attempt produced no better result, so Neville found the bunch of keys.

"Which one?" he asked Isobel.

"That's the front-door key," she said. "But I should imagine the doors are sure to be bolted inside. If so, we had better go through the morning-room door which is round to the left."

They got out of the car, Isobel carrying the empty suitcase. Neville took the largest key and pushed it into the lock of the door. It turned easily and he turned the handle and pushed. The door swung inward.

"Not bolted," said Isobel. "Oh dear, it's so strange — coming home like this to a house that is no longer a home — in which I really have no right to be."

"You have every right until — "

He stopped suddenly, for they were now in a fairly large hall, lighted by a large window on the broad staircase. He looked at Isobel and saw that she too was momentarily speechless. For the large hall was absolutely bare, and the staircase was void of carpet.

"I thought you said that nothing had been disturbed here," said Isobel.

"That's what the solicitor said. Wait a moment."

He walked to a door on the left of the hall and opened it. Beyond was a spacious room, but it was almost as bare as the hall. Only a few — not very interesting — pieces of furniture remained, and on the floor there were the marks where rugs had been spread. The walls too showed squares and oblongs over which pictures had hung. Isobel was now at Neville's side.

"Oh!" she gasped. "The place has been ransacked!"

"It looks like it," said Neville.

In the dining-room the scene was similar. Isobel opened the central drawer of a colossal sideboard, which for some reason had been left.

"All the silver's gone," she said. "Lovely silver too — George the third. Those newspapers must have been brought to wrap things in."

Neville seized a couple of the newspapers. They were dated only a few days earlier.

"This is extraordinary," he said. "No wonder the front door wasn't bolted. They must have removed the stuff that way and then slammed the door behind them. We'd better see just how far this thing has gone before calling the police."

Room after room was entered, and they all told the same story. A lot of poor stuff had been left, but, according to Isobel, almost everything of value had been removed — including a large stock of linen and blankets. But in the bedroom which she had occupied she found what she had come to get. They were sketches in water-colours, strewn all over the floor.

"They evidently didn't consider these to be of any value," she said, as she gathered them up. "Probably they were right."

"What are they?" asked Neville.

"Just sketches for costume — chiefly historical. I — I once thought of taking up fashion drawing as a profession."

"Let me see," begged Neville.

She gave him one of the drawings somewhat reluctantly.

"Not very interesting to a man," she said.

But Neville disagreed, for the sketch revealed most unusual talent. Very soon he was looking at others, and they all bore the sure sign of what he believed to be genius — immature perhaps, but as certain as the sunlight.

"I like them immensely," he said. "And please don't think I'm trying to flatter you. Was there anything else here that belonged to you?"

"Just a few things. A Chippendale table, and a very nice needlework chair — also Chippendale. My mother wanted me to have them, for they came from her old home. But they have gone now."

"I'm sorry I don't understand what has happened. It seems a little significant that the lodge-keeper isn't on view. I should like to find him before I do anything. Shall we look round the grounds? He may be in some outbuilding."

Isobel was agreeable. She packed the sketches into the suitcase and then went with Neville into the garden. Isobel led the way by devious paths through the sylvan grounds. It was nearly all natural, with masses of silver birch trees, millions of wild daffodils, and clumps of valerian and blue-bells. Then a formal patch presided over by a weathered piece of sculpture. A little pond of crystal-clear water, brilliant with uncommon marginal plants. Unexpected corners where honeysuckle spilled over from a stone wall. Neville stopped and looked at his companion. Her eyes were bright, but moist.

"So this was your home," he said.

"Yes."

"How you must have loved it."

"Yes — but long ago. When my brother went it was different. I only want to remember the years before that. My father was a strange man — not easily understood. I think his mind became unhinged when my mother died. Dear little mirror pool! I used to stare down into that when I was very young, and wonder whether I should ever be as beautiful as my mother. It wasn't long before I knew that was but a child's vain dream."

"Are you sure?"

"You should have seen my mother. She wasn't only beautiful in face and form, but beautiful in mind and soul. Oh, I'm talking too much. If we take the path to the left we shall come round to the lodge at the entrance. Perhaps Barding is back there, and doesn't realise we are here."

After negotiating an overgrown path between banks of rhododendrons, they reached the lodge. Neville tried the door again, but found it locked.

"Not there — obviously," he said.

Isobel went into the little garden and stared through the window into the sitting-room. It was empty, and she could see through the open door into the small hall. On the mat just inside the front door were several letters. She came back to Neville, who had been round to the scullery door.

"The other door is locked too," he said.

"Have you a key to this place?" she asked.

"I may have. None of the keys are marked in any way. It's a Yale lock, isn't it?"

"Yes. Oh, there's a Yale key."

"Are you suggesting I should go in?" asked Neville.

"I don't know, but it's rather strange that there are several letters on the inside mat. You can see them through the side window. Would Barding be likely to receive several letters in one postal delivery? And he obviously wasn't at home when that delivery was made."

Neville hesitated to break in. It might well be that Barding was taking a day off — not a very unnatural thing to do for a man placed as he was. Yet there was almost unmistakable evidence that the big house had been rifled. A few moments' reflection were sufficient to overcome his qualms. He tried the Yale key into the lock and found that it turned easily. The door was pushed open and Neville saw the letters — three of them. Two of them were circulars, but the third was typewritten and dated the previous day. Neville turned the envelope over and found the name of Winslow & Winslow printed on the back.

"Posted London at two p.m. yesterday," he said. "But these circulars were posted in Plymouth three days ago. Barding can't have been here for at least two days. This sealed letter is no doubt the intimation that I should be calling. Curious!"

"Let's go in," pleaded Isobel. "I think you have every justification. But we always trusted Barding. I should hate to think — "

Neville nodded and they moved into the small sitting-room. It was quite tidy, except for a coat which was lying on a chair. In the fireplace was some wood ash. It was quite cold. Neville passed through a door and found himself in a bedroom. The bed was made, and a suit of pyjamas were on the pillow. In the scullery there were some dirty crocks. He came back to the bedroom and looked into a wardrobe. It contained a couple of suits, and some odd coats and shoes.

Isobel joined him. She had a pair of spectacles in her hand.

"These were on the mantelpiece," she said. "His reading-glasses, I think. He never used to wear glasses in the ordinary way."

"This is certainly a job for the police," said Neville. "But I think I should speak to Winslow first. Is there a telephone at the house?"

"There was," replied Isobel. "But I noticed that the instrument had gone."

"Do you know where the nearest telephone is?"

"Nothing nearer than Holne, so far as I remember."

"I shall have to run along there. Will you come or would you prefer to wait for me here?"

"I'll wait for you."

"Then I'll lose no time."

They locked up the lodge and hurried back to where Neville had left the car.

"Oughtn't to take me long to get on to London at this time of the day," he said. "Sure you'd rather stay here?"

"Quite sure. Oh, do you realise that I don't even know your name, Mr. Executor?"

"How absurd. It's Brandon. Neville Brandon."

"I'll try to remember."

Neville went off like a shot from a gun, and was very soon in the lovely little village. Within ten minutes he was talking to Mr. Winslow, and the significance of what he said caused the solicitor to doubt the genuineness of the communication. But finally he was persuaded that it really was Neville who was speaking to him, and that what he was saying was true.

"Ransacked!" he wailed. "But Barding was there. How does he explain this incredible thing?"

"He doesn't. I can't find him. The lodge was locked up."

"Then he must be involved. This is, of course, my responsibility, but I can't come down for days, as I have to be in Court all this week. Will you communicate with the police at once? Fortunately I had a detailed inventory of the contents made for the purpose of valuation. I will post this to you. Where shall I send it?"

"To my home address."

"You shall have it."

"What were the contents of the house valued at?" asked Neville. "The police are bound to ask."

"Just over six thousand pounds. You will find the prices in detail in the inventory."

"One more point. I'm about to telephone the police. I suppose the nearest police station is at Ashburton — "

"I shouldn't waste time," cut in Winslow. "Get straight through to County Police Headquarters at Exeter. Ultimately they will have to deal with the matter. This is very bad luck on you, Mr. Brandon, but who could have foreseen such an impudent piece of wholesale robbery? I'll get down as soon as I can."

When he rang off, Neville looked

up the telephone number of the County Constabulary and was very soon talking to an Inspector Adams, who took the details and promised immediate action. Neville went back to the car, but the open door of the local inn was too inviting, so he entered the old-fashioned comfortable bar and ordered a tankard of beer. It was austerity vintage, but very acceptable. The landlord, having caught sight of the luxury car, showed a very natural desire to talk, and Neville deliberately let slip the information that he was interested in Barrowtor House, without revealing what had happened there.

"Used to be a lovely place," said the landlord. "But I'm told it went to rack and ruin during the war. No one to keep up the grounds. Then old Mr. Larkin died, and that made it worse than ever. Someone told me the property was left to his son, who can't be found. Even if he is found it isn't likely he'll keep the place going. I'd like to know what is going to happen to all these fine old houses, without any staff to run them. Just a drug on the market, that's all they are. I remember young Mr. Larkin."

"What was he like?"

"Good-looking young fellow, but wild as they make 'em. Ran away from home when he was about twenty. Never heard of since. There was a daughter too — some years younger. I don't know what became of her. The house was always a kind of mystery house. Old Mr. Larkin was a hermit. No one saw him in years. His father and grandfather lived there before him. The family fortune was made out of wool — when this part of the country had a thriving wool industry. Lordy, how times change! Not thinking of buying Barrowtor?"

"Scarcely," laughed Neville. "I've been trying to find the lodge-keeper — Mr. Barding. But he doesn't seem to be about the place."

"That's funny," replied the landlord, "because Postie told me he hadn't seen him for a couple of days. He used to come here in the evening for a drink and a game o' darts, but he hasn't been here since Monday. That's three days ago. I thought he might have had an attack of rheumatism, but Postie says it can't be that. Maybe he heard that one of his relations is ill. He's got relatives away at Bideford."

Neville finished his beer and declined to be inveigled into discussing his own interest in the matter. He bade the landlord a cheery good morning and then drove back to the house. As he pulled up the car, Isobel approached him hurriedly from the lower garden.

"I've got on to the police — " he said, and then stopped, for Isobel was breathing hard, and her face and eyes told him that she was labouring under considerable emotion. "What's the matter?" he asked. "You look — terrified."

"Yes," she gasped. "I've made an awful discovery."

"Where?"

"In a cupboard on the first landing. It's — Barding."

"You mean — dead?"

"Yes. There is blood all over him. I ran away in a fright. Oh, please come and see."

6

THEY entered the house by the front door, and just before they reached the stairs Isobel stopped and pointed to some dark spots on the floor. Neville bent down and examined the dark brown spots.

"Blood," he muttered.

"Yes. There are some more spots further up."

Neville went forward with her, and just where the lovely old staircase made a turn she stopped him and indicated similar spots. He nodded gravely, and finally they came to a cupboard door.

"In — in there," she said in a whisper.

He put his hand to the brass knob and slowly turned it. It was a broom cupboard, and mixed up with sundry brooms and mops was the curled-up form of a middle-aged man. The head and hair were covered with congealed blood — a terrible sight now. It was abundantly clear to the senses that the body had been there some days, and Neville gasped and quickly closed the door.

"Come down," he said. "This is ghastly."

He took her by the arm and led her down the stairs.

"All right?" he asked.

"Yes. What — what are you going to do?"

"Wait for the police. It's no use telephoning for a doctor. He was murdered days ago."

"Poor Barding!" she murmured, drying her eyes. "And we thought he might have been a party — "

"It's clear he intervened and paid dearly for his intervention. When I was in the village I called at the inn. I learnt there that Barding was in the habit of going there every evening and having a drink and a game of darts. He hadn't been there since last

Monday. This might have happened on Monday night. Barding's habits may have been known to the gang. Perhaps they hoped to get all the stuff away before he got back, but failed. I'm afraid we've landed ourselves in the middle of a ghastly murder mystery. For you especially it has been a bad day. All that bad news and now this harrowing discovery."

"It is almost as bad for you as for me," she said. "I've another discovery too — not — not quite so painful. Phil's personal effects. They're in the old stables — just as they arrived. A kitbag and a box."

"The object of my visit," said Neville. "Everything else has been extra and unexpected — you and the burglary and the — the rest. When I took on this task I imagined that it was the simplest thing in the world. How wrong I was. I'll deal with those effects later. Now what about you? The police can't possibly get here for close on an hour. Wouldn't you rather keep out of this? I could run you back to Ashburton, and get back before the police arrive."

"You want me to do that?"

"It's up to you. If you stay here you will become a witness and be bombarded with painful questions. Where are you staying?"

"I'm not staying anywhere. You — you see, I landed in England only this morning — at Plymouth. I left my luggage in the cloakroom at Ashburton until I could find out — if — if — my father — "

"I understand. You had in mind a possible rehabilitation with your father?"

"Yes. I — I rather hoped that might happen."

Neville felt intensely sorry for her, but the whole thing was puzzling. She had landed in England only that morning — but from where? What had she been doing during the years of her absence? What had caused her to run away and lose all touch with her father and brother? Isobel seemed to be aware of his inner questioning.

"It's a long story," she said. "And not a nice one to tell. Thanks for your offer to take me to Ashburton, but I think it would be better if I stayed and faced the police. After all, it was I who made the discovery, and I don't want you to be compelled to make false statements on my account."

"But it can't make any difference."

"I'd prefer to stay," she said emphatically.

"Very well."

"You came here to go through my brother's effects — why not kill time by doing that? I should like to find some old snapshot albums, full of ancient photographs of the family. The mysterious lady who is to inherit our house, and everything else, will scarcely lay claim to them."

"Go right ahead," said Neville.

The subsequent examination of Philip Larkin's personal effects produced almost negligible results. Most of it consisted of clothing, all very creased and most of it filthily dirty. Presumably his cigarette-case, wrist-watch and other oddments had been stolen by the Germans from the peasant's clothing which he had been wearing when he was shot, but his identification disc had been returned by the farmer who had befriended him. In addition, there was a cheque-book and some photographs of women. Neville was rather glad that Isobel had not offered to help him, for the photographs of the women were on the bawdy side, and they caused Neville to reflect upon Larkin's loose habits in that direction. The value of the whole collection was nil. He stuffed the photographs into his own pocket, and by the time he had finished Isobel was back, with three moderate-sized snapshot albums in her hands.

"So you found them?" he said.

"Yes. May I take them?"

"Of course."

She gave a sad glance at the heap of soiled clothing.

"Is that all?" she asked huskily.

"Yes. Nothing of any value."

"What are you going to do with it?"

"That's up to you. What do you want done with it?"

"There's no sense in keeping it. Couldn't we — burn it?"

"Easily, and I think that is best. There's a little money in his bank account. I wish I could hand that to you, but of course that is out of the question."

"Of course. Oh, please burn it. I — I don't want to be saddened by having it around."

"I think you are wise. I'll do that now."

He found a wheelbarrow and conveyed the whole lot to a spot in the lower garden. Some paraffin, found in a can, aided the burning and very soon nothing was left but a pile of black ashes. He then went back to Isobel, who was seated on a rockery, turning over the pages of one of the tattered albums. Her eyes were red, and he knew she had been crying, and had found relief from her pent-up emotion.

"Time the police were here," he said. "But tell me about yourself. Have you any plans?"

"Yes. I'm hoping to get a job — commercial art or something like that. I've always wanted to do it."

"If it isn't a rude question — have you any means?"

"I'll manage."

"That isn't an answer. You're not likely to find a suitable opening in five minutes. I've an idea you're broke."

She gazed at him indignantly.

"I'm sorry," he said. "I shouldn't have said that. But although you and I are comparative strangers, I and your brother were friends over a long period, so you mustn't expect me to regard you — "

He was interrupted by the sudden appearance of a large car which came rolling up the drive.

"The police!" he exclaimed.

Isobel rose to her feet at once, and

101

they hurried up the steps which led to the terrace and reached the car as two men emerged from the rear part of it. Both were in plain clothes, but somehow they could not disguise the nature of their profession. The latter of the pair came forward.

"Mr. Brandon, I presume?"

"Yes."

"I am Inspector Carson. This is Sergeant Wiggins."

His short and slightly corpulent companion smiled at Neville, and then at Isobel.

"Oh," said Neville. "This young lady is Miss Larkin. This was her home, and we met quite unexpectedly."

Carson stared at Isobel.

"You may remember me, Miss Larkin?" he said. "I came here once respecting a slight accident which you sustained at the hands of a quite crazy motorist."

"Oh, yes," said Isobel. "That was a very long time ago."

"Twelve years, to be exact. And now,

Mr. Brandon, I understand there has been a burglary?"

"I wish it were only that," replied Neville. "But while I was telephoning you Miss Larkin made a startling discovery. The lodge-keeper, whom we had failed to find, has been murdered, and his body hidden in a cupboard on the first landing. I didn't try to find a doctor, because it is obvious he has been dead for some time."

"I had better see the body without delay," said Carson, without the slightest sign of any emotion.

Neville asked Isobel to excuse him and then led the way to the broom cupboard. Sergeant Wiggins opened the door and gave a low whistle at the sight which confronted him. Carson waved him aside and did one or two things to the corpse.

"Dead for two days at least," he said. "Fearful head injuries. Lend me a hand, Wiggins. We'll get him down on that old couch in the hall."

When this unpleasant feat was

accomplished, Carson went through the clothing and produced a few oddments. Finally he was satisfied that he had everything.

"Is there a telephone here?" he asked.

"No," replied Neville. "The instrument has been removed. I had to go to Holne to telephone."

"Wiggins, tell Corry to drive to Holne and get in touch with Ashburton. I'll need an ambulance and a doctor."

Wiggins went outside to give the chauffeur these instructions and was back again in a minute or two. A blanket was found and placed over the corpse, and then the two police officers walked round the house as a preliminary.

"Wholesale kind of job," commented Carson. "Took the good stuff and left the junk. Any idea what the loss is?"

"Yes. I telephoned the solicitor who had an inventory made after the death of old Mr. Larkin. The furniture was valued at six thousand pounds. What is left can only be worth a few hundreds. The solicitor is posting me the inventory to-day. It will give details of the items and that may help in identification."

"Good! I should like to have that as soon as you get it. Where are you living?"

Neville gave him his address, and Wiggins wrote it down in his note-book. Then a table and some chairs were drawn up in the lounge and Carson used this as his temporary office.

"I'm not sure that I've got the state of affairs exactly," he said. "I was aware that Mr. Larkin died and that there was some trouble in locating the heir — who was his son, I believe?"

"That's true. The son was in my regiment and had no idea his father was dead. He himself was missing for many months, but recently the War Office received proof of his death, and he was posted accordingly."

"So you are really acting as his executor?"

"Yes. The house and contents were not sold, but merely valued for the purpose of probate. I came here to-day to examine the personal effects which were sent here by his Commanding Officer. I found them valueless — just a lot of soiled clothing. I decided to burn them."

"And the sister — how did she come into it?"

"I overtook her on the road. Neither of us had any idea that the other was coming here."

"Why was she coming here?"

"To get some sketches which were her personal property. But she hoped to see her father and patch up an old quarrel with him."

"You mean she believed her father to be alive?"

"Yes."

"But he's been dead years."

"She told me she had been away from home."

Carson stroked his long lean jaw.

"I think I'll take her evidence," he

said. "Wiggins, ask Miss Larkin to come here. All right, Mr. Brandon, but don't leave without seeing me again. There may be one or two points that need elucidating."

It was a clear hint that the Inspector wanted to question Isobel alone, and as Neville was leaving the hall Isobel came in with Sergeant Wiggins. She looked pale and tense.

"Nothing to worry about," he said. "I'll be in the garden."

She forced a smile and went on her way. Neville walked into the garden and took a seat in the sunshine. He looked at his watch and found it was nearly one o'clock. He remembered for the first time since leaving home that he had promised to be back to lunch, and to accompany Teresa on her farm-finding exploit. That was out of the question now, and he imagined that very soon his name would be mud so far as Teresa was concerned. But who could have imagined such developments as had taken place in that lovely morning? Truth to tell, it gave him no particular thrill to be mixed up in such a tragedy, for he had seen enough death and suffering to be more than willing to forego any fresh experiences in which violence played a part. Isobel was the one bright spot in the whole sordid affair. There was something irresistibly attractive in her make-up. Physically she was very much what her dead brother would have termed 'an eyeful', but it wasn't merely her physical qualities which intrigued him. She had admitted being wild — like her brother, but in what way the wildness was manifested he was left to guess, and guessing didn't get him very far. Time passed and then, at last, Isobel came to view on the terrace. He waved a hand and she came down to him.

"All over?" he asked.

"Yes. He asked me all sorts of silly questions, which can have no bearing on what has taken place."

"The Inspector probably thinks

otherwise. He seems a fairly efficient chap. Now what about some food?"

"Food?"

"Haven't you heard of food?"

"I'm not very hungry."

"But you can't have eaten anything since breakfast, and that must have been some time ago. It looks as if we are going to be detained for a while. Let's slip away in the car and have a bite. There's that pub in the village."

"I don't think you'll get anything there."

"Well, there's the nice inn at Hexworthy. I know one can get a fair meal there. Now, don't argue. You need food as badly as I do. You get in the car and I'll run and tell the Inspector we'll be back in an hour or two. It'll do you good to get all this out of your system for a little while. Please do."

Isobel smiled and nodded. He saw her into the car and then went to find Inspector Carson. He was no longer in the lounge, but was tracing the blood-spot with a view to finding just where the dead man had been struck down.

"Lunch?" he said. "Why, of course. I had forgotten all about lunch. I hope to have the corpse removed by the time you get back. See you later."

Neville and Isobel decided to go straight to Hexworthy rather than stop and make enquiries in the village, and Neville deliberately drove the car at great speed up the long steep hill which led to the open moor. It had the desired effect, for he saw the girl's tense expression relax as the strong moorland wind blew back her hair and the full sunshine fell upon her.

"There's our moor," he said. "As lovely as it ever looked."

"Yes," she agreed. "For me it's crowded with pleasant memories. My brother and I used to ride ponies here. Did you get to like Phil?"

"Yes."

"Strange," she murmured.

"Why strange?"

"So few people liked him. I thought I was the only one."

"I assure you you weren't."

"Was he a good soldier?"

"Yes. He had a complete contempt for danger. If a volunteer was wanted for any particularly nasty job, Phil was always the first to jump in. Some of the men called him 'Captain Crazy'."

"I can believe that," she said. "But he was weak in some respects — wasn't he?"

"It depends upon what you mean by weak. He was fond of drinks, and any wild gamble, but he had the courage to gamble with his own life. That's how he met his death."

"Tell me," she begged.

"He went out with two men to bring back two others of a machine-gun team who were having a bad time in a ruined house. It was a task suitable only for a handful of men. We were ready to give them covering fire when they returned."

He stopped, and Isobel looked at him.

"Go on," she said.

"They never came back. A few days later we attacked in force. We found the two machine-gunners dead, and we imagined that your brother and his companions had been taken prisoner. Soon after that I was wounded and sent home. The war was over before I was fit again. Then I heard that your brother had not been captured, but had been given shelter by a Dutch farmer. He was shot later when attempting to escape in a peasant's dress. The farmer handed over his uniform and identity disc which he had hidden from the Germans. That's how I came into your life."

"And he never knew that my father had died and forgiven him?"

"No."

"Poor Phil! But I'm glad he made some use of his life. Thanks for telling me."

This simple and brief narration

performed a miracle with her. The expressive violet eyes became alive again and she gave a cry of delight as a Dartmoor pony and its foal suddenly came to view on a blind corner.

"The loveliest things," she said. "In hard winter they used to come right up to Barrowtor and beg for food. Oh, I'm hungry after all."

A few minutes later the Moorland Inn came to view. Neville pulled the car in to the parking place and took his companion into the very pleasant inn. Luncheon was already being served, and within five minutes they were seated at a table where a wide window framed as beautiful a view as could have been dreamed of. It was the usual austerity post-war meal, but welcome enough, and Neville found that the depleted cellars yet contained a few bottles of wine.

"Sparkling Moselle," he said. "That sounds good to me."

"Let me see," said Isobel and took the wine-list. All she did was look at the price. While she looked Neville nodded to the waiter.

"Oh, you shouldn't!" she protested.

"Why not?"

"Because — because I insist on paying my share."

"Nonsense. But if you insist — "

"Oh, let's be frank. I — I can't afford to pay fantastic prices for wine."

"Now listen!" said Neville. "I am an old friend of your brother, and I have invited you to have lunch with me. Won't you grant me that pleasure?"

Isobel was won over, and the lunch as a whole proved an enormous success. Hard as the realities of the situation pressed upon them, they managed for a full hour to engage in pleasant trivialities. Neville found that his companion knew every inch of the surrounding country and loved it all from the barren uplands to the densely-timbered valleys through which the brackish waters of the fast rivers murmured their everlasting music. Ultimately he paid the bill and they re-entered the car.

"Now for Inspector Carson," said Neville. "I wonder how far he has got — if anywhere?"

When they reached Barrowtor a great number of things seemed to have happened during their absence. The ambulance had come and gone, and there was no longer a dead body in the hall. Carson and the Sergeant made an appearance, looking somewhat grimy, and the latter was carrying something wrapped up in a silk handkerchief.

"A clue?" asked Neville.

Carson made it plain that he was not prepared to discuss the result of his activities.

"Hope you managed to get a satisfactory lunch," he said.

"Most satisfactory," replied Neville. "Shall you be wanting us any more?"

"I think not — at the moment. What about that inventory?"

"It should reach me to-morrow."

"At Shaldon?"

"Yes."

"Then I'll pick it up on my way here."

"That's quite a good idea — provided it comes by the first post."

Carson turned to Isobel.

"There's one thing you can do, Miss Larkin. It might help in tracing the stolen goods — and ultimately the murderer — if you would write detailed descriptions of any items which you remember. The inventory may give quite inadequate descriptions. I want to lose no time in circulating the fullest possible descriptions of as many articles as possible. Can you do that by to-morrow morning?"

"Yes," replied Isobel.

"Where can I pick it up?"

Isobel looked perplexed, but Neville, who had been doing a lot of thinking, swiftly came to her rescue.

"I'll have the particulars ready for you, Inspector," he said. "Along with the inventory."

"Good. I'll call — unless you propose coming here."

"I've made no plans yet. I think you had better call. Shaldon isn't much out of your way, if you are coming from Exeter."

"Very well. Oh, I shall need the keys of this house."

Neville handed him the keys, and then collected Isobel's suitcase and walked with her to the car. Isobel looked at him curiously as he placed the suitcase in the back.

"Jump in," he said. "We'll pick up that other baggage of yours at Ashburton, and then — "

"And then — what?" asked Isobel. "I think you had better just drop me in the town and leave me to fix up some place for the night."

"It's a hundred to one against your finding a suitable place. In the meantime my sister and I occupy a house with four spare bedrooms. She'll be delighted to meet you."

"Oh, but I couldn't."

"Why not?"

"You know nothing about me — except

that I am Philip's sister."

"Isn't that enough?"

"Is it?"

"More than enough. You've got a job to do for old Carson. I more or less guaranteed I'd have the goods ready. No conventional nonsense now. When we get to Ashburton I'll telephone Teresa and tell her what to expect. You can add a postscript, and if you don't like the sound of her voice you can run."

Isobel entered the car somewhat diffidently, and on reaching the station Neville found a public telephone box. He was quickly through to Teresa.

"You're a nice one," said Teresa. "You've mucked up everything. I know — you've had a breakdown."

"Dear Angel," said Neville. "Wait until you hear the whole story. The house had been ransacked, and I've spent hours with the police. In addition, I've met a very charming and unfortunate girl. She's Phil Larkin's sister — absolutely stranded, but too proud to admit it.

Nowhere even to sleep. I'm bringing her along and you are going to be exceptionally nice to her."

"Am I?"

"You are. Are you now ready to tell her that you are expecting her?"

"Are you really serious?"

"Never more so."

"All right. Is she going to speak on the line?"

"Yes — immediately."

"I'll hang on."

Neville opened the door of the cabinet and dragged Isobel inside.

"Over to you," he said, and handed her the receiver.

Isobel spoke haltingly at first, and then suddenly she laughed, and Neville knew that Teresa had swiftly put her at her ease. Finally Isobel hung up the receiver, and turned her grateful eyes on Neville.

"I'm not going to run," she said.

7

AND so it was that Isobel came to Fouracres and was immediately taken to Teresa's sympathetic bosom, but it was not until late that evening when Isobel had retired for the night that Teresa heard all the details of that astonishing day.

"You've certainly butted your head into something," she said. "What's the next move?"

"I haven't had time to think about it. Of course there will have to be an inquest, and I expect I shall be called upon to attend."

"The verdict is a foregone conclusion, isn't it?"

"It looks like it."

"And our guest — what is to happen to her?"

"Heaven knows. I'm quite sure she is absolutely broke. What do you think of her, Teresa?"

Teresa pursed her lips in a strange way. She was usually good at sizing up people on first acquaintance, but now she appeared to be in doubt.

"Not easy to get much out of her," she said. "Whenever conversation touched on her immediate past she was quick to go off at a tangent. She was forthcoming concerning her childhood with her brother, but after that there was a kind of drop curtain. Don't you know where she came from?"

"She said she landed at Plymouth early this morning. Anyway, it's no business of ours. For Phil's sake I should like to help her."

"Well, he didn't help her much — signing away a fortune to a dirty little tart. Can't she dispute the legality of that document?"

"On what grounds?"

"He couldn't have been in his right mind at the time."

"But he was. He knew exactly what he was doing."

"He believed that all that was involved was a few pounds. Who's to say he was sober and in his right mind?"

Neville looked at her sharply.

"Very tempting, Teresa," he said. "But I'm not prepared to commit perjury even to procure a fortune for Isobel. No, if the woman comes forward, as I expect she will, it's good-bye to ninety thousand quid. Now what about Isobel?"

"What about her?"

"Can't you persuade her to stay here a week or two? She's trying to find a job, and she might as well make this her headquarters as engage in a futile hunt for decent lodgings."

"Will she expect to be waited on?"

"Of course not."

"So you think. Can she cook?"

"I shouldn't be surprised. She can certainly draw."

"I've yet to be convinced that drawing and cooking are inseparable talents."

"I'm certain she'll pull her weight."

"H'm!" said Teresa. "Well, we'll see."

"Good!"

"Now what about the farm?"

"We'll run out and have a look at the place to-morrow afternoon. But don't hustle me too much, because I want to get this wretched business settled before I make weighty decisions. Good Lord, and John is coming down for the week-end. In the circumstances, would you rather I put him off?"

"Of course not. We'll manage somehow."

Early the following morning Neville collected the two morning newspapers from the front door. In both of them were advertisements for Miss Berenice Waters, phrased as only a solicitor could have done it. Teresa sniffed when he showed them to her, and the sniff spoke volumes. She then gathered up a small tray on which were a teapot and a cup and saucer, and sailed upstairs. She came back a few minutes later.

"Well?" asked Neville.

"She's dressing and will be down in a few minutes. I suggested she should stay, but she declined."

"What!"

"Just that, dear brother. I was quite nice about it, but her mind seems to be made up."

"I'll have a talk with her."

"I doubt if it will get you anywhere, but there's no harm in trying. That must be the postman."

Neville went to the front door, and received three letters from the postman; two of them were for Teresa, but the third — a very bulky long envelope — was addressed to him. On the back of it was the embossed name Winslow & Winslow.

"Two love letters for you," he said to Teresa. "This one is obviously the inventory of the furnishings at Barrowtor. The police want it to find out the details of the missing stuff. Twelve foolscap pages of it, all valued. By jove — some of the things were valuable. Twelve ladderback Chippendale chairs, two with arms — £350. Pale blue Chinese carpet, with flowered design. Size 18 feet by 14. That little item is priced at £400. Nice haul those fellows made. Very few details given of most of the items. That's where Isobel can help."

When Isobel appeared she looked very refreshed from her long sleep. She had done her abundant hair differently, and looked younger than on the previous day.

"Good morning," said Neville. "Did you have a good night?"

"Yes. Absolute oblivion until the sunshine sneaked into my room this morning. Oh, is that the inventory?"

"Yes. It arrived a few minutes ago."

Isobel took the inventory, and a sad expression crossed her face as she scanned the many items.

"I expect you can amplify many of the descriptions," said Neville.

"Oh yes — easily. I grew up among all these things. Most of them were in the family a long time. Shall I make a start now?"

"Oh no. Have breakfast first. Afterwards you can use the study. It will be quiet in there."

"This is a charming place," said Isobel, staring through the window. "Why are you thinking of giving it up?"

"Very little option. Teresa is mad to have a small dairy farm, and farms are dear to buy. Ah, here's breakfast."

At breakfast Isobel ate sparingly, and it was evident that she was feeling deeply the pressure of events. Later Neville took her to the study, and left her there to work on the inventory. Half an hour passed and then she found Neville in the garden, and handed him the document. Against many of the missing items she had made copious additions in very small neat handwriting.

"Good work!" said Neville. "This ought to help the Inspector. But of course the stuff may be a hundred miles away by now. It was certainly a very bold business."

"I can't help thinking of poor Barding. Why did he have to be murdered? They could have overpowered him easily without killing him."

"He was the only person in the world who could identify them. I imagine the job was done at night, and that they imagined they could complete it without waking him up. Let's hope the police will find the persons responsible."

It was an hour later that Inspector Carson turned up, in a big car which contained several other officials. He was pleased to find that the inventory had arrived, and he thanked Isobel for her very valuable additions to the somewhat brief descriptions.

"Have you any idea when it took place?" asked Neville.

"Yes. A little earlier than we at first presumed. Almost certainly on Monday night."

"Four days ago."

"Yes. There is to be an inquest to-morrow, but the verdict is a foregone conclusion, and you will not be needed."

"What about me?" asked Isobel.

"So far as I know at present, that also applies to you, Miss Larkin, since you have stated that you have not seen the murdered man during the past four years. If the coroner should change his mind I will let you know."

"But I shall not be here after this morning."

"Can you give me an address which will find you?"

"Not — not at the moment. I have yet to find accommodation. I'll telephone you immediately I get fixed up. Where shall I ring?"

Carson took a card from his wallet and pencilled a telephone number on it.

"That will find me," he said. "Or at least someone who can take the message. I shall require the inventory, Mr. Brandon. Immediately I have had a fair copy made you shall have it back."

"No hurry," said Neville.

A few moments later the car was gone, leaving behind the smell of its exhaust. Isobel gave a little sigh.

"The sleuths are on the trail," mused Neville. "I wonder how far they will get. Do sit down."

"I ought to be packing."

"Don't you like us?"

The girl stared at him, surprised by the unexpected question.

"What a question!" she said. "You and your sister have been most kind."

"Then why must you rush off at such speed?"

"I have my living to get. You see, I had no idea my father was dead, and I had hoped he would agree to forget the past. Had he been alive, I think he would have done so. You see — he was right and I was wrong."

"That leaves me completely in the dark."

"It was something I did. I don't want

129

to discuss it because it wouldn't do any good. The urgent task is to find work to do, and earn my keep. It was nice of your sister to invite me to stay a while, but if I start that sort of parasitical existence, it might become a habit."

"Parasitical! Phil and I were friends. You talk as if we were offering you charity. On the contrary. I made the suggestion to Teresa, because she has had a very thin time. The man she would have married was killed in action, and she has been living too much within herself. She needs another woman's companionship. Look at these newspapers — full of alluring advertisements for every conceivable type of labour. There's a terrific shortage of labour. Why go looking round for lodgings when you could just as easily reply to advertisements from this address, and at the same time have a bit of a holiday? It may take quite a little time to find just the sort of opening you want. Come, be sensible."

"Do you think it's fair to tempt me? Wouldn't anyone wish to stay in this lovely spot?"

"Then stay. I've a friend coming down to-day, to stay for a few days. Help us entertain him. We really need you."

"I'll stay if you agree to let me help in the house."

Neville's eyes twinkled.

"That was in the back of my mind," he said. "I'm glad that's settled."

John Wallace arrived in time for lunch, and was a little surprised to find another guest in the house. He was even more surprised when Neville introduced her as Philip Larkin's sister.

"I certainly didn't expect that," he said to Neville, after the meal. "Not much like her brother."

"There's a fleeting resemblance."

"Can't see it. How did you get in touch?"

Neville explained how he and Isobel had met, and swiftly put Wallace in touch with the position.

"She must be pretty sore with him for what he did," he said.

"No, I don't think so. She realises that he didn't know he stood a dog's chance of inheriting the estate, and that the whole thing was a ghastly mistake. I gather they have always been the closest friends, and the blow was softened by the knowledge that he died the death of a hero."

"I'll have to watch my step," muttered Wallace. "I can't bring myself to distributing bouquets, and I don't want to hurt her feelings. Pretty, isn't she?"

"Is she?"

"You know darn well she is. Is Teresa still keen about having a small farm?"

"I'm afraid so. I've promised to run out with her this afternoon to see a property which is in the market. Will it bore you too much to come with us."

"I should love it. Is it far from here?"

"Only seven miles. Sounds very attractive, but these things always do — on paper. I expect we shall find a multitude of snags when we get there."

They all set off an hour later in Neville's car. Wallace shared the back seat with Teresa, while Isobel sat with Neville who was at the wheel. It was fine and warm and the collapsible hood was let full down.

"Sure you know the way?" asked Teresa.

"Every inch of it."

But this proved to be an exaggeration, for the route lay through a maze of lanes, in which old sign-posts, dismantled for the purposes of the war, had not yet been replaced. After covering about five miles Neville found himself at the intersection of four different lanes, and completely lost.

"Good thing I brought a map," snorted Teresa. "Wait a minute. Oh, here we are. You're about two miles wrong. You shouldn't have crossed that little river at all, but have taken the left fork on the further side, and then past the mill. You'll have to go back."

"Oh, that's nonsense! Give me the map."

But the somewhat humiliating reverse had to be made, and finally they found themselves at their objective. There lay the little farm in its fifty odd acres, nestling in a green valley, with lazy cattle munching the lush grass, and some chickens wandering about. The farmhouse itself was a black-and-white affair, and on the small side, but the whole made a picture refreshing to the eyes.

"Lovely!" said Teresa. "Herefords."

"Hey?" asked Neville.

"The cows — stupid. But I wouldn't buy them. I've set my heart on pedigree Guernseys. Better leave the car here. Nice place to turn it."

"How much is this lot?" asked Wallace.

"Six thousand pounds, without the stock of course. Oh, let's go and start operations."

They found the farmer in the barn.

He was a red-faced, slow-speaking man, so broad in his speech that Wallace missed half he said. But Teresa never missed a word, and her questions were like machine-gun fire. The farmer had answers to all of them, but they were not entirely satisfactory. In the first place the sole source of water was a well, and lighting was done by paraffin lamps. Sanitation was of the early Victorian order, and boasted of a single outdoor closet. It was soon abundantly clear that to meet the requirements of an attested herd a great expenditure of money would be called for. It took the gilt off the gingerbread, and by the time they completed the round of the farm and entered the farmhouse even Teresa's enthusiasm had received a set-back.

"Such a pity," she whispered to Neville. "It's a lovely little place. If only — "

"If only it didn't lack all that makes life worth living," added Neville. "I feel quite sure that with those things added the present owner wouldn't be wanting to sell."

Teresa nodded and quickly did the round of the small and uncomfortable house.

"This lets me out for a while," said Neville to Wallace. "Teresa's prepared to come down a bit in her standard of living, but not quite to this."

"She may yet find what she wants."

"Yes — at a price beyond our means. I rather think Fouracres has spoiled us."

"It would spoil anyone," agreed Wallace.

They were soon back in the car again, after Teresa had told the farmer she would think it over. But this she clearly had no intention of doing.

"If we could only stick Fouracres in the middle of those fifty acres!" she ruminated.

8

THE days that followed were happy ones for the small party. Trips in the car were alternated by spells of fishing from the boat which Neville kept on the foreshore. He and Teresa knew every cove and secret beach along that incomparable coast, and to Wallace and, in smaller degree, to Isobel their knowledge of the habits of fish was incredible. Nothing gave Wallace more joy than to get among the mackerel, and to haul in the beautiful coloured fish while the motor boat cruised over the heaving sea, and life seemed to be a perfect round.

They bathed from little sea-locked beaches, that were strewn with shells and strange seaweeds, and here after a few visits Isobel collected enough of the comparatively rare cowrie shells to make a necklace, and a whole evening was spent in the tricky work of piercing them. Finally they were strung on silk and Neville had the pleasant task of hanging them round Isobel's admirable neck.

"Now you look like the Queen of Sheba," he said. "They harmonise very well with your sunburn. Let them stay until Teresa and John return, if only to advertise our diligence. I'll bet they find that film dreadful."

"If they had, wouldn't they have come home earlier?"

"I doubt it."

Isobel gave him a sharp glance.

"Oh, you must have guessed," he said.

"Guessed what?"

"I don't think they really wanted to see the film. Wouldn't surprise me if they never got as far as the cinema."

"You mean that John and Teresa have got to like each other?"

"Would that be a foolish notion?"

"No. But I didn't think you had noticed."

"I know Teresa too well not to notice. She's happier than she has been for a long time. Wallace is a very good chap. Absolutely straight and honest and decent. Oh Lord, I've forgotten to lock up the chickens. I'd better do it now."

He went out through the french window, and Isobel switched on the light, for the day was nearly over. Near the switch was a small mirror, and she lingered there a moment to look at the home-made necklace round her sunburnt neck. In a kind of day-dream she heard the telephone ring in the hall, and hurried there to take the message. An observer would have noticed that her face blenched as soon as the receiver was placed to her ear. Then she made one or two monosyllabic utterances, and replaced the receiver. As she walked back to the sitting-room Neville returned by the french window.

"That's done," he said. "Was that the telephone?"

"Y-yes," she stammered. "It was — a wrong number."

"We seem to get nothing else but wrong numbers. Isobel, are you all right?"

"Why do you ask that?"

"You look so pale — somehow quite different."

"I expect it is the strong light after being in the gloaming. Was that the car?"

"Sounds like it. Yes, they have gone straight to the garage. I hope they haven't scoffed up too much of my precious petrol. By jove, you do look pale, you know."

"Nonsense!"

A little later Teresa and Wallace entered the room.

"Ghastly film," said Wallace. "We simply couldn't stand it, so we sidled out and took a run in the car. Found a spot where a nightingale was getting into song, and that beat all the Hollywood crooning into a cocked hat. Why, you've finished the necklace."

"Oh, let me see," said Teresa. "My dear, it's lovely. Just suits your colouring. How many shells did you break punching the holes in them?"

"Only five," replied Neville. "We have now learned the knack, and can supply necklaces complete for a reasonable sum."

"What about a drink?" asked Teresa. "I'm parched."

"Good idea," said Neville. "I'll get something."

"Not for me," said Isobel. "If you don't mind, I think I'll retire."

"Why, it's only ten o'clock," protested Neville.

"All the same, I'm sleepy."

"Just a nightcap then," said Neville.

"Not even a nightcap."

She stifled a yawn and then said good night to them.

"Curious," said Neville, when the door had closed on her.

"What is?" asked Teresa.

"Isobel going off like that. A quarter of an hour ago she was as merry as a lark. I went out to shut up the fowls, and when I came back she was looking pallid and drawn. She had been to answer the telephone."

"Who was it — on the 'phone?" asked Teresa, as Neville poured her a drink.

"Only a wrong number."

"You mean she said it was a wrong number," said Teresa.

"Oh, hang it! That's not a nice thing to say. What's yours, John?"

"Whisky," replied John. "Whoa! By jove, your hand's none too steady."

"He's annoyed with me," said Teresa, "because I made a perfectly reasonable remark."

"I'm not a bit annoyed, but I do think it was uncalled for. It suggested that Isobel was a deliberate liar."

"It suggested that Isobel might have found it convenient not to disclose that someone rang her up. You see, Neville, it isn't the first time."

Neville stared at her from over the top of his glass.

"For the life of me I can't see why she shouldn't receive telephone calls," he protested.

"Neither can I, but apparently she looks at the matter differently. On the previous occasion she also told me it was a wrong number, but I was near enough to hear part of the conversation. I didn't want to overhear, but I couldn't help myself."

"What was it?" blurted Neville. "No, don't tell me. I shouldn't have said that."

John, feeling that the matter was a little delicate, swiftly put the conversation into other channels. For the best part of an hour they discussed the future of England, of Germany, and of the whole human race. Wallace believed in emigration as a solution to England's ills, but Neville, having pondered that proposition on many occasions, shook his head doubtfully.

"As a long-term policy it's sound enough," he said. "But here and now we need all the young men we can get to produce food and goods as never before."

"I'm with you," said Teresa. "And the sooner we get a farm the better."

"A farm with all the mod cons," laughed Wallace. "I envy you the prospects. Heaven knows why I took up soldiering again. Well, with your permission, I'll go to bed."

A few minutes later Neville and Teresa were left alone, and the eyes of Teresa regarded her brother wistfully.

"Still annoyed with me?" she asked.

"You know I'm not."

"Do you want to know what Isobel said on the telephone?"

"No. It was her private business."

"You like her, don't you?"

"What do you mean by that?"

"Just what I say. I'm not blind nor lacking imagination. She's an extremely attractive girl, with artistic gifts, and tons of allure, but — "

"But what?"

"A bag of mystery. She shuts up like an oyster when you attempt to dig into her past. Someone rings her up on the telephone and gives her a fright. I'm going to tell you what I overheard whether you like it or not, because I think you ought to know. She said: 'It's no use. I've told you a hundred times it's over and done with. I won't do it, and that's my last word'."

Her eyes remained focused on Neville's face, to see what his reactions were. All he did was to wince and then finish up what was left of his last drink.

"You know what I think?" she asked.

"No, and I don't want to know."

"Neville!"

"You think I'm in love with her?"

"Aren't you?"

"No. I brought her here because she was poor Phil's sister, and because I've got the very unpleasant task of handing over the family estate to a dirty little tart. You can't expect me to be indifferent about that."

"She may be dead."

"It wouldn't make any difference, because her husband is very much alive and would be the next of kin. He's the worst sort of ruffian, if I'm any judge."

"Does Isobel know all the circumstances?"

"Not quite."

"You mean she doesn't know just how a strange woman comes to be her brother's sole beneficiary?"

"No."

Teresa tossed her head at this exhibition of masculine loyalty. She had heard a great deal about Philip Larkin, and felt she had no cause to respect his memory, even though his last act appeared to be one of great gallantry and self-sacrifice.

"You men are all alike," she commented.

"You think I should disillusion Isobel about some aspects of her brother's life?"

"I think you shouldn't encourage her idolatry."

"Evidently John has been talking to you. He never could bring himself to like Philip."

"Why should he? Larkin was a drunkard and — "

"And a very brave man. But don't let's quarrel about him. He's dead, and the least we can do is to overlook his weaknesses. I'm sorry about the farm. We'll have to try again."

A little later he went to bed, and for a time he sat in a chair enjoying a last cigarette, and reflecting over what Teresa had said. She believed he was in love with Isobel, and he had to admit that there was some ground for her remark, although up to that moment he had not accepted that position. But it was a fact that he was supremely happy in Isobel's company — that he approved of so many things about her — the way she dressed and did her hair; her soft, rather husky voice; her skill with pencil or brushes; and the mischievous light in her eyes which came and vanished like a will-o'-the-wisp. He had believed that he was immune from feminine allure, that for some reason or other sex made no call upon him. Perhaps it had something to do with the war — its fierce impact upon his imagination and sensibility. He had come to admire men at their best, forming numerous close friendships, many of which had ended in a plain wooden cross over a grave in a foreign land, leaving him more and more alone, and more and more cynical. But now there had come a change — all in a few days — and Teresa had been quick to take note of it, and to lay her finger upon the most probable cause.

When he was between the sheets his mind still ranged over this new field of interest, and he found himself wondering idly how the problem of the future could be satisfactorily solved. If eventually Teresa got her farm, it would take their combined capital to buy and stock it, leaving him nothing but his brain and brawn wherewith to support a wife. No doubt Teresa would welcome his help on her prospective farm, but a wife thrown in was quite another proposition. On the verge of sleep he laughed at his own boldness and optimism in allowing his mind to race on far in advance of events, and very soon he was sound asleep.

Morning found him alert and high-spirited. He looked out of the window and sniffed hard at the pearly morn. There had been suggestions of a run in the boat along the coast, with the usual fishing and alfresco lunch on the sand of some secret cove, and all the signs presaged a perfect day. He sang lustily in the bathroom, and plunged into ice-cold water with gasps of mingled pleasure and pain. A rub-down with a very hard towel induced a lobster hue to his healthy skin, and finally he got into a pair of shorts, and a short-sleeved shirt, and sallied downstairs, and out into the sunlit garden. The delicious odours of night-scented stock and tobacco plant still hung heavy on the air, mingling with the more subtle perfumes of the flowers of the day, and the tip of every blade of grass on the nearer lawn supported a sparkling diamond. A slight noise drew his gaze upwards, and he saw John's head and bare shoulders projecting from his bedroom window.

"What a day!" said John. "Any chance of a bathe?"

"No. The tide's wrong. Better have a cold bath instead."

"Not so much emphasis on the 'cold'," protested John. "I hate cold baths. What's the programme? Is it calm enough to do that coastal trip?"

"Yes. But we ought to get away early. Hurry and cover up that ape-like torso while I bring Teresa to consciousness."

"She's already conscious. I can hear her moving about in the next room."

"Good. I'll go and put the kettle on."

He cut a few roses before entering the house, shaking the pearly dewdrops from their fragrant petals. These he placed in a vase which he found in the lounge, and went to the kitchen to add water. He was thus engaged when he noticed an envelope laid out on the top of the gas-stove. Turning off the water tap, he went to the stove and was surprised to find that the envelope was addressed in Isobel's neat handwriting to 'Neville and Teresa'. The flap was not stuck down, and he drew forth a single sheet of folded notepaper.

DEAR FRIENDS,

This is good-bye to you both, with many many thanks for all your kindness. There is a reason why I cannot stay here any longer. I wish I could explain, but it would take too long, and I do not feel up to the task. You have made my brief stay very happy, and I feel painfully aware of my seeming ingratitude in leaving you in this fashion, but try to forgive me. I shall always remember you both even though we may never meet again.

Sincerely,
ISOBEL.

Neville stood for a few moments staring at the writing as if he doubted his own eyesight. Then he went upstairs and rapped on Teresa's door.

"Who is it?" she asked.

"Me — Neville. Can I come in?"

"Yes."

He entered and found Teresa only partly dressed. In the midst of rolling up a laddered stocking she stopped and stared at him.

"You look as if you had seen a ghost," she said. "Oh, surely the post hasn't come yet?"

"No. This was left by Isobel. She's gone."

Teresa wrinkled her brow as she took the sheet of notepaper. She read the farewell message, and gave a little sniff.

"For heaven's sake say something," said Neville.

"There's nothing to say. She appears to have had the last word."

"But aren't you amazed?"

"No."

"Good Lord! Your guest packs her bag and walks off in the middle of the night, and you behave as if you expected that to happen."

"I'm not as psychic as all that, but I believed she was capable of doing the unexpected. I'm sorry, because I was getting to like her very much. She must have crossed by the early ferry and caught the six-thirty train from Teignmouth."

"To London."

"It stops about ten times before it reaches London."

"I'm sure she must have gone to London. That was her original intention. I wonder if the telephone message had anything to do with it?"

"I imagine it did. Well, there's nothing we can do about it."

"She's in trouble."

"Yes — obviously. I'll take a look at her room."

Neville went with her. They found Isobel's late bedroom very tidy. Her two suitcases had gone, and she had folded the blankets and the sheets and placed them in the centre of the bed. The dressing-table was bare, and the wardrobe empty. All that remained to suggest she had recently been there was a little face powder spilt on the embroidered 'runner' of the dressing-table.

"Well, that's the end of her," said Teresa.

"Perhaps she'll drop a card when she finds accommodation."

"Perhaps she won't. Had she any intention of keeping in touch with us she wouldn't have left us the way she did. Hullo, John!"

Wallace was standing in the open doorway, clad in a dressing-gown, and with a towel over his arm.

"Anything wrong?" he asked.

"Isobel has run out on us," replied Teresa.

Wallace gave a low whistle.

"She must have made an early start," he said. "But I slept next door to her and never heard a sound."

"Nobody heard a sound," said Teresa. "She was as quiet as a mouse, but left a note behind her."

"Amazing thing to do," said Wallace. "She told me yesterday that she was looking forward to our trip to-day."

"That was before she received that telephone message," replied Teresa. "Well, I'm sorry, but it can't be helped. I suppose the boat trip is still on, Neville?"

"Of course."

"Good. The next thing is breakfast."

Neville's interest in the projected trip was now considerably diminished, although he did his best to conceal the fact from Teresa and Wallace. All through that pleasant sunlit day his mind would persist in switching to the vanished girl, and the attempt to appear casual was a complete failure. They came back to the house late in the evening, the two men carrying an assorted catch of fish.

"Lovely day," said Wallace. "I feel bloated with ozone, and hungry as a hunter."

"Shall we finish up the cold joint," said Teresa, "or shall I fry some of the fish?"

"Oh no," said Wallace. "You don't want to start frying fish. We'll scrape the old joint. Isn't there a saying to the effect that the nearer the bone the sweeter the meat?"

"This meat ought to be as sweet as syrup," said Teresa. "Come on, Neville, do your share. Get the joint while I make a salad. John, you can put a cloth on the table, and knives and forks."

When finally Teresa came into the dining-room with a delicious bowl of salad, she looked a little troubled.

"What a time you've been," said Neville. "John and I nearly made a start on that hunk of bone."

"I had to tidy myself a bit," explained Teresa. "Neville, I wanted a cigarette, but I can't find my case."

"Didn't you have it on the boat?"

"No. I couldn't find it this morning. But I didn't bother much because we wanted to get away."

"The gold case you had yesterday?" asked Wallace.

"Yes. Father's present to me long ago."

"But you had it last night when we were all together," said Wallace. "I remember seeing you take it from your handbag."

"Yes."

"It'll turn up," said Neville. "Let's make a start. Oh, I remember about the cigarette-case. You didn't put it back in your handbag, but left it on the couch in the lounge. I picked it up and put it on the mantelpiece just after you went to bed."

"It isn't there now," said Teresa.

Neville looked at her fixedly.

"Are you sure?" he asked.

Teresa nodded and then proceeded to serve the simple meal. There was a silence for a minute or two, and then Wallace coughed in a nervous kind of way.

"I hate to admit this," he said, "but I — I've mislaid my wrist-watch."

Two pairs of eyes instantly surveyed him.

"What do you mean by mislaid?" asked Teresa.

"I was under the impression I left it in the bathroom last night, but it wasn't there when I used the bath this morning."

"Not there!" gasped Neville. "Why on earth didn't you tell me?"

"Well, I wasn't quite sure — at the time."

"But you are now?"

"I think — "

"Don't beat about the bush," interrupted Teresa. "You mean you are sure you left it there — don't you?"

"Yes."

"I thought so," said Teresa grimly.

"Just what are you thinking, Teresa?" asked Neville.

"I was thinking that it's a nice coincidence when a cigarette-case, a valuable gold watch, and a lady vanish — "

Teresa stopped as she saw her brother's face tighten up, as it invariably did in any unpleasant situation. She put out her hand and touched him on the arm.

"Sorry," she said. "Perhaps I shouldn't have said that, but things don't simply vanish into thin air. What do you think, John?"

"I think the best thing we can do is to engage in a thorough search. I'm quite capable of picking up things absent-mindedly and laying them down somewhere. But let's finish this excellent meal."

Later the search was started, and not a single possible hiding place was overlooked. Not only was it a failure, but before they had finished

Teresa discovered that two other objects were missing. One was a gold medal presented to her father by a garden-planning association, and the other was a gold Apostle spoon which had been in the family for several generations. Neville was now convinced that during the past twenty hours a robbery had taken place, but not yet was he prepared to name the thief.

"After all, the house was left unguarded all day," he pointed out. "Certainly we locked all the doors, but I'm not sure that all the windows were fastened."

"That's right," agreed John. "I found the window on the half landing partly open."

"It would mean climbing over the porch to get through that," said Teresa.

"The thief, whoever he was, seems to have a mania for gold," commented John. "So far as I am concerned it serves me right for being so careless. As a matter of fact I got that gold watch in exchange for five hundred cigarettes, so my loss is negligible."

"The best thing we can do is ring up the police," said Teresa.

Neville winced at this suggestion. To bring in the police would undoubtedly place Isobel under suspicion.

"You don't want to do that?" asked Teresa.

"No. Damn it, Isobel was a guest here. John, what value do you place on that watch?"

"Five hundred cigarettes. It was a swindle anyway. If you — "

"You'll have to allow me to replace the watch."

"I'll be damned if I do. Let's forget all about it. I'm having a marvellous time and I don't care two hoots about the loss of the watch. Teresa, you can sit down and have a smoke while Neville and I show you how beautifully we can wash up."

Teresa accepted a cigarette from him, and then sat down and became sunk in reflection. One thing now seemed to her abundantly clear. Neville who, to the best of her knowledge, had never been in love, was now up to his ears in it, and the woman who had brought about this minor miracle was almost certainly a clever adventuress and thief.

9

MR. AUGUSTUS TAMLING sat in the back parlour of a dirty little pub in Soho and scanned the columns of a racing journal while he worked his way through his third pint of mild and bitter. He was the only person on that side of the bar, and he needed its relative privacy. From time to time he gazed at the clock on the wall, and his whole attitude was one of gnawing impatience. The door opened and a man in a loud suit entered.

"Hullo, Gus!" he said. "Is Sid around?"

"No," replied Gus. "Did you want him?"

"Nothing important. If you see him tell him Black Knight isn't running in the three-thirty."

"Do you know anything?" asked Gus.

"Yes, Darling's selected. Tell him that. I just got it through from Newmarket."

"Okay! Have a drink?"

"Not now, thanks. I'm in a bit of a hurry. How are things with you?"

"Not too bad. Not too bad at all."

"Good! Well, don't forget to tell Sid. So long!"

The visitor departed and Gus had recourse to his racing journal again. He marked some 'runners' with a pencil, gazed at the clock again, took another gulp at his beer, and lighted yet another cigarette, which he smoked at tremendous speed. His cruel black eyes moved curiously in their sockets, and the hard muscles in his jaw pressed up through the skin. That he was deeply moved was obvious. He had in fact been in that condition for over a week — ever since Neville Brandon had called at the flat in Glass Street, and as the days passed his emotion grew more and more unbearable, for reasons which were hidden deep in his mind.

At last the man he was waiting for arrived. It was Sid Toller, weedy and pallid and sinister as ever. Gus sprang up from his seat at the sight of him.

"Get me a drink first," gasped Sid. "I bin tearin' me guts out gettin' 'ere. Couldn't get a bus or a taxi."

Gus finished up the drop of beer that was left in his pint mug, and then rapped on the counter at the serving hatch. The barman's head came to view.

"Two pints," said Gus.

The beer was drawn, and after Gus had paid for it the hatch was closed. Gus carried the two pint mugs to the table, and handed one to Sid, who was fanning himself with his hat.

"Cheers!" said Gus.

Sid took a long gulp, wiped his mouth with the back of his hand, and sighed.

"Well?" snapped Gus. "Did you get the lowdown on everything?"

"Sure I did! Oh boy, you're going to have a surprise. It was a chap named Philip Larkin who left Berry that money — "

"We know that."

"You don't know everything. Philip Larkin's will hasn't been proved yet, but his father's will has. The old man died in 1943, and left everything he had to his son — Philip. I've been to Somerset House and seen the will. How much do you think he left?"

"Brandon said it was a goodish sum."

"It was. Have a guess."

"Three thousand pounds?"

Sid laughed almost hysterically.

"Cut it out!" snarled Gus. "How much?"

"Hold yer breath — ninety-two thousand quid."

Gus did hold his breath literally. For a moment or two he was utterly speechless.

"You look ill," said Sid. "Why don't you laugh?"

"Ninety-two thousand pounds! Are you kidding?" asked Gus at last.

"Never more serious in me life. Best thing you can do is find Berry and make it up with her before she sees that ad. in the newspapers. How do you know that she hasn't already seen it, and has put in her claim?"

Gus shook his head.

"How do you know?"

"She would have to be identified, and that means they would communicate with me — being her husband. But ninety-two thousand quid! That's a hell of a lot of money."

"You're telling me," said Sid. "Any idea where Berry is now?"

"Yes."

"Where?"

Gus was silent for a few moments, and then he spoke through his clenched teeth.

"With a greasy-headed swine who calls himself Achilles. He's a Cypriot or something, and was a waiter at the Pyramid Club. He's taken her to one of the Greek islands. Can't remember the name."

"But you told the fellow who called — "

"Never mind what I told him."

"But there are millions of Greek islands. It would be like looking for a needle in a haystack."

"All the better."

"What yer mean?"

Gus pushed a finger down his collar, which suddenly seemed to be too tight for his large neck. Then he took the pint pots and had them refilled. Sid was watching him intently, with his rat-like eyes.

"What's on yer mind, Gus?" he asked.

Gus blew the froth from his beer and took a long draught before replying.

"Remember Suzy?" he asked.

"Suzy Cameron?"

"Yep."

"Could anyone forget her? But why do you ask?"

"You always said she was a bit like Berry."

"So she was. Same yellow hair,

and — Say, what is all this?"

"Suzy would do a hell of a lot for me. Before I met Berry, Suzy and I had some good times together."

"And after," said Sid with a grin.

"Why not? Berry turned out to be — But that don't matter. What matters is ninety thousand quid — enough dough for all of us to sit pretty for the rest of our lives. It's as good as in the bag too, if we play our cards right."

"How do we play them?" asked Sid.

"I want you and Flo to identify Berry when called upon."

"Now I get it," said Sid. "It's neat, but dangerous."

"Do you expect to scoop up ninety thousand quid without a spot of danger?"

"What will our cut be — me and Flo?"

"Five thousand of the best."

"I like that," expostulated Sid. "Do you call that fair?"

"You've never had five hundred quid in your life, let alone five thousand."

169

"I can still do my arithmetic," said Sid. "And five from ninety-two is eighty-seven. It may be even more than ninety-two because there's no telling how much money the son may have of his own. Like to make another bid?"

"I can wait for Berry — if you drive me too hard."

"Who's driving you? I'm only suggesting a fair cut, and if you call five per cent fair I don't. Look at the risk. Suppose Berry did get to hear of this, and then found that she was too late. Nice spot me and Flo would be in."

"She'll never know."

"How can you be sure?"

"She knows that if she ever came to this country I'd wring her blasted neck."

"It's ten per cent or nothing doing."

Gus looked murderous for a moment, but then he nodded his head and Sid gave a little sigh.

"That's a bargain," he said. "But there may be snags. Have you thought of that?"

"I've thought of nothing else day and night since that fellow called."

"What about him? How do you know he hasn't seen Berry?"

"If he did it must have been years ago. Look, I've got these snaps of Berry, taken just after we were married, and here's one of Suzy. Have a look at them."

Sid took the snaps and scanned them.

"You're right," he admitted. "You can hardly tell one from t'other."

"Of course I'm right. I've got the marriage certificate too."

"What about relations — Berry's, I mean?"

"She told me she was left an orphan at ten years of age, and lived with an aunt who died when Berry was seventeen. I've been down to Reading where Berry was born, but I couldn't find the dump where Berry had once lived with her parents, because it had been hit by a bomb. Couldn't find anyone who knew anything about her.

Why should they — after over twenty years?"

"What about the registrar who married you?"

Gus laughed scornfully.

"They have twenty marriages a day in that office," he said. "He wouldn't know her from Eve."

"But there's the signature — in the register."

"I can fix that. In fact, it's fixed already."

"I don't get it."

"You will. We'll run up and see Suzy now. It's about her getting-up time, and I want to be sure she's doing her lessons."

Less than a mile away Susan Cameron was sitting at a table in a tiny and ill-ventilated flat doing her 'lessons'. She was a somewhat rusty blonde, of uncertain age, and she was clad in little more than a diaphanous nightgown. The table was littered with sheets of paper on which was a single signature, repeated hundreds of times — Berenice

Ethel Waters. She smoked endlessly as she wrote, and at intervals took a sip from a glass of gin. The specimen signature which she was so laboriously copying was scrawled across the bottom of an old letter, and her later efforts were a very praiseworthy imitation.

The gin in the glass ran out and she refilled the glass from a squat black bottle, and cursed as she spilled some of it on to one of the sheets of paper. She commenced writing again, and then suddenly she sighed loudly and flung the pen across the room. It hit the mantelpiece and rolled into the grate. She scowled at it as she sat well back and blew rings of blue smoke towards the dirty ceiling. Then the doorbell pealed. She rose from her chair, slipped on a coatee, pushed her hair into place, and went to the door. Outside were Gus and Sid.

"Morning, lovely!" said Gus. "I've brought an old friend to see you."

Suzy nodded at Sid, and the two men passed along the narrow passage into the little sitting-room. Gus at once became interested in the signatures.

"Not bad," he said. "Not at all bad. Hey, where's the pen?"

"In the fireplace," retorted Suzy. "I'm sick of writing that damned name. I can do it with my eyes shut."

"Oh, you can, can you?" said Gus. "Well, here's the pen. Just try."

Suzy sat down again and took the pen. Gus covered her eyes with his hands.

"Now write it," he said.

Suzy did so, with Gus watching each letter as it was formed.

"Won't do," he said. "The 'r' isn't right. If you have to write that name you won't have a specimen to help you out. Practise on that 'r'."

"Hell I will," said Suzy. "Not any more this morning. I'm going — "

"You're going to sit right here and get that signature dead right."

"Who says so?"

"I do. You damned little fool! Don't you realise what it means to us?"

174

"I realise all right. But when do I get some money?"

"When we're through of course."

"But I want a spot to go on with. I've promised myself a new hat and costume, and I guess I've got writer's cramp. You can wait here while I dress, and take me out to lunch. Then if you buy me a hat and costume I'll come back and write till I bust."

"You'll stay — " thundered Gus.

"Easy!" said Sid. "Maybe she's right, Gus. Give her a break. I'm hungry too."

"You would be," snarled Gus. "All right, Suzy. Get some covering over those limbs, and make it snappy."

Suzy squealed with delight, and tripped into her bedroom. Gus gathered up all the signatures and set fire to them in the grate.

"Can't be too careful," he muttered.

"I suppose you can trust her?" asked Sid.

"You bet I can. What about Flo?"

"I can deal with Flo."

"I wonder."

"What yer mean?" snapped Sid, hurt by this innuendo.

"Well, sometimes I think it's Flo who wears the trousers in your set-up."

"Maybe she thinks she does, but you've never seen her eat out of my hand when there's any dough around. You can trust Flo like you could yer own mother."

"I never could trust my mother," growled Gus. "It was she who sent me to the reformatory."

He prowled round the untidy room like a caged animal. The news which his crony had brought was certainly stupendous. He had reckoned to make some money out of this situation, but in his wildest dreams he had never reached such dizzy heights as now. All through his criminal career he had played for comparatively small rewards, and had taken many risks merely to keep alive. What risks would such a man take to secure for himself immunity from the need to scheme and plot any more. Already he saw himself set-up for life. With so much money he could buy service. He had but to lay his hands on the cash and the rest was comparatively easy. Not all the world was open to him, but there were still vast expanses in the sterling area where he could take his money, and there lose himself for ever. There was South Africa with its sunny climate, Australia, New Zealand. How different life could be with nearly a hundred thousand pounds at his command. There were many reasons why he wanted to cross the ocean, and some of them were sufficiently weighty as to give him nightmares.

"Why don't yer sit down?" asked Sid, who was relaxing on the short couch.

"Because someone has to do the thinking, and I do it better walking about."

"But I thought all the thinking was done."

"You'd better think again."

"I'll tell you one thing," said Sid,

after a pause. "You'd better make sure that Berry hasn't been in touch with them solicitors before you start the ball rolling."

Gus shrugged his shoulders at this unnecessary advice. He had no respect for Sid's thinking powers. But Sid could be useful in certain contingencies, and one never knew when they might arise.

At last came Suzy, nicely powdered and rouged. She had a splendid figure, and her dress was calculated to enhance her physical attractiveness, but Gus sniffed at the heavy scent, and cast a glance at her lengthy display of legs.

"You're right," he growled. "Time you had a new frock. You look like a blasted whore."

"What do you think you look like?" retorted Suzy. "I'll tell you one of these days."

"Oh, cut the gags," pleaded Sid. "Let's get going. My inside is crying out for food."

They left the flat and were soon on the bustling street.

10

AT Fouracres the days had passed pleasantly enough, despite the unexplained missing articles. Teresa was of opinion that Neville should notify the police, but she refrained from pressing the matter since it was obvious that Neville was most reluctant to take that course.

"Poor old Neville!" she said to John. "To have his first love affair nipped in the bud like that."

"Then you think Isobel took those things?"

"What other solution is there? She left us hurriedly, and has remained silent ever since. I think Neville knows she is guilty, but can't bring himself to accept it. If he really believed in her innocence he would have gone to the police."

"If he loved her you can't blame him."

"Perhaps not. But I hate to think she got away with it. I hate to think that she has caused Neville so much unhappiness."

John nodded, for his own feelings were similar. Outwardly Neville was putting up a show, but it was not at all convincing. If one caught him unawares he invariably seemed to be sunk in a brown study. Then, one morning, a curious thing happened. Neville was looking at one of the cheaper daily newspapers brought in by the daily 'help'. Suddenly he came upon a fashion drawing, which caused him to draw in his breath with a hissing sound. He knew that drawing — the bold charcoal lines and the initials I.L. It had been among the bundle of drawings which Isobel had taken from her old home. It signified that she had sold at least one of them, and was fulfilling her desire to be a fashion artist. He said nothing to Teresa or John about this, but later in the day he pronounced his intention of going up to London on the afternoon train.

"Oh, have you heard from the solicitors?" asked Teresa.

"No, but I propose calling on them. In any case it's a ghastly trip to do in one day, so I shall stay the night, see the solicitor first thing in the morning, and return to-morrow evening. I hope you don't mind, John."

"Of course not," replied John. "But oughtn't I to come with you? I feel I've rather oustayed — "

"Rubbish! You haven't seen anything yet. Stay at least until the end of the week. Talk to him, Teresa."

"He ought to know he can stay as long as he can — unless he gets bored."

"Bored!" ejaculated John. "This is the most marvellous spot on earth."

"Then that settles it," said Teresa. "Where will you stay, Neville, in case I want to get in touch with you?"

"The Tivoli. It's nice and quiet there. But I'd better ring up first and see if they have a room."

The call was made and Neville was successful in booking a room. At two o'clock he was in the fast train, and by half-past six he was in London. There the weather conditions were very different. It was raining hard and the streets were running rivers. He joined the queue for taxis, deposited his suitcase at the hotel, and then walked in the rain to a newspaper office in Fleet Street. There he asked to see the editor, but was told that he was not available. The sub-editor was in his office but wished to know what was the business of the caller.

"It's private, but rather important," said Neville. "Please tell him I won't keep him a minute or two, and that I'm not trying to sell him anything. It concerns one of his contributors."

There was some delay, but finally he was conducted up to an office on the fourth floor, amid the smell of printer's ink. There he found a youngish man busy with proof, and smoking furiously.

"What can I do for you, Mr. Brandon?" he asked.

"It's about Miss Larkin — one of your contributors."

"Oh, Miss Larkin — the fashion artist. What about her?"

"Can you possibly give me her address?"

"That's most unusual. If you wish to get in touch with Miss Larkin the correct procedure is to write to her here, and the letter will be forwarded."

"I know. But this is important. I particularly want to see her to-night, so a letter is not a bit of use. She's a friend of mine, and until recently she stayed with me and my sister — in Devon."

The young man made a mark with his pencil on a bit of proof, and then looked up.

"It would be breaking all the house rules," he said.

"What's a rule if it can't be broken — occasionally. Come, be human."

The young man went to a nest of

files and took out a card. He laid this face upwards on the end of the desk, and Neville saw that it bore Isobel's name, and an address. Swiftly he pencilled the address on the back of an envelope.

"Thanks a lot," he said.

"Remember — I didn't tell you."

"Of course you didn't. Good evening!"

A quarter of an hour later Neville stood outside a slim tall house in Bloomsbury, staring at the number through the drenching rain. This was the address beyond question, and at that moment the place looked most uninviting. He mounted a few steps and entered the doorway. Inside, on the wall, was a list of the occupants. Three of them were boldly painted, but the fourth had recently been painted out, and the otherwise blank space bore only a small card. On the card was Isobel's name — as occupant of the fourth-floor flat.

He mounted the stairs two at a time, and finally reached the fourth, and top, floor. Here there was a door, with a fanlight, and a card similar to the one he had seen downstairs. A little breathless, he pushed the bell button. There was silence for a few moments, and then he heard the noise of a latch, and the door slowly opened, revealing Isobel's head and shoulders.

"Oh!" she gasped.

"Forgive me," he pleaded. "I found out your address and couldn't resist the temptation to look you up."

From her expression he was quite unable to determine whether she was pleased or annoyed.

"You — you surprised me," she said. "Oh, do come into my garret. It's pretty grim, but all I could get."

He followed her into a combined bed-sitting room, which was divided by a pair of old curtains, not completely closed. Isobel drew them together as he took a seat. He saw that she had been working, for on a drawing board was an unfinished sketch in charcoal. The furniture was old and sparce, and the walls badly needed distemper. On the floor were three threadbare rugs, and on the right was a door.

"There's a small kitchen through there," said Isobel. "Just big enough to house the gas-stove, and a bath, which has a flap to serve as a table. For all this I pay three guineas a week — and lucky to have it, so I am informed. But how did you find me?"

"I saw one of your sketches in a newspaper. I recognised it as one which you brought from Barrowtor."

"And you went to the newspaper office?"

"Yes."

"Oh, they shouldn't have told you my address."

"I wasn't actually told it. In fact they refused to give it, but I found out."

"That was clever of you. All the same, I didn't — "

"You didn't want to see me?"

"That's not quite true. I've been very lonely since I came here, and you — you know I'm glad."

"You don't look very glad. Isobel, what's wrong?"

"Nothing — except that I had to come down to earth. I couldn't go on enjoying your hospitality. I simply had to make a start, and I've been lucky to get one of my sketches accepted, with the promise of further work."

"I congratulate you on that, but was it necessary for you to go as you did, without even a good-bye?"

"Yes. I ought to have gone before. Oh, please, please try to understand. I have to learn to stand on my own feet. You and Teresa were so good to me. I was in danger of taking the line of least resistance — of becoming a parasite. In time I hope to get out of this hovel, but one has to make a start."

"Of course. I admire you for that. But I've missed you terribly. Somehow things haven't been the same since you left."

"You're just trying to be nice. Bless you for that."

"I'm not trying to be nice. I'm just

telling you the truth."

"Neville."

"Yes."

"It's lovely seeing you to-night, but I'm sure it would be better if in future we went our separate ways."

"Why are they necessarily separate?"

"Because — because I'm a career girl. I want to make a name for myself, and that means hard work — "

"It surely doesn't mean hiding yourself from your friends?"

"It may. I don't know."

"Well, give up work for an hour or two and come out and have a meal."

"Why do you tempt me?"

"In order that you will fall. Come on, put on a mackintosh, and we'll find a place where there's music and bright lights. I'm starving, and I bet you haven't had a meal since lunch."

"That's true."

"Come on then."

Isobel seemed to brighten.

"Snatching a poor girl from her bread and butter," she complained.

"All right. Just give me a few minutes to tidy myself. Sorry I haven't any cigarettes. They're too expensive."

She went through the dividing curtains, and Neville lighted a cigarette, and picked up the drawing-board. He was admiring the bold lines of Isobel's unfinished sketch when the door-bell rang.

"I'll go," said Isobel, from behind the curtain.

After a few moments she appeared, with her hair down, and a dressing-gown over her shoulders.

"I expect it's my neighbour from downstairs," she said. "She's a lonely soul and likes a gossip. But this time she is going to be disappointed."

Neville heard the door open, and then there came a kind of strangled gasp. He laid down the drawing-board.

"Get out!" cried Isobel angrily. "How dare you — ?"

"Take it easy, honey," said a thick male voice. "No need to get sore. Come on, now!"

There came a sound like a sharp scuffle, and a sharp cry of pain. Neville rose to his feet and almost leapt into the small passage. There he saw a wild-eyed fellow clutching Isobel by the arm and almost dragging her towards the sitting-room. The girl's face was livid with pain and rage. The man's gaze switched from his prisoner to Neville.

"Who the hell are you?" he snapped.

Neville felt his gorge rise.

"Take your hands off her, or I'll take them off for you," he said.

"Oh, you would, eh?"

Neville took a step forward, but stopped dead at the sight of Isobel's convulsed face. Clearly she wished to prevent any active intervention on his part. Suddenly she shook her arm free.

"It's — all right, Neville," she gasped.

"I'll say it's all right," growled the man. "Who is he anyway, and what is he doing in your flat?"

Isobel paid no attention to him.

Rubbing her arm, she stared into Neville's face.

"He's my — my husband," she said.

Neville took this almost knock-out blow like a trained warrior.

"I see," he muttered. "I never dreamed you were married."

"Well, now you know," said the husband. "So you can beat it, and the sooner the better."

Neville looked at Isobel.

"Is that what you want?" he asked.

She hesitated and then shook her head.

"It's what I want," said the husband. "I'll go inside and wait while you get rid of him. Then I've a few things to say."

He passed Neville and vanished through the doorway, closing the door behind him.

"I'm sorry about all this," said Neville. "Why did you keep it from me?"

"Because I was ashamed to tell you. He was the reason why I ran away

191

from home. My father hated him, and refused to consent to our marriage. I had to choose between my father and Roger Algood, and I chose wrongly. He turned out to be all my father said he was. After two years of terrible unhappiness I left him — in Ireland. I came to Plymouth on a cattle boat."

"What are you going to do now?"

"I don't know. I can't think — at the moment, but one thing I do know. I will never go back to him. That is what he wants me to do."

"Would you rather I left you together?"

"No. Please don't go, Neville — not yet."

Neville found himself in a dilemma. He tried to think what the legal position was. Had the husband some legal right there, or could he be forcibly ejected like any other intruder on premises rented, and paid for, by his wife? In the few seconds available to him he was quite unable to arrive at a decision.

"All right," he said. "Let's go and join him."

They entered the sitting-room, and there they found the intruder lighting a cigarette. He still wore his hat, and he glared to observe that his wife was not alone.

"I think I told you I had something to say to you," he said to Isobel.

"You can say it while Mr. Brandon is present," she said.

"Damn Mr. Brandon! What is he doing here, anyway? Perhaps he intended to stay here?"

"Keep your insults to yourself," said Neville. "Or I may feel disposed to kick you down the stairs."

"I should advise you not to try," snarled the husband. "It's you who may be kicked out with impunity, so watch your step. I'm here, and I mean to stay here until my wife is ready to come home with me."

"I'll never do that," said Isobel. "You're a drunkard and a brute, and when I left you I told you it was for good."

"And I told you that I wouldn't

stand for it — that I'd follow you to the end of the earth if need be. I didn't have to do that, but you've led me a nice dance, and now that I have found you I don't intend to lose sight of you again. So tell your boy-friend to beat it, and then we can talk business."

"The boy-friend has no intention of beating it," snapped Neville, aggravated by the insulting reference. "He has a few questions to ask you. Did you ring up Isobel at my home?"

"I did. Any objection?"

"Many objections." He turned to Isobel. "Did he ring you up on the night before you left Fouracres?"

"Y-yes," replied Isobel. "I didn't know you knew."

"Is that why you left in such a hurry?"

"Yes. He told me that unless I met him early the next morning he would come to the house and make a scene. I — I wanted to prevent that."

"So you met him?"

"Yes. I got on the train with him, but at Exeter I managed to get away."

"So when he telephoned that last evening he was close at hand?"

"Yes — in Teignmouth."

"I see," said Neville thoughtfully. "Yes, I think that explains quite a lot."

The remark seemed to have a significance which missed Isobel, but the husband's mouth moved curiously as Neville's eyes became focused on his face.

"I've had enough of this," he said. "Are you going to get out?"

"I am not. It is you who is going to get out."

"Think you can throw me out, eh?"

"I think I could, but I'm not even going to try. Why should I bother when a policeman can do the job better."

"Neville!" cried Isobel.

"I know what I'm doing. Is there a telephone here?"

"Downstairs — in Mrs. Titterman's flat. But you can't — "

"He's mad," said the husband.

"But not blind," snapped Neville, moving towards the door. "If I call a policeman it will be to arrest you for robbery."

Isobel stared at him in astonishment, but Algood looked not so amazed.

"I told you he was crazy," he said. "He doesn't know what he's saying."

"I know quite well what I'm saying, and so do you. Isobel, would you feel safer if this man were in jail?"

"Yes. Oh no — no. I only want him to go — and never come near me again."

"There is no guarantee that he will leave you alone — short of iron bars."

"But I don't understand," pleaded Isobel. "What has he done that you can send him to prison?"

"When we came into the room he was taking a cigarette from a small cigarette-case. That case was stolen from Fouracres the night — or day — before you left. It belongs to my sister. A gold watch went at the same time. I think I saw it just now — well up on his left wrist."

"I saw a watch — when — when he gripped me," stammered Isobel.

"I am certain he visited the house while we were on that boat trip. He could have climbed in through the window on the half-landing. He got safely away and later he telephoned you."

"That's a damned lie!" shouted Algood.

"Then show me that case — and the watch."

"I'll see you in hell first," raved Algood. Then he stooped and picked up a fairly heavy poker.

"Neville!" cried Isobel in alarm.

The infuriated husband came at him in a mad rush. In a flash Neville picked up the stout chair in front of him, and took the poker blow on the seat of it. Then he drove forward with his improvised shield and pinned Algood against the wall. Three legs of the chair came flush against the wall, but the fourth pressed hard into Algood's stomach. He tried to aim another blow, but now all Neville's thirteen stone was behind the chair, and Algood's eyes rolled in agony. The poker fell from his nerveless grasp, and Isobel picked it up and laid it on the table near Neville.

"Careful!" she gasped. "You're killing him."

"He'll eventually die much more violently."

After a few moments the intense pressure was relaxed and Algood slid to the floor. Neville put the chair down, and within ten seconds was in possession of the cigarette-case and the watch.

"Do you recognise these?" he asked Isobel.

"Yes," she panted. "Oh, but I didn't know."

"I know you didn't." He took the poker from the table. "All right, Mr. Algood, you can get up."

Algood struggled to his feet, moaning

and breathing hard.

"I'll — get you for this," he grunted.

"Shall I call the police?" asked Neville.

Isobel shook her head, with tears gathering in her eyes.

"Then get out — and get out quick," he said to Algood. "If you come here again I'll give you in charge."

The crestfallen man staggered to the door, where he halted for a moment to indulge in a spate of obscene language. Then he slammed the door with a noise which shook the whole house, and Neville uttered a sigh of deep relief.

"Lucky spotting that cigarette-case," he said. "But for that I shouldn't have noticed the watch. Oh come, dry those tears. It isn't your fault that he's what he is."

"It's humiliating," she said, as she dried her eyes. "What am I to do now?"

"Carry out our programme, which he so rudely interrupted. Get into that frock."

"Do you really want that?" she asked.

"Of course. You'll feel better when you've had a decent meal."

"All right. I won't be long."

Neville sat and pondered over the unexpected happening. At last he was able to understand Isobel's queer behaviour — her frequent changes from gaiety to gloom, her reluctance to talk about the immediate past, and her elusiveness whenever he had attempted to cross the line of mere friendship. It was a heavy blow to his hopes and ambitions, but at the moment at least his sympathy outweighed his personal disappointment. At last came Isobel, looking attractive in a frock which he had not seen before. Her face was a trifle pale, but her eyes were bright and as alluring as ever.

"Ready now," she said.

"Where shall we go? Any preferences?"

"None. I am a stranger to London."

"I don't think we could do better than my hotel. It has a restaurant and I know the ropes there. There's music too, which is rare in London these days."

"I'm in your hands."

"Come on then."

They were lucky in getting a taxi almost outside the house, and within ten minutes they were in the restaurant of the Tivoli. Albert — the head waiter — recognised Neville immediately, and came forward to give him personal attention. He found them a table in an alcove, from which the small string orchestra was visible, but where privacy was almost complete.

"I think there's a message in the office for you, Mr. Brandon," he said. "I'll send the boy to get it."

"Thank you."

"This is lovely," said Isobel. "I like the lighting and the colour scheme. How did you find it?"

"Oh, I've known it for years — before the war, when I was very young and adventurous. Albert has been here all the time. He's Swiss, and what he doesn't know about head-waiting isn't worth knowing. I've left the food to him, because he is infallible, and I rather fancy we shall fare better than some."

"Is that the terrible thing known as favour?"

"Special attention reserved for old customers."

Isobel soon found that Albert was as reliable as his reputation. The excellent soup was followed by breast of chicken in casserole, and with this came the message mentioned by Albert. It was scribbled on a page from a telephone message pad. It proved to be a request from Mr. Winslow for Neville to ring him up as soon as possible, at his private address.

"He's the solicitor to the estate," said Neville. "It may be that he has some news. I expect Teresa told him I was staying here. Well, he'll have to wait until my inner man is satisfied."

It was between the ice and the coffee that Neville begged to be excused and went to the telephone box. He was absent only a very short time, and then came back to find Albert serving the coffee.

"I hope the dinner was to your liking, Mr. Brandon?" said Albert.

"Very much so. Albert, you're a wizard."

Albert smiled in his quiet way, and vanished.

"Well, things are moving at last," said Neville. "Winslow has heard from Berenice Waters — or rather Mrs. Tamling, as she now is. She will be at Winslow's office at ten o'clock to-morrow morning. It's as well I happen to be in town."

"I wonder what she's like?" mused Isobel.

"So do I."

"But you've seen her, haven't you?"

"Only once, and that was in the evening, years ago, and in a bad light."

Isobel was silent for a few moments, as she stirred her coffee.

"Was he in love with her?" she asked.

Neville shook his head emphatically. "Then what made him leave her the estate?"

"A foolish whim. It was the last night of our embarkation leave, and we had had a few drinks. He seemed to have an intuition that he would never come back. You have to remember that at that moment he had no idea that his father would die and leave him everything."

Isobel's wide eyes disturbed his simulated calm.

"I won't lie to you," he said. "She was no good. I'd give my right arm to undo that will, but I don't think it can be done. It is a fact that the intention of the testator must be taken into consideration when interpreting a will. Phil's intention doubtless was to leave her what possessions he had. It might be argued that he did not know that his father would make a new will in his favour, and that a great sum of money was at stake. On the other hand, the defence might put in a plea that he could not possibly know that his father would disinherit him, and that it was his intention that the woman should get everything that had accrued to him at the time of his death. I propose to go into that with Mr. Winslow."

"You're thinking of me, aren't you?" asked Isobel.

"Of course."

"You needn't. One thing is certain — my father intended that I should get nothing. I'm content to abide by his wishes. He gave me a choice and I chose. What have I to quarrel about?"

"A great deal. You made a mistake, but thousands of women have made similar mistakes. It's a rotten thing that — "

"Please, Neville!"

"All right. But would you like to see the prospective owner of Barrowtor?"

Isobel hesitated for a moment.

"Could I?" she asked.

"I don't see why not. Shall we call it a date?"

"Yes."

"I'll call for you, at about a quarter to ten."

They were silenced by the orchestra, which commenced to play the Peer Gynt suite. Neville strove to give the excellent music his rapt attention, but from time to time his glance went to Isobel's face. In the soft lighting he found much there to entrance him, and he wished more than ever that he had not to keep the appointment on the following morning with the lucky but unworthy claimant to the Larkin estate.

11

AT a few minutes before the appointed time Neville and Isobel arrived at Winslow's office and were forthwith conducted into his presence.

"This is Miss Larkin," said Neville, introducing Isobel. "Possibly you remember her?"

"Why, yes — I think I do," said Winslow, shaking hands. "But you have grown up a bit since then. It must have been ten years ago since I was at Barrowtor."

"Just ten years. But you haven't changed a bit," said Isobel.

"Perhaps not to outward view, but I feel those ten years very much."

"Miss Larkin would like to see the claimant," explained Neville. "Have you any objection?"

"Not the least. I heard from her

yesterday afternoon — over the telephone. Apparently she did not see the advertisement for some days. Her attention was drawn to it by a friend. Over the telephone she sounded just a little — common."

"I think you'll find her common enough," said Neville.

"I begged her to be punctual, so she should be here at — "

He stopped as the buzzer sounded on his desk, and picked up the receiver.

"Mrs. Tamling?" he said. "Oh yes, show her in."

The claimant entered the room a few moments later, and the two men rose. Winslow welcomed her with a word and a smile, and then introduced Neville and Isobel. She uttered a husky "pleased to meet you" and then made herself comfortable in the chair which Winslow provided. Neville's mind flashed back over the years — to that fateful evening when he had set eyes on Berenice Waters. He had but the vaguest memory of the yellow hair and the straight nose, and rather close-set greenish eyes, but he had no doubt this was the same woman.

"Now, Mrs. Tamling," said Winslow. "What was your maiden name?"

"Berenice Waters."

"Where were you born and on what date?"

"I was born at Banner Street, Reading, on April the twelfth, 1918."

"What was your mother's maiden name?"

"Cadding — Emily Cadding."

"When did you first meet Mr. Larkin?"

"I can't quite remember. It was some time in 1941, I think."

"Did you see much of him?"

"No — only a few times."

"Do you remember the last time you saw him?"

"Yes. It was then he told me he was going abroad."

"Do you remember Mr. Brandon?"

The woman stared at Neville for quite a few moments.

"He seems familiar like," she said. "But I can't say that I remember seeing him in any partic'lar place."

"Did Mr. Larkin lead you to expect that he was going to name you as beneficiary under his will?"

"He said something about it, but I thought he was kiddin' — I mean I thought he was having a joke."

"Can't you remember the circumstances of your last meeting with him — where it took place?"

"No, I can't. I've had a lot of trouble since then."

"What sort of trouble?"

"I got married a year or so afterwards, and it was a bit of a wash-out as you might say. I ran away from him, and haven't seen him since."

The statement that she had seen Larkin a number of times was not in accord with Neville's information, but he suspected that she made that claim to cover up the unpleasant facts. Notwithstanding, he felt he must say something.

"Mrs. Tamling," he said. "I was with Mr. Larkin on the one and only occasion when you met him."

"Oh!" she gasped.

"Do you still maintain that you met him a number of times?"

"Yes," she said. "If he told you that was the first time he had seen me, it was a lie."

Neville shrugged his shoulders, and gave way to Winslow.

"When were you married?" asked Winslow.

"May the 24th, 1943."

"Where?"

"Paddington Registry Office."

"Where did you live after the marriage?"

"At Kew — a bungalow in Rylands Road."

"What was the name of the bungalow — or number?"

"I don't think it had a number. It was called Moonstone."

"Have you your marriage certificate?"

"No. I tried to find it, but couldn't.

I don't know what has become of it."

"Mr. Tamling has it," put in Neville. "He showed it to me."

"We shall need to have that," said Winslow, "and a copy of your birth certificate. Do you know where your husband is living now?"

"I think he is at the house where I had a flat before I was married."

"Have you communicated with him since yesterday?"

"No. I don't want to see him."

"But he will be necessary for identification purposes. Who else is there who can identify you?"

"There's a Mr. and Mrs. Toller who knew me before I was married. They had a flat in the same house at No. 27 Glass Street. I don't know if they are there now."

"What about other relatives?"

"I haven't any. I was an only child and was left an orphan at an early age."

"I have no reason to doubt that you are the person named in Mr.

Larkin's will," said Winslow. "But you will appreciate that the matter of identification is very important. I think the first step is to get your husband and Mr. and Mrs. Toller here. I shall also need the marriage certificate and a copy of your birth certificate. Will you see your husband personally, or would you rather I got into communication with him."

"Oh, you, please. I don't want to have anything more to do with him. He treated me shocking."

"Have you anywhere to stay in London?" asked Winslow.

"Not yet. I came straight here from the station."

"Well, please let me know where you are staying so that I can get in touch with you — after I have contacted your husband and the Tollers."

"I will. Oh, about the will — is there much money to come to me?"

"A very considerable sum. You are a very lucky woman, Mrs. Tamling."

"You're telling me! Fancy him keeping his promise. Was — was he killed in the war?"

"Yes."

"Poor chap! He said he reckoned he wouldn't come back. How much did he leave?"

Winslow looked across at Neville, but Neville's face was like a sphinx.

"The estate should realise over ninety thousand pounds," said Winslow.

The claimant gulped, and her greedy eyes gleamed.

"That — that's a lot," she said.

"Yes, indeed. It includes a large house on Dartmoor. In due course you had better let Mr. Brandon know if you wish to keep the property. Oh, I should explain that Mr. Brandon is the executor under the will."

"You told me that over the telephone. What about Miss Larkin. Isn't she to — to get anything?"

Winslow shook his head slowly.

"Unfortunately, no," he said.

"Oh, but that's not fair. I don't

want to take all that money and leave her — "

"It's very kind of you, Mrs. Tamling," said Isobel in frigid tones. "I presume my brother knew what he was doing."

The claimant sniffed.

"All the same, if there's anything you want — " she commenced.

"The only thing I want is to know just what part you played in my brother's life," said Isobel. "I can't believe he was in love with you."

"Why not?" demanded the claimant.

"Because with all his faults he was a man of education and culture. Mr. Brandon said you only saw my brother once — "

"That's not true. Just what are you trying to make me out to be, eh?"

"There are several names for it."

"Please, please, ladies!" protested Winslow.

"She started it," said the claimant. "I was only trying to do the right thing."

"Yes, yes — of course. But you

must remember that Miss Larkin has suffered a very grievous loss. Oh, one thing more — I should like to have your signature, Mrs. Tamling. First your married name, and then your maiden name."

He produced a sheet of notepaper and a pen, and the claimant wrote her name very boldly and deliberately.

"Thank you," said Winslow. "I will now get in touch with your husband, and with Mr. and Mrs. Toller. Perhaps we can arrange an early meeting with a view to establishing identity. That, of course, is a mere routine matter. Mr. Brandon, I presume you will be available for a meeting to-morrow, or the next day?"

"Yes," replied Neville. "I am anxious to be rid of my responsibility."

"Very well then. I need not detain you any longer, Mrs. Tamling, but please let me know your address as soon as possible."

"Within an hour, I hope."

"Good!"

Mrs. Tamling rose, and after a nod at Neville and a glare at Isobel, she was shown out. Winslow came back to his seat.

"Did you recognise her?" he asked Neville.

"I think so. I certainly remember the yellow hair. Mr. Winslow, I presume that if she establishes her identity to our satisfaction, there are no grounds for contesting the will?"

"There are two possible grounds. One — that the testator was not in his right mind, and, two — that it was his intention only to leave the woman such property as he possessed in his own right, excluding property which he might inherit between the making of the will and the time of his death. As to the first, are you prepared to swear that he was not in his right mind at the time he signed that will?"

"No."

"Then that leaves us with the alternative, and I must say I don't think we could get away with it. But

I'll get a good opinion on that. Would you be prepared to contest the will on those grounds, provided opinion was favourable, Miss Larkin?"

"No," said Isobel.

Neville looked at her with surprise.

"Oh, come!" he begged. "That woman has no moral right to all that money."

"Nor have I," said Isobel. "One thing is perfectly clear. My father never wished me to have anything. Had he done so he would have made a different will. He forgave Phil, but not me. I wanted to see her, but not to get anything out of her, or to fight her in the High Court."

"In that case there would appear to be nothing we can do," sighed Winslow. "It's all very, very tragic and unsatisfactory."

A few minutes later Neville and Isobel were out in the street which was now flooded with sunshine. Isobel seemed to have no immediate plans in her mind, so they walked aimlessly towards Trafalgar Square, and from there crossed to the Admiralty Arch and entered the park. Near Buckingham Palace there were crowds of people — most of them obviously visitors.

"Come to see the changing of the guard," said Neville. "I remember being brought here as a boy by my father. Lord, what a kick I got out of it. Soldiers seemed such romantic figures then, but now I wouldn't care if I never saw another man in military uniform."

"The soldiers aren't to blame," said Isobel. "Your father died for his country, and so did Phil."

"Yes, but it's all wrong. The way to settle disputes is round a table. Fighting men and machines are anachronisms."

They did not stay to see the military spectacle, but passed through the crowds and back to Isobel's flat by devious ways.

"Now I must work," said Isobel. "Shall I see you again?"

"As often as you like, and it can't

be too often. It looks as if I shall have to stay in London for a few days, and London is a place in which one can be very lonely. You're worried, aren't you?"

"Just a little."

"About — your husband?"

Isobel winced.

"Don't call him that," she begged. "I want to try and persuade myself it never happened."

"Do you think he will worry you again?"

"Yes. When he sets his mind on a thing it isn't like him to let go. I can't think how he found me."

"Can't you get rid of him — divorce him?"

"I've no grounds — except cruelty."

"Has he ever ill-treated you — physically?"

"Yes."

"The swine! Isobel, I think I should have held him while he had those stolen articles in his possession, and then called in the police. Why not change your address?"

"Where could I go? You've no idea how difficult it is to find any place which I could afford."

"Why not come back to Devon? Teresa and I never wanted you to leave. It's different now because you have made a good business contact. You could draw just as well down there, and come to town when it was necessary."

Isobel shook her head after a short pause.

"You're a dear, Neville," she said. "But it wouldn't do."

"Why not?"

"It just wouldn't. If Algood pesters me again I shall go to the police, and ask them for their advice and help."

"Well, think it over," begged Neville.

"I will. At any rate, it is nice to know there is a place of refuge in case of dire necessity."

"I'll call round at about seven this evening."

Isobel nodded, and a few moments later Neville was striding towards his hotel. When he arrived there he was informed that a gentleman was waiting to see him in the lounge, and he was surprised to find it was Inspector Carson.

"Ah!" said Carson. "I got your address from your sister. We've made a move forward in the Larkin case — I should say the Barding murder."

"A clue?"

"We think we have traced some of the stolen property. Of course we circulated full details, and I got some help from Scotland Yard. It was their investigations which brought me up here. But I badly need Miss Larkin to identify the stuff we have located. Have you any idea where she is? Your sister thought you might have."

Neville opened his eyes at this remark. How on earth had Teresa arrived at such a conclusion? Was she psychic?

"Yes, I know where Miss Larkin is,"

he said. "In fact, I left her only a short while ago."

"Splendid! That should help matters a lot. The stuff we have traced is a bundle of old silver. The articles bear the initials J.S.L. Miss Larkin had added those initials to the items in the inventory. The stuff is at Scotland Yard at this moment. Where can I find her?"

"I'll take you to her," said Neville.

Isobel was found hard at work, and Neville apologised for the early interruption. Inspector Carson then explained the situation, and Isobel agreed to go with him to Scotland Yard.

"Does that include me?" asked Neville.

Carson concurred, and a few minutes later they were in the office of a C.I.D. official. He was introduced as Detective-Inspector Ransom and was a comparatively young man.

"Here are the articles," he said, producing a suitcase. "Seem to be a complete set of Georgian silver. Rather a handsome lot."

Isobel gave a little gasp as she took up a spoon and a fork, and examined the monogram.

"They're ours," she said.

"You are quite sure?"

"Oh yes. When I was living at home it was always my job to clean them."

"I think that's good enough. The man who received them is well-known to us as a fence."

"A what?" asked Isobel.

"A man who works with thieves and disposes of stolen property," explained Carson. "Is he still here, Ransom?"

"Yes. We brought enough pressure on him to induce him to tell us how he came by the silver. Half an hour ago we picked up the man who sold it to him. I think we'll have him in. It's possible you may know him, Miss Larkin."

He pushed a button, and a uniformed Sergeant entered the room.

"Oh, Groves," he said. "Bring in Harrington."

"Very good, sir."

"Do you know anything about Harrington?" asked Carson.

"Quite a lot. He operates on the black market, but usually with uncontrolled commodities. Hitherto he has not been involved in house-breaking so far as we know. I've been watching him for months. Actually I can put him away at any moment, but I've been hoping that he will lead me to a man who is known as Kubla Khan."

"A bit poetical, isn't it?" asked Carson.

"Yes. Rumour has it that he lives like Kubla Khan, and that half the black marketeers in London are in his service. Some are inclined to think he is a myth, but I don't take that view. If I could lay my hands on that man I could clean up a regular nest of these pests. This business may prove to be a windfall to me. Harrington is not the sort of man to relish the prospect of jail, and he may talk."

The detained man was brought in.

Neville expected to see a scowling ruffian of the criminal type, but instead Mr. Harrington was the best-dressed man in the room. His age might have been thirty, and he was of an athletic type, with curly hair and a ready smile. Up to that moment he had not been told why he was under arrest.

"Look in the suitcase, Harrington," said Ransom.

Harrington did so.

"Nice lot of silver," he said calmly.

"Yes. Stolen from a house on Dartmoor, and sold by you to Harry Letts. Do you admit that?"

"No. Letts is trying to make me a scapegoat. He's never liked me, and this is his idea of scoring off me."

Ransom shrugged his shoulders.

"What do you think we are?" he asked. "Listen, Harrington — what we know about you would fill a big book. It does in fact fill a big file. But up to now you have operated mostly within the law. This time is different. In the house from which that stuff was taken a man was killed. So this isn't really a matter of theft. It's murder."

"You know I don't believe in violence," he protested.

"I know nothing of the sort. But in any case you can be involved without having done the job yourself. This is a show-down, Harrington, and if you take my advice you'll tell me exactly how you came possessed of that silver."

Harrington's calmness seemed to be leaving him. Two little lines appeared in his forehead, and his throat moved convulsively. Ransom turned to Isobel.

"Do you know this man, Miss Larkin?" he asked.

"No."

"Of course she doesn't," said Harrington. "I've never seen her before in my life."

"Are you still going to deny that you sold the silver to Letts?" asked Ransom.

"No, I'm not."

"So you are getting some sense.

Where did you get it?"

"At the house you mentioned," blurted Harrington.

"How did you know the house was unoccupied?"

"I was tipped off."

"By whom?"

"That's neither here nor there. I admit I did the job. It sounded easy — and I took it on?"

"Alone?"

"No."

"Who was with you?"

"I can't tell you that."

"You must have had a large van?"

"I did."

"Where did you get the van?"

"It was provided for me. I picked it up in Exeter."

"Lying about the streets, I suppose?" said Ransom sarcastically.

"There was a man with it, but he was a stranger to me."

"Didn't he go with you to the house?"

"No. I went with my friend."

"Then either you or your friend must have killed the lodge-keeper."

"You're wrong. We never saw any lodge-keeper. We took all the stuff the van would hold, and got safely away."

"What then?"

"I left the van at the place where I picked it up. Then I and my pal caught the next train back to London."

"When you left the van, did you see the man who was with it when you took it over?"

"Yes. He gave me my cut."

"You mean this silver?"

"No. Hard cash."

"How much?"

"A hundred quid — out of which I had to pay my pal."

"Then how did you get the silver?"

"We hid it in our clothing. I reckoned a hundred quid wasn't much for a job like that, so I decided to make a bit on the side."

"What became of the rest of the booty?"

"Haven't an idea. I had my instructions and I carried them out."

"Who gave you those instructions?"

Harrington shrugged his shoulders.

"A nice story," sneered Ransom. "You don't know who the van belonged to. You don't know the man who paid you, and you can't tell me who planned the job. But a man was savagely murdered, and at the moment you're in a bad spot."

"I've told you the truth," said Harrington, with some emotion. "I've never slugged anyone. Not in my line. If you know so much about me, you ought to know that."

"I know a lot of things," said Ransom. "I know that you are associated with a man who calls himself Kubla Khan."

Harrington gave an involuntary start.

"Was it he who gave you that job to do?" asked Ransom.

"It might be, but I didn't get it from him."

"Someone who acts as his agent?"

"A letter was left for me at a certain place."

"Have you got that letter?"

"Not likely. I tore it up when I had read it."

"So it was Kubla Khan?"

"I said it might be. I've never seen him."

"Do you expect me to believe that?" asked Ransom scornfully.

"Have you ever met anyone who has seen Kubla Khan? He's just a planner. Nobody ever gets within three moves of him. If you put me on the rack I couldn't tell you any more. London's full of men who work for him, and mostly they don't even know it. They get their slice and are satisfied."

Ransom turned to Inspector Carson.

"Anything you want to ask him?" he said.

"Yes," replied Carson. "What sort of a van was it that was used?"

"Small furniture van. It had a Ford engine, and was painted green. No name anywhere."

"Did you see the number plate?"

"No. I was too keen to get the job done to worry about that."

"And you saw nobody at the house all the time you were there?"

"No one at all. When we swung in through the gate I switched off the engine, and the van went a good way on its momentum. I was warned to do that."

"How did you enter the house?"

"I broke a window on the ground floor, and then unlatched it and opened the front door. Everything went without a hitch."

"Yet a man was killed."

"I tell you I know nothing about that."

"And you refuse to tell us the name of the man who accompanied you?"

"I don't squeal," muttered Harrington. "At least leave me one small virtue."

Carson indicated that he had finished with the prisoner.

"All right," said Ransom. "You will be charged in the first place with larceny," he said to Harrington. "But I warn you that a more serious charge may follow."

Harrington was led away, and as soon as the door closed after him Carson turned to his colleague.

"Do you believe his story?" he asked.

"Partly. He may be speaking the truth about Kubla Khan. That fellow is a slippery customer. Well, Miss Larkin, at least you have got your silver back, although I can't hand it to you at the moment."

"It isn't mine," said Isobel.

Carson gave Ransom a sharp glance as if to indicate that that subject was a trifle painful.

"Well, Miss Larkin," he said, "I must thank you for coming here and identifying the silver. Shall I motor you back?"

"Thank you," she said, "but I think I would rather walk."

"As you wish."

A minute later Isobel and Neville were out on the street.

"Sorry I interrupted the great work," said Neville. "I suppose you want to go straight back to it?"

"Yes, I must. It's been very interesting. The first time I've ever seen a professional crook. I wonder if he really did kill poor old Barding?"

"I think the police know more than they are willing to tell. I'm sure that Carson has some sort of a clue, and that Harrington is in a tight corner. He certainly doesn't look like a murderer, but one can't go on looks. Ransom seems to be more interested in Kubla Khan. I suppose that's his particular pigeon. Who was Kubla Khan?"

"Don't you remember Coleridge's unfinished poem?"

"Can't say I do."

Isobel quoted:

In Xanadu did Kubla Khan
    A stately pleasure-dome decree;
Where Alph, the sacred river, ran
    Through caverns measureless to man

Down to a sunless sea.
So twice five miles of fertile
ground
With walls and towers were
girdled round:
And there were gardens bright
with sinuous rills
Where blossomed many an
incense-bearing tree;
And here were forests ancient as
the hills,
Enfolding sunny spots of greenery.

"What a memory!" exclaimed Neville.

"Not so wonderful, considering I once recited it at a children's party. You see, Coleridge was born at Ottery St. Mary, so we always considered him a local celebrity. Shame on you for your ignorance, being also a Devonian."

"I'm afraid poetry isn't my strong point — or wasn't. Tell me some more."

Isobel laughed — that ringing little peal that was such a joy to hear, perhaps because it was so infrequent.

"People would think I was mad if I recited poetry on the public highway," she protested. "But I should like to convert you to the ways of the muses."

Neville thought he was not averse to being converted by such a tutor — in some more private spot. A little later they parted, and he went on his way with the music of Coleridge in his ears, but on his face a somewhat dour expression as he remembered the existence of the man she had married.

12

FOUR days later Mr. Tamling walked briskly to the flat of his alleged wife. Things had gone exceedingly well in the interim, and he was elated to the skies. He and his accomplices had been to the office of Mr. Winslow and there had met the claimant to the Larkin estate. Suzy had played her part with commendable skill, exhibiting just the right amount of embarrassment at the sight of her 'husband' and joy at the reunion with Flo and Sid. Winslow had a copy of the birth certificate, and Tamling had brought with him the original marriage certificate. All three witnesses lost no time in identifying Suzy. Neville was present, but not Isobel. There were innumerable questions, all of which were answered apparently to the satisfaction of Winslow and Neville.

Yes, Mr. Tamling had cause to be elated.

When he rang the bell at Suzy's flat she came at once and let him in. Suzy was now wearing a new evening frock, and seemed to be conscious of her enhanced appeal. On the table in the sitting-room were some glasses and several bottles of drink.

"Where are the others?" she asked.

"They're coming along. It's that damned Flo — she's always late. Say, you're looking good."

"I feel good," said Suzy. "Things seem to be going all right, don't they?"

"Not so bad. I told you it would work out."

"So you did. You're a bright one, Gus."

"Damned good thing I thought of the signature. He must have checked up on that, or he wouldn't have asked for it. Let's have a drink now while we're waiting."

"Sound idea. Whisky?"

"Yep."

Suzy poured out the drinks, and lighted a cigarette.

"Mud in yer eye!" she said.

"Diamonds in yours," replied Gus. "You've done damn well, and I'm proud of you, old gal."

"Me of you too — you genius."

They drank in silence for a moment or two.

"When are we likely to handle the dough?" asked Suzy.

"Can't say. May be some time yet. These legal matters always take time. But there's one thing we've got to do."

"What's that?"

"Make it up. Patch up our quarrel."

"What quarrel?"

"The one they believed took place. It's natural enough in the circumstances. Next time you see that solicitor, or Brandon, just drop a hint that you're thinking of living with me again, then, if we're seen together it won't matter. Was that the bell?"

"Yes. You go."

Gus went to the door and found Sid and his wife there. Sid had an evening paper in his hand, and wore a curious expression.

"Come in," said Gus. "You're late — as usual."

"All Flo's fault. She took hours shoving stuff on her face."

"You could do with some stuff on yours," retorted Flo.

"Where's the heiress?"

"Don't be funny," retorted Gus. "Hey, Suzy — here they are!"

Suzy beamed at them as they entered, and got busy with the drinks. Flo's gaze went to the new frock.

"Smashing," she said. "I want one like that, Sid."

Sid made no response, but he accepted the drink from Suzy and then handed the newspaper to Gus.

"Seen that?" he asked. "Some scribbler got a scoop."

Gus took the newspaper, and stared at the large headlines in the centre column. 'War hero leaves large fortune to casual acquaintance.' There was a quarter column of letterpress, broken by a photograph of Suzy.

"What the bl — !" he commenced.

"What's wrong?" asked Suzy.

Gus shoved the newspaper at her.

"Look at that, you nit-wit!" he rasped.

"Oh, it's all about me," said Suzy. "I wonder where they got all that from?"

"Didn't I tell you not to talk to anyone?" raved Gus.

"Ease up!" snapped Suzy. "I haven't breathed a word to anyone."

"You didn't, eh?"

"No."

"Then how did they get this photograph of you?"

"I wouldn't know. Oh, yes I do. I was leaving that solicitor's office when a man with a camera stopped and looked at me. I didn't know he was taking a photograph. He didn't ask me anything."

"What's all this?" asked Flo. "Does it matter?"

"Matter? Of course it matters. This paper has a million circulation. Some-one might see it who knows Suzy, and might get suspicious. Why the hell didn't you turn your head away?"

"I didn't have time. Besides, how was I to know he was a Press reporter? Blame yourself for not warning me that someone might do that."

"That's right," said Sid. "Be fair, Gus. Them reporter chaps are pretty slick. It's clear this chap got the lowdown on the business from someone in that office, and saw a story in it."

"You're making mountains out of molehills," said Flo. "It isn't a very good photograph, anyway, and might easily be the real Mrs. Tamling. If you ask me, there's nothing to it. Fill this glass up again, Suzy. Too damn small by half."

★ ★ ★

It was on the morning following that Mr. Winslow received a most violent shock. He was opening his morning mail at his office when he came upon a letter which caused him to draw in his breath with a hiss. He read the epistle again, and then pushed the bell. His lady secretary entered the room.

"Oh, Miss Jones," he said. "Ask my brother to come in."

The junior partner joined him a few moments later, and found his elder brother looking distinctly agitated.

"Anything amiss?" he asked.

"Just a letter shoved in the letter-box — without a postage stamp. Run your eye over that."

His brother took the single sheet of notepaper and then felt in his pocket.

"Hang!" he said. "I must get my spectacles."

"Never mind. I'll read it. It says:

'The writer has reason to believe that the claimant to the estate of the late Mr. Larkin is not Miss Berenice Waters. Miss Waters had appendix operation 1926 – 7 at Royal County

Hospital, Reading. Suggest enquiries should be made.'"

The junior partner stared at his brother.

"Who is the writer?" he asked.

"No signature and no address."

"Hm! Do you think there is anything in it?"

"I rather wish there were, but for all we know the claimant may be able to show us a very nice surgical scar in exactly the right spot."

"She might, but it's not quite the sort of thing that you or I could ask her to do, much as you would doubtless enjoy it."

"Speak for yourself, Herbert. I think the first thing to do is to check up that statement by telephoning the hospital."

"Yes, I think you're right. Have we a telephone directory covering Reading?"

"I think we have."

"Then ask Ethel to look up the number and to ring the hospital. She'd better ask for the secretary, and then put him through to me."

A few minutes later Winslow was talking to the secretary. He was told that he would be rung back as soon as possible. There was a lapse of half an hour and then Winslow received an answer to his enquiry. It was that Berenice Waters had undergone an appendix operation on May 4th, 1926. She was then in her eighth year, and had stayed in the hospital for three weeks.

"So far, so good," said Winslow senior. "Mr. Brandon told me he was going home to-day, but now I think he had better come here. There may well be nothing in this, but it calls for investigation."

Neville was surprised to receive the request to go along to the solicitor's office. He was actually on the verge of leaving the hotel for the railway terminus, and Isobel had called to say good-bye.

"Something has happened," he said. "That was Winslow. He has received a mysterious letter which calls for immediate attention. It looks as if I am destined to be kept here indefinitely. One thing is certain — I shan't be able to catch the ten-thirty. Will you come with me and see what all the excitement is about?"

"If you would like me to."

On reaching the office Neville left Isobel outside, but Winslow caught a glimpse of her, and came to the door to greet her.

"No secrets from you, Miss Larkin," he said. "Do come in and take a seat."

When Isobel was seated, Winslow produced the letter and passed it to Neville.

"Good Lord!" ejaculated Neville. "Have you checked this?"

"Yes. It is true."

Neville handed the letter to Isobel, who quickly scanned the short message.

"Is there still a doubt, then?" she asked.

"That is inevitable in a case like this,

but I must confess that the claimant's answers to all questions have been satisfactory, as have the documents produced. All the same, this matter seems to call for additional proof. What do you think, Mr. Brandon?"

"I agree with you."

"The question is just how to tackle it."

"What about the police?" asked Neville.

Winslow was silent for a moment, and then shook his head.

"A bit too drastic," he said. "It isn't as if we knew the person who sent the letter. But anonymous letters are the curse of our profession, and one can only act on them with the greatest discretion. I think the best plan would be a frank admission of the receipt of this letter, and leave it to the lady to take the obvious step."

"You mean to submit to a physical examination?"

"Yes. Perhaps Miss Larkin would be willing to help us in that event?"

Isobel looked a little uneasy.

"I'll be honest," she said. "I don't like the woman."

"One can understand that," said Winslow. "But if she herself suggested that you should settle the matter to our satisfaction?"

"All right," replied Isobel. "I'll do that."

"Good. I'll get a message to the claimant, and try to get her here in an hour. I'm sorry, Mr. Brandon, if it delays your return to Devon, but it will save a lot of valuable time if we can get this matter sifted without delay."

"That's all right," said Neville. "I can catch the afternoon train. Miss Larkin and I will return in an hour."

"That's splendid. I shall hope to have her here by then."

Neville and Isobel filled in the time with a walk and a cup of coffee in a quiet little restaurant, and Neville was surprised to observe Isobel's reluctance to do what she had promised.

"Cheer up," he said. "It shouldn't

take a second or two. I know you hate her, but for all concerned it is better to get the matter settled. I deplore the whole business as deeply as you, and shall be glad to have it off my mind. I wish now I had never taken on the job. Why, why did Phil do so crazy a thing?"

"I don't mind her getting the cash. What hurts me is the thought of her living at Barrowtor — using the furniture and the things which I remember so well."

"She won't be able to use much of that, unless the police locate the stolen stuff. But my bet is that she will sell the house as soon as she gets possession. Can't imagine that sort of woman settling down to a country life. Well, it's time we got back to the office."

They found Winslow alone, but he said he was expecting the claimant at any moment, as it was already past the time agreed upon. Isobel and Neville were scarcely seated when the buzzer sounded.

"Mrs. Tamling?" said Winslow. "Yes, show her in."

A moment or two later the receptionist appeared at the door, and made way for the claimant. Behind her was Gus.

"Good morning," she said, smiling at Winslow. "I hope you don't mind my husband being present? You see, we — we have patched up our old quarrel."

Nods were exchanged and then the couple took two of the vacant seats. Winslow seemed a little embarrassed at the unexpected addition to the party, and was evidently wondering just how this ugly-looking fellow would react to the present situation. He played about with some documents, and finally produced the letter.

"Ah, here it is," he said. "I thought I had finished with the question of identity, but a point has cropped up, and I am hoping it is a matter which can be settled without delay. Mrs. Tamling, I want you to carry your mind back to the time when you lived at Reading. Would you say that you had good health in those days?"

"Yes — very good," said the claimant.

"Were you ever a patient in a hospital?"

Neville felt certain she was about to shake her head when Tamling took a hand in the business.

"There was that operation for appendicitis," he said, gazing at his alleged wife.

"Oh, that," she replied. "I thought you meant real illness. I soon got over that. I've never been ill since."

"I congratulate you," said Winslow. "I was compelled to ask you that question, because it came to my knowledge that you had undergone that particular operation. I presume you have no objection to settling that point?"

Suzy looked at Tamling for a lead.

"But it is settled," he said. "I don't quite get the hand of this. She's been identified by three different persons, including myself, and you have the marriage certificate, and a copy of the birth certificate. What more can there be?"

"Very little, I agree. But it would be very satisfactory to me and to the executor if your wife would consent to be examined."

Suzy gave a little gasp, and Tamling gave a fine exhibition of surprise and annoyance.

"This is preposterous," he shouted. "Are you suggesting that my wife should take off her clothes and display — "

"Really, Mr. Tamling, you are exaggerating the matter. Outside there is a ladies room, and Miss Larkin is willing — "

"She may be willing, but I'm not," said Gus. "My wife has provided every proof that any reasonable person could desire. I call this damned indecent. Berry, we'll get out of here, and I'll get some good advice — "

"Oh, Gus," pleaded Suzy. "Don't you think — ?"

"No, I don't. Come on!"

He stood up, and almost pulled Suzy to her feet.

"Wait!" said Neville. "This is ridiculous. What has been suggested is quite ordinary routine, especially in view of the fact that someone has written an anonymous letter. Your wife can give the lie to the innuendo contained in that letter in a very few moments. I personnaly shall be glad to discharge my duty as executor under the will, but this last bit of proof is essential."

"So you think," said Tamling. "I'm going to take the matter elsewhere. Good day to you!"

Suzy gave a little sigh as he escorted her to the door, and a few moments later the door closed with a resounding bang. Winslow looked at Neville.

"They're frauds," he said. "No sane person would risk losing a big fortune all because of a triviality. The person who sent that letter was right. There's only one thing to do, and that is to notify the police."

Neville bit his lip. He had rather wanted that unexpected sequel, but now he saw the whole matter being prolonged. Isobel looked bewildered.

"If the woman is not Tamling's wife, why should he say she is?" he asked.

"That's quite a nice point," replied Winslow.

"It is indeed," said Neville. "If Tamling is so sure his wife is not coming back he must have good grounds for it. Yes, I think this is where the police take a hand. I've met a Detective-Inspector Ransom in connection with the theft at Barrowtor. Shall I go and put the matter to him?"

"That might be a good idea," said Winslow. "You'd better take the anonymous letter with you, for he is almost sure to ask for it."

An hour later Neville was closeted with Inspector Ransom, having first taken Isobel back to her flat. Ransom listened attentively to what he had to say, making notes as Neville proceeded.

When Neville had finished, Ransom rang a bell and gave a clerk some instructions. Within a few minutes the clerk came back with a large file, in which was inserted a slip of paper to mark a place. Ransom opened the file and gave a little grunt.

"He's here," he said. "That's the fellow, isn't it?"

Neville gazed at the photograph of Augustus Tamling. With it were columns of details, and a set of fingerprints.

"That's the man," he said. "So he's been convicted?"

"Twice, and on both occasions for larceny. The first occasion was ten years ago when he served a sentence of twelve months. The second occasion was two years ago when he went to prison for a further twelve months. Ah, here's an interesting point. On the second occasion he was given away by his wife, and he was fully aware of the fact. Yet now we are asked to believe that he has had a reconciliation with her. That doesn't sound very convincing. I think we shall have to pick up the alleged Mrs. Tamling, also Tamling himself, and the two other persons who testified to the identity of the wife. I should like to retain this anonymous letter, since the writer may well prove to be a member of the gang who for some reason has decided to double-cross his associates. Where will you be staying this evening?"

"I had hoped to go back to Devon, but in the circumstances it looks as if I had better stay on. You can get in touch with me at the Tivoli Hotel."

"Good. You'll be hearing from me."

Neville heard sooner than he expected. He was having dinner at the hotel when a message was brought to him. He went into the lounge and found Ransom there.

"Sorry to interrupt your meal," he said. "I've got Tamling and his two associates — Toller and his wife. But the woman has vanished."

"Vanished!"

256

"Yes. Tamling had a nice story. When they got home his wife said she wasn't going to lose a fortune because of her husband's ridiculous attitude, and that she was going back to the solicitor's office to submit to the suggested examination. Of course she didn't go there. I've got men watching her flat, but I very much doubt if she will come back. The whole thing is a cooked-up story. Tamling saw he was in a mess, and that the best thing to do was get rid of the woman, to prevent our proving that she was a fraud. The Tollers naturally vouched for his lies. I'm holding them for a bit, but I can't do much until I can trace the woman."

"What a pity we let them go," said Neville.

"Yes. If you had telephoned me quietly it would have been a different matter. But here's an extraordinary coincidence. I had that letter examined for possible fingerprints. It bore several, but one of them — the best, because it came over the gummed part of the flap — was the fingerprint of the man I want most to meet — the man known as Kubla Khan. I already had a fingerprint of this man, and he left it in similar circumstances. What he did was quite clear. He obviously has a dislike for licking down envelopes, and when sealing them he wets his index finger and runs it along the gum. Naturally this leaves a small amount of wet gum on his finger, and in pressing down the flap this gum is transferred to the outside. He actually made the same blunder twice, which is astonishing in a man of his undoubted talent. So one thing is clear — the robbery and murder at Barrowtor, and this claim for the Larkin estate, are in some way connected. Kubla Khan stepped in at the psychological moment to double-cross Tamling and his alleged wife. I should like to know why."

"So should I," replied Neville. "I had imagined that my task was going to be a simple one, but it gets more and more complicated. Did you question Tamling about Kubla Khan?"

"Yes, and the others. They deny all knowledge of him, and of course still swear that the missing woman is Mrs. Tamling, née Berenice Waters."

"Then you can do nothing until you locate the woman?"

"I can put the fear of God into the Tollers, in the hope that they will squeal."

"They're not likely to do that with prison staring them in the face."

"I'm not so sure. I propose to introduce them to Mr. Harrington this evening. Somewhere there must be a link-up."

"Perhaps; but I'm tired of it all. Whatever happens, I must return to Devon in the morning."

"That's all right. But keep in touch with Inspector Carson, who has the case in hand at the Devon end."

Neville promised to do this. After his interrupted meal he tried to get in touch with Isobel, but found her flat locked up when he called. So he pushed a note under the door informing her that he was leaving on the ten-thirty train the next morning, and would meet her under the clock at the railway terminus at ten if she could manage it. He was under the clock at the appointed time, but Isobel was not there. He lingered until a few minutes before the train was due to leave, and then had to give up the hope of seeing her.

In the train he pondered her failure to meet him. It seemed to him that at least she had had time to telephone him at the hotel to tell him she could not keep the appointment. He could not help feeling that during the past few days Isobel had grown curiously unresponsive, and at moments had given him the impression that she wanted him to go. He did his best to view the matter from her point of view. She was married to a drunken thief who had made it quite clear that he would never give her the freedom she might desire. She was intent upon carving out a career for herself, which doubtless could be achieved more easily outside any domestic entanglement. Never had he believed that she would be willing to engage in any extra-marital set-up, but what of friendship? Did she feel in her heart that friendship was no acceptable alternative to the outlet of deeper passions, and for that reason resolved to pursue a solitary course? It looked very much like it.

As the fast train entered the greener country, his spirits began to rise. It was pleasant to see the lazy cattle in the fields, and to catch glimpses of lime-washed cottages and farmsteads, for in his blood was the deep love of the countryside — especially the English countryside, which was different from all others. Then his mind turned to Teresa and Wallace, left so long to their own devices. What had they been doing while he had been absent? There no doubt in his mind that Wallace was fascinated by Teresa, and he believed that Teresa was no less intrigued by the well-built, dependable young soldier. It pleased him to reflect that something might come of that mutual admiration.

13

THE sun was shining brilliantly as he crossed the ferry between Teignmouth and Shaldon. There was a full tide flowing in, and he turned his gaze up the lovely estuary towards the impressive Dartmoor hills. Never had they looked more beautiful nor more peaceful, and he let forth a little sigh of immense satisfaction to be home again in the land which he loved.

On landing, he waited at the garage for the hire car which was out on a trip, and finally he entered it and was driven up the narrow winding lane which led to Fouracres. As it entered the drive he saw Teresa and Wallace having tea on the lawn in front of the house. They waved their hands to him, and a few moments later he had dropped the suitcase in the porch and was drawing a garden chair up to the table on which was spread delicious strawberries and cream and sundry other attractive eatables.

"No fatted calf for you, my lad," said Teresa. "What on earth have you been doing in that sinful city? First you were coming, then you weren't. Then you were, and then you weren't. Now you barge in here without even a warning, just when we had given you up as lost."

"I wired you from Waterloo. Didn't you get it?"

"No. That was a waste of money. Telegrams take days."

"What a country!" He turned to Wallace. "Sorry, old man. It just couldn't be helped. All sorts of unexpected things happened. Oh, I've got something for you. This."

He drew Wallace's lost watch from his pocket and laid it on the table.

"Whew!" whistled Wallace. "Where did you get that?"

"You'd never guess. You too have

been remembered, Teresa. Here is your cigarette-case."

Teresa's question was written plainly in her eyes, but Neville shook his head.

"It's a long story," he said. "Give me some tea first."

Teresa passed him a cup of tea, gazing at him shrewdly.

"If it wasn't Isobel, who was it?" she asked.

"Her husband," he said, and drank half the tea before she recovered from her surprise.

"Are you serious, Neville?" asked Wallace.

"Most damnably serious. You see, I really went to London to see Isobel — just as you guessed, Teresa. I traced her through a sketch which she got published in a newspaper. I found her, and — oh well, you may as well have the whole story."

They listened attentively while he narrated what had happened during his absence. Half-way through, Teresa passed him another cup of tea without a word, and when he had finished there was a long silence, broken ultimately by Teresa.

"That seems to have nipped something in the bud," she said sympathetically.

"Yes. You were right about that, Teresa, but I didn't realise it at the time. The arrival of the husband was a nasty blow."

"I can't think why you didn't hold him and give him in charge," said Wallace. "It would have saved Isobel from being pestered."

"I wish I had."

"And what now?" asked Teresa.

"Heaven knows. The next move is with the police. Why, oh why, did I have this business thrust upon me?"

"Take my advice and hand it to the Public Trustee," said Teresa, "or you may have it hanging round your neck for ever."

Neville shook his head.

"There may yet be a chance of saving something for Isobel," he said.

266

"Suppose, for instance, that the real Mrs. Tamling is dead — "

"Then the estate would go to her husband."

"Not if she died before Phil Larkin."

"That's true," mused Wallace. "What an unholy mess he made of things. Even death didn't put an end to his nuisance value. No, I won't shut up, Neville. You were influenced by his devil-may-care disposition — his utter disregard for danger and death, but after you were knocked out I saw a great deal of him, and disliked him more than ever. I'm glad I was never friendly with him, because it saves me from any delusions."

"Who are we to judge him?" asked Neville. "Most of us have had our mad moments. At any rate he certainly didn't know there would be all this bother after his death. So let's leave him at rest."

"Suits me, old man," replied Wallace. "Anyway, I'm grateful to you for the recovery of my watch."

"Forget it," said Neville. "And what have you two been doing during my absence?"

"Eating and washing up, and looking for the ideal farm," replied Wallace, with a laugh. "We found it too, didn't we, dear?"

The endearment slipped from his lips before he could stop it, and Teresa's wide eyes reproved him.

"Dear it was — damned dear," he stammered. "Just a matter of fifteen thousand quid."

Neville tittered and then laughed out loud.

"You really can't get away with that," he said, and then seized Teresa's hand. "What have you been wearing on that finger to cause that impression?" he asked. "You must have taken it off when you saw me arrive. Confess, you cheats."

"You win," sighed Teresa. "We meant to keep it secret — for a bit."

"All your fault, Nev," said Wallace. "You left me here alone for days with quite the nicest girl in the world, and what more could I do than prove that my intentions were, in the words of the poet, strictly honourable? Are you very annoyed?"

Neville's reply was to grip his friend's hand, and then to lean over the narrow table and kiss Teresa on the cheek.

"No news could be more welcome," he said. "It's a bit like losing on the swings and gaining on the roundabouts. When did all this happen?"

"Yesterday," replied Teresa.

"And how does it affect the farm idea?"

"Not at all. I only agreed to become engaged provided John would consent to work eighteen hours a day on a farm when he is free of the Army."

"When will that be, John?"

"Within a year, but of course I don't intend to put off marriage until then."

"The idea is that we shall be married on John's next leave," said Teresa. "After that I shall keep the farm warm for him."

"When you get it," Neville laughed.

"Oh, I'll get it. Somewhere there is just the thing I want, at a price I — or rather we — can pay. Neville, now that you know the awful truth, let's all run over to the Golf Hotel to-night and celebrate the occasion, for in two days John has to return to his unit."

"That's a date," said Neville. "But is there any more petrol left in the car?"

"No, but I've fixed that."

"How?"

"Never mind how. Now I'll have to clear up. John, you can come and give me a hand while Neville has a bath."

"Who said I needed a bath?" asked Neville.

"My eyes bear witness to the fact. The trains are filthy these days. Come on, lazybones."

The ensuing celebration was an unqualified success — just what Neville needed to chase away the last ragged edge of his gloom. Almost for the first time in his life he became mildly tipsy, and Teresa forgave him, feeling that she and Wallace were mainly responsible. When they were ready to leave for home Teresa took over the wheel.

"I'm certain you can see double," she said to Neville. "At any rate, I'm not taking any chances."

"Rot!" he protested. "I could drive this car through the eye of a needle. You two can spoon in the back while I — "

"We can spoon just as well in the front," said Wallace, "while you have a nap in the back."

"All right, but if you think I can't drink a couple of glasses of champagne without getting binged you're making a big mistake. I'll bet you lose the way."

The remark was made in jest, but actually it came true about half an hour later. Neville, in the back, awoke from a doze to find the car stationary, and Teresa and Wallace with their heads together over a road map.

"Hey, what's wrong?" he asked.

"We're off the road," replied Teresa.

"You can go to sleep again. We'll put the matter right."

Neville, with his head clearer, let loose a peal of laughter.

"Just what I said," he teased. "I'll get out and have a look round."

He got out into the cool sweet air, and realised that it was nearly dark. Overhead the stars were visible, and in the west there were the last lingering red bars of the sunset. But the road was lined by thick timber, and visibility was reduced to that narrow avenue.

"Heaven knows where you've got to," he complained. "I don't know this road at all. Didn't you take the left fork at the reservoir?"

"Did we?" asked Teresa of Wallace.

"I can't remember any reservoir."

"Well, have you passed any signpost recently?"

"Not for miles. I thought you knew this country well."

"What country?" asked Neville. "How do I know what you two have been doing while I was pleasantly dreaming.

You may have gone round in circles."

"We were talking," explained Teresa.

"I'll bet you were. Better drive on a bit and see if we strike a signpost."

He got back into the car and Teresa drove slowly forward. The road grew narrower and very pot-holey, and soon it was pitch dark.

"Look, there's a light," exclaimed Teresa.

"Where?" asked Wallace.

"Away on the left. Oh, it's gone now."

"Reverse a bit," said Neville. "We may be able to spot it again."

The car was reversed for about a hundred yards and then Teresa again saw the light. It shone through a gap in the timber and appeared to be about half a mile ahead of them, but slightly to their left.

"This road must lead to it," said Neville. "Unless we have missed a left turning."

"I'm sure we haven't passed any turning," protested Teresa.

"Then carry on — very slowly."

Teresa did this, and about a quarter of a mile further on they came upon a turning so narrow that Teresa hesitated to put the car into it.

"You wait here," said Wallace. "I'll go up there and see if I can spot the light again. Nev, the electric torch is in the door pocket near you, I think."

"I'll come with you," said Neville, as he handed Wallace the torch.

"No. You'd better stay with Teresa. I won't be a minute or two."

"I'll keep the headlights on and then you won't get lost," said Teresa.

Wallace got out of the car and walked up the lane. Suddenly it turned to the left, and he had recourse to the torch. The trees on either side formed a green tunnel, but after a few moments he found a wooden gate, and saw before him a lighted window, very high up, and what appeared to be a large building. He hurried back to the car.

"It's a house," he said. "I think we must be at the back entrance. I'm going up to find out just where we are. Back in a few minutes."

"All right," said Neville. "We'll have a cigarette."

Wallace soon found that he was right in his conjecture. The path inside the gate led him through a waste of garden, and to the rear part of a large house, built of the local stone, and evidently of great age. Part of the building was overgrown with creeper, and the wide stone terrace had grass growing between the paving stones. He passed round to the front and found there an elaborate portico with stone columns. Here there were no lights at all, and he feared that everyone was in bed, and that he would receive a chilly reception. Notwithstanding, he mounted the wide steps which led to the front door and pulled the old-fashioned bell chain. From inside he heard the clanging of a bell, and after a few moments a light appeared inside and illuminated the stained glass above the front door. Then the door itself opened, and a very old man in a short dark coat came to view.

"I'm sorry to bother you," said Wallace. "But I've lost my way and should be glad if you could put me on my road. I want to get to Shaldon. My car is in the narrow lane at the bottom of the garden, and I happened to see a light here."

"Shaldon," said the old man reflectively. "Can't say I know the place."

"It's across the Teign — opposite Teignmouth."

"Oh, yes. I remember now you mention it, but you must be a long way away, and I don't quite know how you get there. If you'll come inside I'll make enquiries."

He stood aside and Wallace entered a large hall, which was now lighted by a huge chandelier which was suspended from the ceiling. To the left was a broad staircase, and to the right a number of doors, one of which was open and led into a very long secondary hall.

"Do take a seat, sir," said the old man. "I'll be back in a few moments."

Wallace sat down on a long seat and cast his eyes around the place. At some time it must have been a most imposing entrance hall, but it now looked as if it was yet another victim of the war, and seemed to be crying out for attention. He got the impression that troops must have been quartered there, for there were signs of the awful chocolate paint which the Army invariably used while in requisitioned houses. From a distance he could hear the low murmur of voices which made weird echoes, and then from above him he heard a door slam. Higher up the stairs there appeared additional illumination, and then suddenly a figure appeared. It was that of a woman, and she came down to the half landing and made for a door. Wallace only saw her profile, for she did not turn her head in his direction, but that profile caused him to hold his breath, for it was exactly like the profile of Isobel Larkin. But that was not all. The dressing-gown which she was wearing was exactly like one he had seen at Fouracres, and that walk, and the way she held her shapely head — ! Before he could get his breath she had vanished through the door, and at the same time the old man returned — shuffling his way across the worn carpet.

"You seem to be on the wrong road," he said. "Where did you come from?"

"The Golf Hotel at Hartridge."

"Then you're miles out of your way. You should have turned right five miles back. That would bring you to the reservoir. From there it's twelve miles to Shaldon. You'll have to reverse your car, follow the lane for two miles, then the first left and the first right."

"First left, first right," repeated Wallace.

"That's right, sir."

"Well, I'm very much obliged."

"Not at all, sir. These roads are very tricky after dark. They haven't put all the sign boards back yet."

He went to the door with Wallace, and as they reached it Wallace turned his head for a moment, to gaze up at the half-landing. But he saw only the stairs and the closed door.

"Well, good night!" he said.

"Good night to you, sir. Glad to be of service."

In a few minutes he was back at the car, and in his absence Neville had taken the wheel.

"Hey!" he said.

"All right. Fresh as a lark now. What's the worst news?"

"Back two miles then the first left, and the first right. It will bring us to the reservoir which you mentioned. After that — "

"I know the road from there. You'd better get in the back with Teresa, and hide your two heads in shame."

Wallace obeyed the first part of this injunction, and found it rather nice to snuggle up against Teresa in the semi-darkness. For a minute or two there was dead silence except for the hum of the car engine, and then Teresa pushed her elbow into Wallace's side.

"Don't go to sleep," she said. "You'll probably have to get out soon to investigate signposts."

"I'm not going to sleep," protested Wallace. "I'm thinking."

"That must hurt a lot."

"It does. Do you remember a rather attractive dressing-gown which Isobel wore at Fouracres at times?"

"What on earth are you burbling about?" asked Teresa.

"A black dressing-gown with some fancy trimmings in gold."

"What about it? I'm not sure I like you dreaming about other girls' dressing-gowns."

"Then you do remember?"

Neville turned his head slightly.

"Did they give you anything to drink at that house?" he asked.

"You'll think they did — when you hear what happened. Nev, I'm absolutely certain I saw Isobel in that house."

The car gave a swerve as Neville's face came almost fully round.

"Steady!" cried Teresa. "You'll have us in the blessed ditch."

"My fault," said Wallace. "But it's true — or I'm crazy. I was sitting on a bench in the hall waiting for the butler to come back with information when she appeared. She had come from the first floor and was walking across the half-landing to a door. I only saw her sideface, but I'll swear it was she. She didn't appear to notice me, and in a few moments she had passed through the door."

Teresa was staring at him in the dim light that was shed by the illuminated panels of the dashboard, and Neville had brought the car down to a crawl. Wallace could now see the reflection of his face in the driving mirror. It was lined with incredulity.

"You must have been mistaken," he said.

"It's possible, but my sight is pretty good, and she had switched on a light before she came down. Then there's the dressing-gown — "

"Isn't it likely that a dressing-gown similar to Isobel's started that thought in your mind?" asked Teresa.

"No. That was secondary. It was her face — her profile — which struck me first, and her light brown hair was done in that sort of halo which Isobel favoured. Oh, I know it sounds crazy. That's why I didn't mention it at once. It gave me a shock, I can tell you."

"The odds against it are about ten million to one," said Teresa. "Who lives in that house anyway?"

"I don't know."

"What is it called?"

"That too I don't know. There was only a small wicket-gate the way I went, and it had no name on it. The main entrance must be on another road."

Neville shook his head as he got the

car into quicker action.

"It's too improbable," he said. "I rather think that we all had a drink too many at that hotel."

Wallace made no response, and in due course they came in sight of the reservoir, and from there it was an easy run home. Before they went to bed, Teresa made a pot of tea.

"Help to clear our heads a bit," she said.

"Mine doesn't need any clearing," replied Wallace. "I shall still continue to believe that the girl I saw was Isobel."

"Suppose I disillusion you?" asked Neville.

"How?"

"Isobel has no telephone in her flat, but there is one in the flat below. What was that woman's name — Mrs. Tit — something."

"Tittermouse?" suggested Teresa.

"Mighty near it. It was Titterman. We have a London Telephone Directory, and that should give her number. I'm going to convince you that you were dreaming."

He found the directory and turned over the pages of the last volume.

"Here we are," he said. "Mrs. Annie Titterman. There oughtn't to be much delay at this time of night."

"But, Neville, she won't thank you for waking her up — if she's asleep," protested Teresa.

"I'll be very apologetic."

He picked up the telephone receiver, asked for the number, and was told to hang on.

"No delay at all," he said. "Now, John, what's the betting I don't speak to Isobel herself?"

"I'm not a betting man."

"That air of certitude is vanishing."

"No, for once I'll indulge in a little depravity. I'll bet you five bob you don't speak to Isobel."

"Wait a moment. She might be out."

"You should have thought of that before. But is the bet on?"

"Yes."

A minute or two passed and then Neville was told by the operator that he was connected.

"Is that Mrs. Titterman?" he asked.

"Yes," said a clear voice. "Who is speaking?"

"My name is Neville Brandon, and I am a friend of your neighbour — Miss Larkin. I'm sorry to trouble you, but I should like very much to speak to Miss Larkin. Could you possibly get her down to the telephone?"

"I'm sorry," said Mrs. Titterman. "But Miss Larkin isn't at home. I think she went away yesterday. At any rate she hasn't been in all day. Actually I have only just been up to her flat to give her a parcel which the postman left with me this morning, because he couldn't get an answer. There is a bottle of milk still outside her door."

"I suppose you have no idea where she can have gone?"

"None at all. She didn't say a word

to me about going away. I presume she must have got some urgent message. Is there any message I can give her when she returns?"

"Oh no — thank you. Sorry to have troubled you."

Neville hung up the receiver and stared across at Teresa and Wallace.

"What — what did she say?" asked Teresa.

"Isobel apparently left the flat yesterday, since her morning milk is still outside her door. The postman too came with a parcel and was unable to deliver it. It's all rather extraordinary."

"I don't know," mused Teresa. "Isobel may have gone to stay with a friend. There's nothing extraordinary in that."

"No. But does the friend live in that house which John visited, and can it be her husband?"

"Why not? That may well be a solution. But how amazing for John to have hit upon that very place!"

"If Isobel went with her husband, it can only have been by force. He's a drunken sot — "

"But still her husband. Oh, Neville, let's forget all about it. Who knows what may have taken place? She may have changed her mind. There may have been a rehabilitation. You haven't drunk your tea."

Neville gulped down the almost cold tea, and then Wallace adroitly changed the conversation.

14

ON the following morning Wallace left for London, en route for Germany.

"Hope the old car will make it," he said. "My mother is staying at Bristol, so I shall go that way and say good-bye."

"Does she know about your engagement?" asked Neville.

"Not yet. That's my little surprise for her. When she gets back to town I want Teresa to call and see her. She's really a darling, and I feel sure Teresa will love her."

"The point is, will she love me?" asked Teresa.

"At least as much as I do. You will call, darling, won't you?"

"Yes — of course."

"Then — then all that remains is to say good-bye."

They said it in front of Neville, with a warm hug and an even warmer kiss. Neville noticed that Teresa now wore her ring and that her eyes were a little moist.

"Come — come back soon, John," she murmured.

"I will."

A grip of Neville's hand and he was gone, with his car sending out clouds of suffocating smoke. Neville took Teresa's arm and led her into the house.

"Oh dear," sighed Teresa. "Life is nothing but meetings and partings."

"And reunions," added Neville.

"You didn't think this would happen to me, did you?"

"I always hoped it would."

"How strange to remember that a few weeks ago I was quite certain I was destined to be a spinster for ever."

"Did that prospect appal you?"

"Just a little. You see, I've always wanted children. Now I hope I'll have dozens."

Neville laughed and then grew pensive. Teresa thought she knew the cause, but decided it was better not to mention it.

"That girl ought to be here," she said. "She just comes and goes as she thinks fit. I've a good mind to sack her and chance getting someone else."

"Raising her wages might be a better idea," said Neville. "She can get fifty jobs."

"But she had an increase of wages three months ago, and it didn't make any difference. That sounds like a car coming up the drive."

Neville peered through the window, and saw the car approaching. He knew it by the long radiator and mass of chromium.

"It's Inspector Carson," he said. "Probably on his way to Barrowtor. I'll go to the door."

By the time he reached the front door Inspector Carson was on the doorstep.

"Morning, Mr. Brandon!" he said

cheerfully. "Thought I'd drop in to tell you of some new developments. My colleagues at the Yard haven't wasted much time."

"I'm glad to hear that. What has happened?"

"They've got the woman — and her accomplices."

"Accomplices! Does that mean she is a fraud?"

"Absolutely. She couldn't produce a surgical scar, and under pressure she gave the whole show away. When they knew that she had squealed the Tollers also broke down. The woman's name is Susan Cameron, and she admits having lived with Tamling for a period. Tamling coached her in her impersonation — taught her how to forge his wife's signature, and put her in possession of all the details of his wife's past. The Tollers had to be given a rake-off because they knew the real wife and would be called upon to identify the substitute. It was a nice little plot, but it failed."

"It very nearly succeeded," said Neville. "But why did Tamling not try to find his real wife?"

"Thereby hangs a mystery. There is good reason to believe that Tamling knew that his wife was dead, and that suggests the possibility of murder. There are strong motives too, because it was Mrs. Tamling who got him sent to jail. Excavations are taking place at the bungalow at Kew where Tamling lived with his wife for a period. No one saw the wife after he left the bungalow, so far as we know."

"How ghastly!" ejaculated Teresa.

Carson nodded his head.

"What about the anonymous letter?" asked Neville. "Do any of the gang know who wrote that?"

"They swear they don't. We know it was written by the man who is known as Kubla Kahn, and Ransom used that information in the hope of drawing one of them into telling us where Kubla Khan can be found. But not a word was forthcoming. All of them denied having had anything to do with the fellow, and they all denied knowledge of Harrington. Harrington too swore they were strangers to him."

"What did Tamling say in his defence?"

"The only thing he could say. He swore his wife had run off with another man, and was in some foreign land. He didn't see why he should lose all that money because his wife couldn't be found. He thought, in fact, that she was dead, and that her death might never be proved in his lifetime. He was tempted and he fell."

"And now they're looking for her body — but not in any foreign land?"

"That's the size of it."

"Then actually it doesn't get you any closer to solving the mystery of Tom Barding's murder?"

"No. As I see it, the two things are not related."

Neville shook his head in his perplexity. If the two things were not closely related, how came it that Kubla

Khan sent the anonymous letter?

"Have you a clue to the murder of Barding?" he asked. "Or is that a question I shouldn't ask?"

"It is," said Carson. "But I'll be candid. There is a clue and it doesn't point to Harrington."

"But he admitted he had an assistant."

"Yes, and nothing will induce him to name him. I'm all for trying out a bluff — charging Harrington with murder. That might make him talk. But the Yard is a bit fussy about such things. Still, they may yet come to it. Is Miss Larkin here by any chance?"

"No. I think she is at her flat in London."

"She wasn't there this morning. Ransom tried to get her, but failed."

"Why should he want her?"

"I don't know. He telephoned me to tell me what had happened, and asked me if I knew where she was. I told him that if she wasn't at her flat I had no idea."

"That applies to me too," said

Neville. "But reverting to Tamling — and what you suspect. If he murdered his wife he will hang, of course?"

"Not much doubt about that."

"In that event, what becomes of the estate? Presuming it can be established that Larkin pre-deceased her?"

Carson stroked his long jaw reflectively. "The line of inheritance would appear to be Mrs. Tamling, then Tamling, and then heaven knows who. But I'm not well-informed in that matter. You and the solicitors will have to iron it out. Kind of unholy muck-up if you ask me."

"Unholy is right," agreed Neville. "Well, it's no use anticipating, for this business seems to take a delight in going its own way. What is happening at Barrowtor? You have the keys and — "

"I've a man living at the lodge. If you have cause to visit the house, he has instructions to admit you. But I'm on my way there now, if you feel like coming along."

But Neville declined the invitation, and a minute or two later the Inspector left. Teresa, who had listened to the conversation, looked at her brother.

"Why didn't you tell him about the house where John called last night?" she asked.

"Because I have yet to prove that John was mistaken."

"How do you propose to do that?"

"By calling there in person."

Teresa expressed her surprise with a lift of her eyelids.

"Is that wise?" she asked.

"One can be too wise — or cautious. If Isobel is really in that house, it suggests dirty work."

"On the part of her husband?"

"Yes. The last thing he said was that he would never leave her alone. I am convinced she did not go there voluntarily."

"Are you trying to tell me that he kidnapped her in London and brought her all the way to Devon against her will?"

"Why not?"

"Because, short of drugging her, he couldn't do it."

"I'm inclined to agree. You haven't met the man she married, and I have. I believe him to be capable of any villainy."

"But, Neville, when John saw the woman he believed to be Isobel she was moving freely about the house. Doesn't that upset your theory a little?"

It did, but at the moment he was not prepared to admit it. All night that strange story of Wallace's had surged through his brain, and it had gained credence by the result of the telephone call.

"I'm not leaving anything to chance," he said. "At any rate I propose to have a look at the house, in broad daylight, even if I refrain from calling."

"I think you're mad," said Teresa.

"Because I happen to care what becomes of Isobel?"

Teresa met his gaze and then repented.

"I'm sorry," she said. "One thing I had overlooked — the most important thing. You're deeply in love with her, aren't you?"

"Yes."

"Despite the husband?"

"Damn the husband! She herself would not have me call him that. She admitted that he had beaten her, and swore that she would never go back to him. Why should we consider him? What rights has he now over her? He has forfeited every right the law ever gave him."

"But, Neville, has she ever given you real encouragement?"

This was a poser.

"Yes," he said slowly, as if the words were being dragged from him. "But not in so many words. But what are words?"

"A great deal — sometimes. She may have cause to hate her husband, but that doesn't mean that she would welcome interference."

"No more, Teresa," he begged. "My

298

mind is made up."

"In that case, I'll stop carping. When will you go?"

"Almost at once. I want to look up the road on the large-scale map."

A little later he did this. Knowing the route to the reservoir on the high moorland, it was a simple matter to trace the two turnings which they had taken, and to estimate the mileage. The map showed a property just at the right spot, and he found that there was a secondary road to the south of it. Against the small black square which represented the house there was the word 'Overlands'.

"This is quite obviously the place," he said to Teresa. "That's where we stopped the car, and that's the narrow track up which John went. But the main entrance is on another road. Just on the eight hundred foot contour and well-wooded. About the highest point in the neighbourhood."

"Yes, that's it," agreed Teresa. "Shall you be back for lunch?"

"Probably, but don't wait for me."

Neville went to his bedroom to put on a tie, and ten minutes later he was on his way. It was a mile short of the reservoir that he found the road which led to the south side of the house, and he decided to take that in preference to the tortuous lane which they had previously traversed. It led him to the delectable village of Presting, and here he stopped the car to buy some cigarettes at a small shop.

"Is there a house near here called Overlands?" he asked the wind-tanned old man who kept the shop.

"Aye, zur. It be up over. Two mile or more from yere."

"Can I see it from the road?"

"Used to be able to when I was a lad, but not now. The trees have grown so tall. Them were young plantations then, planted by Sir Robert Dykes. Now it's a proper forest."

"Does Sir Robert Dykes still live there?"

"Not he. He died forty year ago.

300

His son went on living there until the war came. Then he joined up and was killed. The Army had it for a bit, but when the war was all over they left, and the property was put up for sale. Nobody wanted it — proper white elephant it were. Who'd want a house with twenty bedrooms these days, and where would you get the servants? Mr. Western, the agent, told me he couldn't give it away, but at last he managed to find a buyer. He was an ex-Naval officer — a sick man who thought the good air might help him get better. I've never seen him, but Postie says his name is Captain Cardinal and that he is nearly always in a wheel chair. It's lovely enough up there in summer, but in winter there's a wind strong enough to blow you off your feet. Are you making a call there, sir?"

"I may," said Neville. "I once knew someone who was a servant there."

"Not many servants there now I should say. I was going to warn you if you was minded to call."

"Warn me?"

"About the dogs. The Captain keeps dogs — several fierce Alsatians, and they bain't always tied up. Postie was nearly bitten once and he told the Captain that if he didn't keep the dogs tied up he wouldn't deliver any more letters. The Captain said he would see to it, but he didn't, and so Postie only delivers as far as the lodge. I don't blame him either."

Neville laughed and took his change from the pound note which he had tendered.

"I happen to like dogs," he said. "So perhaps they'll treat me kindly."

"Not them. They ain't dogs — but wolves, so Postie says. Good morning to you, zur!"

"Good morning! Shall I see the lodge?"

"Aye. On the left from here. But the house is about a quarter of a mile up the avenue."

Neville went back to the car and

was soon moving again. The road went winding through the timber, and about two miles further on he found a road on his left marked 'Private'. A hundred yards up this was a lodge built of granite, and a pair of immense wrought-iron gates adjacent. The gates were open, giving access to a broad avenue, lined with immense elms. Here the land rose steeply and the avenue appeared to go round in a wide bend, limiting visibility to some two hundred yards. Neville drove the car on a bit, and off the road. Here he stopped and pondered his next move.

The surrondings were delightful. Here the trees were all conifers, and the ground was deep with brown pine needles and fir cones, with shafts of sunlight striking through the myriad branches. Through gaps he could see an ancient stone wall, which rose about ten feet, but in which there were gaps and many loose stones. This, he guessed, formed the boundary of the estate.

The question was — should he drive

boldly through the gates and invent some excuse for calling, or adopt more cautious tactics? He saw it would be a simple matter to clamber over the wall at some spot where the masonry had fallen, but in the long run this might prove unwise, for, if he were observed, suspicion as to his object would undoubtedly be aroused. As an alternative he might walk to the house and plead that his car had ceased to function and that he wished to telephone to the nearest garage for assistance. That would have the advantage of giving him access to the house, and perhaps Captain Cardinal himself. But if this plan was to be put into effect it seemed to him desirable that the car should be out of order. He thought for a few minutes, and then opened up the box which contained his battery, and loosened the terminal joint, thus cutting off the main supply of current. He tried the self-starter and satisfied himself that it was out of action.

A minute or two later he was outside the lodge, and here, to his disappointment, he found a telephone line, but it appeared to come from the house, and he hoped it would prove to be a local line. He pushed a bell button on the door, and to his relief got no reply. Then he started up the steep drive. The giant elms were backed by great masses of rhododendron bushes, which had recently bloomed, and blocked his view in all directions until he reached the wide bend, when the expansive gardens and the house came to view. Despite much overgrowth, there was a fine display of blossoms along the various terraces under the big house. In a way it reminded him of Barrowtor, but on a larger scale, but the house itself was far different. It seemed to comprise about three different periods, the later of which was definitely ugly. On the western wing was a tower built in the style of an eastern minaret, and utterly out of keeping with everything else, and the preponderating effect of the whole thing was one of shocking neglect and inevitable decay. In places the tenacious ivy had overgrown certain windows so that they became almost obliterated.

Ultimately the road flattened out and wound round to the right, to terminate in a wide space in which stood the main entrance. He mounted a few steps and entered the outer porch. Inside were some seats and a great double door. Finding a bell pull he operated it, and waited. No response came for a minute or so, and he tried again. After a few moments the right-hand door opened, and an elderly man stood before him.

"Good morning!" said Neville cheerfully. "I'm very sorry to trouble you, but my car has broken down outside the lodge. I wondered whether you would be kind enough to let me use your telephone to speak to a garage which could send me help."

"I'll see, zur," said the old man.

"Please come in, and I'll ask the master."

Neville stepped inside, saw the broad staircase mentioned by Wallace, and sat on what he believed to be the same bench. The old man vanished for a few moments and then returned and conducted Neville to a door on the right.

"Captain Cardinal will see you," he said, and then tapped on the door and opened it.

"This is the gentleman, sir," he said.

Neville found himself in a very large room, containing some splendid oak panelling and huge ceiling beams. Before him was a man sitting in a wheel-chair, with a newspaper on his knees. He was bearded and wore dark spectacles, and there was a heavy rug wrapped round his legs.

"Good morning!" he said. "Trouble — eh?"

"I'm afraid so. My name is Brandon, and I am on my way to Plymouth. I had time to kill, so I came this way from Shaldon. I hate main roads, and this country is new to me. My car died on me not far from your lodge. Electrical trouble I think, for I can't get a spark out of her. I thought you might be kind enough to let me use your telephone to ring up a garage."

"Certainly — if you will wait a minute or two. My secretary is in the middle of a trunk call. Do take a seat."

Neville took a chair near the central table, and the cripple pushed his chair to a corner bureau and brought back a box of cigarettes.

"Smoke?" he asked.

"Thank you," said Neville, and took a cigarette.

As he lighted it the sun which had been obscured for some time suddenly emerged into a clear patch of sky and illuminated the wild rambling garden as if it were a stage-set.

"Lovely spot you have here," said Neville.

"Yes, but just a trifle lonely, and

quite beyond my means to maintain as it should be. We struggle with the plants and flower beds, but nature always seems to win. Fond of gardens?"

"Very."

"I wasn't until I came here. The war smashed me up a bit, and I was told I needed plenty of fresh air. Any rate I get that. The place is miles too big for me, so I keep most of the rooms locked up and try to forget them. I suppose I ought to introduce myself. My name is Cardinal — Matthew Cardinal, late Royal Navy. I presume you were in the forces?"

"Yes. Unfortunately I was destined not to be in at the finish. I too was smashed up a bit, but I'm all right now."

"Good! I hope to get on my feet one of these days. Makes a man feel so damned useless in one of these contraptions."

There came a rap on the door and a sleek fellow, in a well-cut lounge suit, entered.

"I've finished with the trunk call, Captain," he said. "Groves told me to let you know — "

"Oh, yes, Tony. Mr. Brandon here has car trouble, and wants to ring up a garage. Who is there who would be likely to come here at once and get the car going?"

"The nearest repair garage is at Bovey. Williams is quite a good mechanic, but one can't always get him at once."

"Well, we can try. Take Mr. Brandon to the instrument and let him try his luck. Then come and take me out onto the terrace. I can't manage that step. We really must do something about that. See you before you leave, Mr. Brandon."

Neville nodded and went off with the secretary. The telephone was sited in the inner hall, and after telling him the number of the garage, the secretary went back to his employer. It seemed a shame to bring a mechanic a number of miles on a faked mission so Neville took the receiver off its rest, but kept the rest pressed down. He then gave the number, waited a few moments, and then began to talk to an imaginary person. It was quite a nice piece of make-believe, and when he saw the secretary coming back he ended by saying: "That's fine. I'll meet you by the car in half an hour."

"Everything all right?" asked the secretary.

"Yes. A man is leaving in a few minutes. I have arranged to be at the car in half an hour. I am very much obliged to you."

"Not at all. I hope it will be a simple matter to put right. Captain Cardinal is on the main terrace if you wish to see him before you leave."

"I should like to thank him."

"Then you can either go through the morning-room — that door to the left — or through the lounge."

"Thanks. I'll find my way."

Neville purposely went through the morning-room. It was much smaller than the lounge, but had the same kind of French windows leading to the terrace. The furniture was sparse but good, and the decorations were dingy, as elsewhere. He looked for signs of a woman's presence, but found none. Finally he opened the long door and stepped out into the warm sunshine. Cardinal was sitting in his wheel-chair, in front of the lounge, reading his newspaper, but he put this down when he heard Neville's footsteps.

"What luck?" he asked, as Neville approached him.

"Quite good. The garage is sending a man up. I have arranged to meet him by the car. He said he would be there in half an hour."

"That's fine! Now you can see my problem."

He waved a hand to indicate the expansive grounds which terminated in thick timber. There were no less than four terraces, all in Italian style, with a great assortment of statuary, and tall terra-cotta jars overflowing with geraniums and other flowers. Below them were arbours and shady walks, two ornamental ponds joined by a stream, and a willow-pattern scene. Away to the left was a spacious pavilion, along the front wall of which trailed an immense wistaria. Only the main terrace was in any kind of order.

"You've certainly taken on a tough proposition," said Neville.

"It was all I could get, and I got it cheap because nobody else wanted it. But the timber's worth money."

"It is. I wonder the Government hasn't taken it."

"They wanted to, but I raised hell. I suppose you're finding things a bit difficult after the Army?"

"Quite difficult enough. If I don't get into some sort of useful work soon, I expect they'll start directing me. What lies behind the tall yew hedge yonder?"

"A rather nice Dutch formal garden, with a central fountain. The fountain isn't working because the motor pump is out of order. There are some unusual ornamental fish in the pool. You can go round that way if you're interested. The footpath will lead you out to the main drive."

"I think I will," replied Neville. "It was very good of you to let me use the telephone."

"Not at all. I see so few people here that an occasional breakdown is a godsend to me. Well, I hope that mechanic will soon get you moving. If it's going to be a long job, come back and have a drink."

"Thanks," said Neville. "I'll go now."

"Good-bye, and good luck!"

"Good-bye!"

Neville walked down the wide terrace towards the yew hedge, passed down some steps, where there was a fine statue of Mercury in bronze, and then entered the formal garden. This, like the terrace, was well-kept and most beautifully planned. The central pool was elliptical and contained a grotesque leaden figure, at the top of which was a jet which normally spilled water over the water-lilies, but it was now dry and silent. He approached the stone parapet and gazed down into the water, where innumerable ornamental carp gleamed like jewels and moved lazily in their element. Evidently they were used to being fed, for several of them came to the surface quite close to him, and opened their square mouths to blow bubbles and move round gracefully in diminishing circles. It was a fascinating place, and he reclined for a few minutes in a stone seat and watched more fish joining the expectant throng. And while he watched, he pondered the situation, and was fast coming to the conclusion that he was on a fool's errand. Wallace had seen a girl — possibly a visitor — and in bad lighting had mistaken her for Isobel. One had to remember too that Wallace, who drank very little, had taken several glasses of champagne. He could see no cause to link Isobel with Captain Cardinal in any way. The odds against such a thing were enormous. Still, the trip had not been void of interest, and he did not regret it.

He looked at his watch and found that time had passed quickly. The best thing to do now was to get back home and have lunch with Teresa. He climbed the several shallow terraces, and was about to leave the exquisite garden by a second entrance when something red lying amid the flowers caught his eye. He halted and peered closer. It was an empty book of strip matches, with an advertisement on the flap. It was the advertisement which caused him to draw in his breath hard, for it said 'Lunch and dine at the Tivoli' and then gave the address.

He picked up the empty book, and his mind went back to the night when he and Isobel had dined at the Tivoli. They had both run out of matches, and he had asked Charles for a light. Charles had produced a book of strip matches, advertising the house, and had presented them to Isobel. The significance of this could not be overlooked. If the girl who looked like Isobel was just a coincidence, what was to be said of this discovery? No, one had to draw a line somewhere. Wallace was right after all. Isobel had been here. There was no other explanation that was acceptable.

If she had been here the previous evening in all probability she was here still. If that was so, what was her object? Why should she suddenly leave London to visit this remote spot, at a time when she and he were meeting regularly? Was this why she had failed to meet him at the railway station after he had left the note at her flat? Had she, as a matter of fact, already left for Devonshire?

A few moments' pause and he was adopting the other side of the argument. By what right was he investigating Isobel's movements? For all he knew she might have good reasons for visiting the house — reasons which might have nothing to do with her criminal husband, whom he had dragged in to excuse this attempted intervention. She might have known Cardinal in the past, and the fact that he had purchased the derelict estate suggested that he had connexions in the west-country. Cardinal himself had appeared to be both charming and honest.

He was now following the narrow path, which twisted like a serpent through the lower garden, and brought to view many attractive, if somewhat overgrown, features. But now his mind was turned inwards to his confused thoughts. Sorting these out, it seemed to him that he had accomplished his professed bare object — to find out if Wallace's statement was true. Further than that he dared not go without making a fool of himself.

Suddenly he found himself out in the drive up which he had come. He descended the hill, and finally found the car where he had left it. Uncovering the battery, he screwed the main cable down hard, and started the engine. Reluctantly he drove the car into the road and set it moving in the direction of home. He had covered about a mile, and was in the narrowest part of the road, when he saw a woman approaching. He slowed down the car as there was barely room for a pedestrian to pass, and then gave a little gasp as he recognised the walker. It was Isobel! Quickly he put his foot down on the brake, and stopped the car within a few yards of her. A moment later he was outside the vehicle.

"Neville!" she gasped. "I — I thought I recognised the car. What are you doing this way?"

"I might ask you the same question?" he laughed.

She regarded him with very definite nervousness.

"I — I have a friend who lives near here."

"At Overlands?"

"Yes. How did you know?"

"A little bird told me. Oh hell, there's a car coming up behind, and

I'm blocking the lane. Do get inside and I'll drive to where the road is wider."

She hesitated, and then did as he suggested. They drove on for half a mile, and then Neville was able to take the car off the road on to a patch of open land.

"That's better," he said. "Now we can talk. I tried to see you on Tuesday night at your flat, but it was locked up. So I scribbled a note and slipped it through the letter-box. It was to tell you that I had to come back to Devon the next morning."

"I didn't get it," she said. "I left London that afternoon. I tried to telephone you, but the woman downstairs was out, and when I reached the railway terminus I had only just time to catch the train."

"You're not in trouble, are you?"

"Oh no. Why do you ask that?"

"You look so pale."

"I had a headache and thought a walk would cure it. Neville, how did you know I was at Overlands?"

Neville told her how it had all come about, and watched her expression of incredulity.

"Of course it was an amazing coincidence — Wallace hitting upon that very house to enquire the way. I couldn't believe him — at first."

"Is that why you came out here — to prove it?"

"Yes. I got it in to my head that Algood was mixed up in it. I persuaded myself that he had taken you away from London by force. He swore he would never leave you alone."

"Well, he has. I suppose Captain Cardinal told you I was staying with him?"

"No. Not knowing how the land lay, I used a stratagem to see him. Your name was never mentioned?"

"Then how did you know I was really there?"

Neville took from his pocket the exhausted match-strip.

"I found that in the Dutch Garden

when I was coming back to the car."

"I see," she ruminated. "It was very clever of you."

"You're annoyed a little, aren't you?"

"Not really. But it isn't nice to feel that one is being shadowed — even by one's friends."

"I'm sorry," he said. "But you have never mentioned Cardinal to me."

"I had almost forgotten him. Like you, he saw that drawing of mine in the newspaper and recognised it. He sent a letter to the newspaper, and it was forwarded to me. He told me he had been injured in the war, and was a cripple. He asked me to come and see him — for old time's sake — and I decided to leave at once."

"Was it so urgent?"

She gazed at him reprovingly, but this time he did not apologise.

"Was it?" he repeated. "Does he mean so much to you?"

"I gathered from his letter that he was very lonely and on the edge of a nervous breakdown. Why do you look at me like that?"

"Because — Oh, I don't know. Yes I do. The fact is, Isobel, that I love you. You must listen. I know you are married, but you yourself have admitted that that marriage was a ghastly failure — "

"Neville!" she begged.

"You must listen. I've loved you ever since that day when we met in such strange circumstances, and it was my unhappy lot to inform you of the death of Phil and your father. When Algood turned up it was a nasty blow and silenced me for a bit. But I have got used to Algood by now. In view of what has happened he can mean absolutely nothing to you."

"Less than nothing," she murmured.

"Then set my heart at rest."

"How?"

"By telling me you love me, and that you'll marry me when you are free of that brute."

"But I may never be free!"

"If you were free — "

"What's the use? It will never happen. I know him better than you. He'll never give me grounds for a divorce. Much as he loves money, I'm certain that in this matter he can't be bought off. That's why I am convinced that it would be better if we were not to meet again."

Neville's mouth twitched.

"You've been trying to say that for a long time, haven't you?"

"Yes. You and Teresa have been kind to me, and I don't want to hurt you or her. Oh, Neville dear, don't you realise that this can never come to anything. I fear I am a *femme fatale* — "

"What nonsense! I know the facts and am facing them. They don't prevent our being lovers — "

"But they do. I'm afraid of Algood — not so much for myself as for you. He's a murderous brute — capable of anything. His jealousy is something you can scarcely imagine. You saw what happened in my flat — "

"I did. He got much the worst of it, and the next time he tries anything like that I'll have him jailed. You still haven't answered my question. Will you marry me when you are free to do so?"

"Give me time, Neville," she begged. "My mind is in a flurry. I can't think clearly just now. Take me back to Overlands and then — then I'll see you in a day or two."

"Why go back to that mausoleum at once? Make this day a holiday, Isobel. Let's go and have lunch somewhere, and spend the rest of the day on the moors, or by the sea?"

"But I am expected back to lunch, and, remember, I am a guest of Cardinal's."

"You could telephone from some place and beg to be excused. Please do this for me. I won't mention the contentious matter again — not to-day. We'll just play around like a couple of children — with no cares in the world. Say 'yes'."

This appeal seemed to have some effect, for Isobel stared out at the sunshine on the green hills. He took one of her hands and pressed it. Nor did she attempt to withdraw it, and a new light appeared in her eyes.

"All right," she murmured. "But I must telephone first."

"Bless you! Where shall we go — moors or sea?"

"Moors. All the beaches will be crowded. Go where you like, but stop at the first public telephone."

A quarter of an hour later Isobel made her telephone call, and came back to the car looking a little more relieved.

"All right?" asked Neville.

"Yes. I told him I had run into an old friend whom I hadn't seen for a long time. That was an exaggeration, but it really does seem a long time."

"Years," he corroborated.

The car rolled on over the undulating uplands. Neville knew most of the roads, but Isobel knew them better, and more or less dictated the course.

"Far from the madding crowd," she said. "I don't want to see anything but the sky and clouds and earth."

"And me, I hope?" he laughed.

"Don't flatter yourself," she replied. "Oh, but it's good to feel free, even if one isn't."

"Aren't we just as free as we feel?"

"That's a philosophical question. Look, there's a buzzard hawk — and there's another. There he goes — the big one — down — down. I fear there's going to be a ghastly murder."

It was amazing to watch the way her spirits were reasserting themselves. The pallor which had hardened her cheeks had gone, and now they were suffused with pink, and her eyes were like jewels. Again she directed him.

"Just where are we going?" he asked. "I know the other road, but not this one."

"The other road would take us close to that stark prison at Princetown. I don't want to look at prisons. I think this should bring us out to Dartmeet. It seems so long ago since I was there."

After many twists and turns they came to the lovely confluence of the rivers, but already it was packed with char-à-bancs, and Isobel gave a little sigh.

"Don't stop," she begged. "We'll find seclusion somewhere."

They found it in the lovely country beyond Huccaby, where the river burbled in the wind, and the myriad bees from a nearby bee farm plundered the blooming heather. Neville had forgotten all about lunch in the thrill of being alone with Isobel. They walked to where the brackish water rushed between the great boulders, and sat on nature's soft and alluring carpet.

"You love all this, don't you?" he asked.

"Yes. There's no other country for me. The moor is in my blood. When I'm away from it I can smell it. No matter where I went, it would draw me back — some day."

"As it did on that day when I found you plodding up that steep hill?"

She nodded and pitched a stone into a deep pool.

"How long have you known Cardinal?" he asked, after a long pause.

"Oh, since I was a child."

"So he's a Devon man?"

"Yes."

"Where did he get so badly smashed up?"

"In the Mediterranean — I think."

"His legs chiefly?"

"Yes."

"Will he ever walk again?"

"I don't know. What — what did you think of him?"

"He was quite charming. Seemed very glad to talk to someone. I can't help thinking it's a mistake to bury himself in that big house. I gathered he doesn't hope to be able to keep it in any sort of order. I suppose he's shy of his disability?"

"Very."

"But can he get good medical

attention where he is?"

"He says he does."

She had turned her head away, and when he looked closely at her he saw that there were tears in her eyes.

"Isobel!" he cried. "I didn't imagine you would feel it so keenly, or I shouldn't — "

"It's all right," she said, dabbing her eyes with a handkerchief. "But you see — in the past we were very great friends."

"I understand. Did you tell him who it was whom you had met so unexpectedly?"

"No."

"I'm glad, because I feel a bit conscience-stricken. You see, I pleaded that my car had broken down and asked to use his telephone. Actually I didn't put a call through to the garage he recommended because I didn't want to waste anyone's time."

"I had no idea you could be so deceitful."

"Well, now you know the worst

about me. I don't even jib at lying where your welfare is concerned."

"But I don't want you to perjure your soul for me. I'm really not worth it."

She shook her head as if in remonstrance, and then surveyed her shoes.

"Do you think I should look idiotic if I paddled?" she asked.

"Who's to notice it — except me?"

"The water looks so inviting."

"It does, but it's as cold as ice. It always is up here, as you should know. Most of it comes from deep springs."

"Who's afraid of cold?" she snorted, and commenced to take off her shoes and stockings.

A few minutes later she was standing in the water up to her knees, screaming in mock agony, and attempting to keep dry the edge of her skirt.

"I told you so," he said.

"It's painfully lovely," she gasped. "Reminds me of ice-cream gulped down too fast when I was a child. Ah, it's getting better."

"You mind how you step," he warned. "There are deep pools all over the place."

"It's all right. I can see the bottom. I'm going across to the other side."

"You can't," he protested. "It's quite deep in the middle."

But already she had made a start, feeling for footholds on the submerged rocks. He expected that at any moment she would slip and get drenched to the skin, but she made the passage, and climbed on to a rock where she sat with all the grace of a sculptured water nymph.

"Aren't you coming back?" he called.

She reached for the water with her toes, and kicked up a rainbow.

"No. I think you're safer at a distance."

But a little later she came back, and sat by his side, with her wet shapely legs drying in the wind and sun. He tried to keep his mind off her — to draw all the happiness he could from the pleasant surroundings, but she was as intriguing as a wild flower — and far more disturbing.

"There's something I haven't told you," he said. "While you have been away Scotland Yard has been after you."

"Scotland Yard!"

"That bright young Inspector wanted you in connection with the arrest of Tamling and the rest of the gang."

"Arrest!"

"He found the woman, and satisfied himself that she was not Tamling's wife. Under pressure she confessed that it was all a plot engineered by Tamling. He and the Tollers had already been arrested."

"Why — why didn't you tell me this before?"

"I had more important things to tell you."

"But the woman — the real wife — where is she?"

"That's the immediate problem.

Inspector Carson said there were grounds for believing that Tamling murdered her."

"You — you mean before he knew she was heiress to an estate?"

"Of course. If he did that he certainly cooked his own goose. The idea of passing off a substitute was a natural expedient, but that anonymous letter did the trick. Do you know who sent it?"

Isobel stared at him.

"Our old friend, Kubla Khan — Ransom's pet bugbear."

"But how does he know that?"

"By a clever bit of fingerprint work. He already had a fingerprint of Kubla, and the envelope in which the letter was contained bore another. Ransom was as pleased as a dog with two tails, but the gang deny all knowledge of Kubla, and the exact connection remains a mystery."

Isobel looked at him with great seriousness.

"Suppose the real Mrs. Tamling is

never found, or is proved to have been murdered, what becomes of the estate?" she asked.

"Don't ask me. It gives me a headache. Lovely to be away from it all for a bit."

Isobel sat with her fists clenched.

"Somehow I knew that woman was a fraud," she said. "But she knew all the answers so well."

It was hours later when they got back to the car. Having missed lunch, they found a remote cottage where they were successful in getting tea, and after that very protracted feast they explored an old tin-mine and finished up at the neolithic settlement at Grimspound, where they sat and watched the sun declining in the west.

"Goodness, it's late!" said Isobel. "The hours have simply flown past. I must get back to Overlands. Thank you, Neville, for a marvellous day."

"It's I who should thank you. I've just about enough petrol left to get home — thanks to Teresa, who seems to have got into the black market. Ready?"

"Yes."

They walked over the springing turf to where Neville had left the car.

15

DARKNESS had fallen by the time Neville came in sight of the lodge gates at Overlands, and the sky was sprinkled with the first stars.

"Better stop here," said Isobel.

"Oh, nonsense! I can drop you further up the drive — close to the house."

"No — no, please."

"Very well — if you insist."

"It would be better."

He already had the nose of the car inside the gates, but he stopped it there, and Isobel got out.

"When shall I see you again?" he asked.

"I — I promised to stay another day or two."

"Then come over to Shaldon and spend one night with us. I could fetch you."

"I'll telephone you — to-morrow."

"Is that a promise?"

"Yes."

She was standing at the open door, and Neville put out his hand. As she took it he drew her towards him, hesitated and then kissed her on the lips. For a moment her wild eyes stared into his and then she drew herself away.

"Good-bye, Neville!" she said brokenly, and hurried off.

For a little while the headlights of the car illuminated her, and then she was gone. Neville sighed and commenced to reverse the car. There was scant room for the operation, and it took a few moments before he was facing in the right direction. A touch on the accelerator pedal and he went rapidly up the short connecting private road. As he made the right turn into the main road, his headlights came round, and fell full on the figure of a walking man, who was about to turn into the connecting road. He had but a split second to avoid him, but in that split second he recognised the walker. It was Mr. Algood!

He drove on for a hundred yards or so, then put the car onto the green verge and switched off the engine and his headlights. Here was a situation quite unexpected, and he paused for a few moments to collect his wits. But a short while ago Isobel had intimated that she had had no further trouble from her villainous husband, and now here he was, like the bad penny. There was no doubt in his mind that Algood was making for the house. There was indeed no other possible objective in that direction. By some means or other he had discovered that his wife was there. What was to be done?

Probably the most sensible thing would be to continue on his course and leave Isobel to deal with the matter, with the assistance of her friend, Cardinal. But his whole being rebelled at the idea of abandoning her in the face of this threat. Rightly she feared this creature, and, doubtless, with good reason. This was no time for cogitation, but for action.

Taking a torch from the pocket of the car, he locked the doors and then hurried back to the turning, up the connecting road and through the lodge gates. At the top of the drive he could see a pencil of light moving round the sharp bend. In a moment it had disappeared, and he moved to the grass verge, directed his own torch before him and ran swiftly forward. On reaching the bend, he found he had gained appreciably. It was lighter here and he could see dimly without the aid of the torch. Algood was making for the open space before the main entrance.

Neville took to the timber, dodging from tree to tree, with Algood continuously in view, and a minute or two later barely fifty yards divided them. Algood now halted and seemed to be regarding the entrance. But he made no attempt to go up the steps to the door. Instead, he moved round the house, towards some extensive outbuildings. Neville crept forward, but now kept his distance. What was the fellow up to? If he wanted his wife, why didn't he go boldly up the steps and ring the bell? Was it possible that he did not know his wife was there, but only suspected it, and that he was getting the lie of the land as a preliminary?

Then suddenly there came the sharp warning bark of a dog, followed by horrible snarling and more barking. These noises were obviously getting closer, and Neville recalled what the man in the village shop had said. Algood had stopped dead. He was still using the torch, and, as Neville watched, two enormous dogs came to view. They saw the man with the torch and went straight for him. Algood sprang sideways towards some double doors. Frantically he pulled on a handle, and the door moved along just sufficiently for him to squeeze himself through the opening. As he closed the door, the two infuriated animals reached it and pawed at it, with their teeth gnashing. Slightly above Neville's head was the stout bough of a cedar tree. He pulled himself up on it and pressed close to the large trunk. The two dogs kept up their hellish noises, and a little later the front door opened and two men came to view. Neville, peering round the tree trunk, recognised one of them as Cardinal's male secretary, Tony, but the second man was a stranger to him, and this man carried a sporting gun.

"Rex! Rover!" he cried. "Come here! What is it, boys?"

The dogs ran between him and the double door, barking less furiously now, but still highly excited.

"Was that door locked, Tom?" asked Tony.

"I think so."

"They wouldn't make all this noise for nothing. Try the door."

The man with the gun slid the door a few inches.

"Damned if it isn't open!" he

growled. "Could anyone — ?"

"Wait there while I get the dogs away. I'll be back in a minute."

He seized the two reluctant animals by their collars and bundled them up the steps and through the front door. Then he came back and shone a torch on the door of the building. Approaching it, he waved Tom aside.

"Stand by," he said. "We'll soon sort this out."

He put a hand to the door and pushed it right back.

"There he is," said Tom. "Behind the van. I can see his feet."

Tony rapped out a command, and a few moments later Algood appeared. Tom trained the gun on him.

"Turn that gun away!" he snarled. "I was going to make a call when those two mad animals came at me. I had to take cover. Why do you let things like that run wild?"

"What were you doing up here?" asked Tony. "You must have passed the front door."

"It was the only place where I could get away from those crazy brutes. I had to take a chance."

"Who are you, anyway?"

"My name's Algood, and I came to see my wife."

"Then you must have come to the wrong address. There's no one of that name here. In fact, there's no woman in the house at all."

"I happen to know there is."

"A nice story," sneered Tony. "You were prowling round the garage. You're coming inside to give a proper explanation befor I make up my mind whether to call the police or not."

Algood laughed scoffingly.

"You'd better keep the police out of this," he said.

"What do you mean?"

"Just what I say."

"All right, Tom. We'll take him inside," said Tony. "Keep that gun trained on his back, because I don't trust him."

They marched the prisoner to the

front door, and Neville pressed his body close to the trunk of the tree and held his breath, for they had to pass within a few yards of him. After a few moments he heard the door close, whereupon he slid to the ground.

The conversation which had passed intrigued him. Why had Tony sworn there was no woman in the house? It was possible that he did not know Isobel under the name of Algood, but why deny her presence there? Then there was Algood's suggestion that they should keep the police out of it. Why had he said that?

He looked towards the garage, and saw that the door was incompletely closed. Tiptoeing towards it, he shone his torch inside and saw a large green van alongside a huge American saloon car. His heart beat fast as he recalled a statement made in his presence at Scotland Yard by the man who had admitted stealing the silver from Barrowtor. He had said that the van which had been placed at his disposal to remove the furniture had been green in colour, bearing no name, and with a Ford engine. He nipped inside and lifted the bonnet of the van. There was the Ford engine!

Suddenly he heard footsteps, and realised that someone was approaching the door, which he had closed after him. He dived behind the saloon car, since that offered better cover, and a few moments later he heard a key turned in the lock, and the sound of retreating footsteps. It was only then that he realised the place had no windows, and that he had been idiot enough to get himself locked in. He went to the door to make sure about this, and very soon found that his conclusions were correct.

"Damn!" he muttered.

The ray from his torch wandered over the dank walls of the place which appeard to be old stables, at some recent time converted into a spacious garage. To the left of the green van there was a bench against the wall, with some tool racks over it, and above these there were some ventilation slits. He went in the opposite direction and found a lot of old garden clutter — iron seats and mouldy sunshades. Here there was a door, but it was fastened on the other side and was immovable.

His predicament was exasperating, and he sat down on the running-board of the saloon car to consider what to do. If he banged on the door hard enough no doubt someone would hear and start to do something about it, but explanations would be difficult, and he had the feeling that this Captain Cardinal was not all he was reputed to be. Why this van?

He stood up and went to the back of the vehicle. The two doors were clamped together with a heavy bar, and this bore a large padlock. He climbed into the driving cab, and found a small glass window behind the driver's seat. Through this he shone the torch, to find that it was full of boxes stacked almost to the roof, and coming within a few inches of the window. His suspicions grew apace. What was a private house doing with a large removal van full of what appeared to be merchandise?

A little later he discovered something else. The licence attached to the vehicle did not correspond with the two number plates, and on examining the plates he saw that these had recently been changed, for the bolts which held them were without rust and greasy to the touch.

How could one fail to be impressed by these various items? Was this not just the sort of isolated spot where a man — or a gang — could carry on some kind of racket without being suspected? And one had to remember that Algood had hinted that it would be inadvisable to call the police. What did it all add up to — and where did Isobel come into it — if at all?

Looking over the tools, he found a crowbar with a fine hard edge. It caused him to consider ways of escape.

The door, he imagined, must lead to another of the outbuildings, in which there might be windows or at least some form of exit. The point was — could he force the heavy door without making enough noise to invite unwanted attention? He took the heavy tool to the door, and inserted the broad edge between the lock and the jamb. The implement was a good two feet long, and slowly he let it have all his weight and strength. The narrow space widened as the wood was sprung, and now he could see the steel tongue of the lock — a good half inch of it. But it still held the door firmly.

He desisted for a few moments and then tried again, getting a deeper grip with the claw of the crowbar. But again he failed, for the tongue of the lock seemed endless. On the third attempt he was successful. The tongue cleared the plate by a fraction, and now he needed another tool to hold the tongue free while he pulled the door open. He went to the bench and brought back a broad flat screwdriver. The crowbar was again brought into service, and when the tongue was free he pushed the blade of the screwdriver between it and the plate, and then discarded the crowbar and tugged on the door-knob. The door moved towards him, and was finally free. To his surprise, it did not lead to another building, but to a flight of descending steps. He mopped his brow and hesitated.

Second thoughts suggested that whatever happened he was scarcely likely to worsen his position. To be caught red-handed was the last thing in the world he wanted, and that must surely take place if he stayed where he was. So down he went, directing the ray of the torch before him. There were sixteen steps, and then a long narrow passage. He counted the paces — twenty. Then another door. He listened outside, but heard not a sound. Then he tried the handle. The door resisted him, but it was only the spring control. He pushed his way through, and shone the torch forward. The door closed slowly on the heavy spring, and as the latch clicked into place he heard the sound of a loud bell from some unlocatable part of the building. He knew it was an alarm, but he was unable to move for a moment, for the torch revealed great piles of crates of different shapes and sizes piled in a huge chamber. But a sense of his personal danger turned him round. He tugged on the door, but found it at least as firm as the other one, and now he had no crowbar to aid him. The bell was still ringing hard, and he realised that it was operated in some way by the heavy spring and the automatic closing of the door. Here indeed was the climax — unless he could work a miracle. Then the bell stopped ringing.

Like a rabbit, he went scurrying through the narrow alleys between the piles of crates and bales. Some of these bore labels of a well-known cigarette firm, others — much smaller — were quite obviously crates of whisky. Farther on there was a pyramid of wrapped motor tyres, which completely obstructed further progress in that direction. He stopped and listened. There were footsteps in the distance — coming nearer and nearer, and then suddenly the whole place became illuminated.

"That's better," said a voice. "You'd better go round to the right, Tom. But if you see him, don't shoot. Harry, you stay by the stairs. I'll take the left side."

"Okay."

Neville saw before him a single pile of large tyres, standing shoulder high. He stepped on to a smaller pile, and gazed down the indiarubber well. Quite close was a large carton half full of boxes of cigarettes. He seized this and placed it about half-way across the top of the larger pile of tyres. Then he climbed up and lowered himself inside the tyres. Putting the palms of his hands upwards he contrived to jockey the carton right across the top of the tyres. Lowering his body as far as he was able in the restricted space, he listened intently.

"Nothing round this way," called a voice which he recognised as Tom's. "Think that alarm went off by accident?"

"No, I don't. But go round to the door and see if it is fixed. That will prove it."

Slow footsteps were now coming towards Neville's hiding-place, and then Tom's voice came back again.

"The door's fixed all right."

"Then he must be here."

The last voice was so close that Neville could hear the intake of the speaker's breath, and the air inside the closely packed tyres was rapidly becoming unbreathable. There was a tickling in his throat, and he wanted to cough.

"What are you doing, Tom?" asked the voice from somewhere above him.

"Coming round your way."

"You needn't. I can see everything from here. Go to the bay and look in there."

"Okay, but it's mighty queer."

There was a long silence, during which Neville felt he must choke, and then the voice which had been so close to him was heard a little farther away. "Well?"

"Not a smell of anyone. I still think it was an accident. How could anyone get in here?"

"Through the garage — idiot."

"But I locked it after we had caught that other swine."

"Yes, but not at once. You there, Harry?"

"Sure I am. Can't you see me?"

"I can now. Run up to the garage and make sure that door is locked. Better still, look inside."

"What do I do if he's there?"

"Shoot him if he starts any trouble. But I think he's still down here."

By this time Neville was on the verge of passing out. Raising his hands he succeeded in moving the carton, and drew into his lungs the fresher air. His mind began to work again. He gathered that the stairs were now unguarded, and that they offered a possible means of escape. From the direction of the voice above him he concluded that the owner of it had climbed up on the larger pile of tyres. The question was — could he see the stairs from his present position? He raised his head through the orifice which he had created, and by peering round the edge of the carton he saw a man, with his back to him, squatting on the tyres. It was Tony — the sleek secretary — and in his hand was an automatic pistol. The position of Tom was uncertain. He had but the vaguest idea of the direction of the stairs, but, at any rate, forward progress was out of the question. What he wanted to hear was Tom's voice, and after a few minutes' wait it was heard — well away to his left.

"Not a sign of the swine," he called.

"Well, stand fast. When Harry comes back we'll bring the dogs down. They'll find him quick enough."

This remark acted as a spur to Neville's indecision. He prised himself through the opening, and succeeded in getting to the ground without making a sound. On hands and toes he retreated the way he had come, but then took a turn to the right, and from the end of a narrow passage through the vast collection of goods he saw the stairs immediately ahead of him. Half-way down this he came upon the bare wall, and up this went an electric cable — to vanish through the ceiling. The stairs were but twenty yards away, but he believed that from his elevated position Tony could see them, and had them covered. But the electric cable had given him an idea. He slipped his hand into his pocket and found there a knife with two strong blades. He opened the larger blade, and then wrapped his handkerchief round the handle. A couple of powerful strokes and he was through the lead covering. He slipped the end of the smaller blade under the flex inside, took one last look at the stairs to register the direction, and then drew the knife through the flex in one savage stroke. There was a blinding flash of light and the place was plunged into darkness. All he felt was a faint shock, and the next instant he was moving swiftly towards the stairs.

"Tom!" cried Tony.

"Hey, what's wrong?"

"I don't know. Have you got a torch?"

"No."

"You damned fool! Get round to the stairs."

But Neville was already there. He felt his way up them, and was at the spot where they turned to the right, when a pistol flashed and a bullet struck the wall not very far away.

"There he is!" cried Tony.

Neville went up the last dozen stairs and found a door slightly open. He passed through it, and saw a key on the farther side. This he turned, pocketing the key afterwards. Now he felt savage. A shot had been fired at him. The real battle was on. He dashed along a short passage. It led to what appeared to be a kitchen. There was a light inside and the radio was on. He could see no outlet here, so he turned to the right and went down a lengthy passage. As he did so, he heard thunderous sounds from behind and realised that either Tom or Tony had reached the door which he had locked and was hammering on it. At the end of the passage was another door. He opened this and found himself in the main hall, with the front door only a little ahead of him. But before he could reach it a door on the left opened, and who should come to view but Algood.

"What!" said Algood. "You again!"

"Get out of the way," said Neville.

But Algood's hateful eyes had gone to the wall, on which was hanging an old sword. He snatched it from the nail and brandished it ferociously.

"Captain Cardinal!" he shouted.

Neville moved towards him, but at

that moment the front door opened and a man with a shotgun entered.

"This is the fellow who is causing all the trouble," said Algood. "He's always causing trouble. Watch him!"

"I'm watching him," said the evil-looking man with the gun. "If he moves a step — Ah, here is the Captain."

Through the wide side-door came Captain Cardinal in his wheel-chair. He gazed from Neville to the other two, and gave a short laugh.

"We seem to be having an exciting evening," he said. "Harry, you can dispose of that weapon, and get along to the kitchen. What's all that infernal noise?"

"Sounds like Tom and Tony trying to get to us."

"Well, go and do something about it. I'll ring for them if I need them." He turned his benignant gaze to Neville. "I suggest you explain this curious situation," he said. "Better come inside. You too, Algood."

Neville looked at the scowling Algood,

and then accepted the invitation, and passed into the room which he had entered earlier that day. Cardinal wheeled himself in, and Algood followed, still carrying the ugly sword.

"Now, Mr. Brandon," said Cardinal. "What is the meaning of all this?"

"I saw this man making for the house as I was — passing this evening."

"Did that appear remarkable to you?"

"Yes, because I happened to know that his wife is here, and that she is not very anxious to see him."

"So you are a friend of Mrs. Algood?"

"Yes."

"And you think that entitles you to object to her husband visiting her?"

"Yes."

"I must say that is rather curious reasoning. When you came here this morning, had you some ulterior motive?"

"Yes. I wished to find out if she was here."

"So the whole story of your car

breakdown was false?"

"Yes."

"But why? If you believed Mrs. Algood was here, why didn't you ask about her?"

"I thought it might be possible she was being kept here against her will."

Cardinal looked at him incredulously.

"You mean — kidnapped or something like that?" he asked.

"Well, that was possible."

"By me? Oh, come!"

"Not by you, but by the man she was stupid enough to marry."

"I won't stand any cheek — " commenced Algood, but was interrupted by a knock on the door, followed by the entry of Harry.

"What is it?" asked Cardinal impatiently.

"This fellow must have the key of the basement. The door's locked and Tom and Tony can't get out."

"Idiots to let themselves get trapped. Brandon, have you got the key?"

Neville produced it and threw it at

Harry, who caught it and scowled. Cardinal waved him out.

"Now," he said. "Let's get to the bottom of this. You say you thought Mrs. Algood might have been kidnapped, not by me, but at least with my assistance or knowledge?"

"Yes."

"Well, you were wrong. I had never seen Algood until he arrived here this evening. By some means or other he discovered that his wife was staying here. Really, I don't see where you come into this, Mr. Brandon — "

"I'll tell you," interrupted Algood. "This fellow has been pestering my wife for some time now. Running after her, and taking her out to meals. It's true Isobel and I had a bit of a tiff, but that's all blown over and — "

"You liar!" said Neville. "She lived in deadly fear of you, and you know it."

Algood waved his scimitar threateningly.

"Put that ridiculous thing away," said Cardinal. "You have no idea how foolish you look."

Algood dropped the weapon to his side.

"You can't blame me if I get the impression that it is you who are not telling the truth," said Cardinal to Neville. "Within the last few minutes I have observed to my satisfaction that the rift between Mrs. Algood and her husband was only a small one. They are leaving together to-morrow morning."

"I don't believe it," snapped Neville.

"In that case I had better convince you. Algood, ask your wife to come here, and leave that sword where you found it."

Algood went out, and Cardinal sighed.

"I should have been in bed by now," he complained. "But it has been one interruption after another. What induced you to believe that Isobel was staying here?"

"That is my business."

Cardinal shrugged his shoulders,

obviously resenting the short, curt reply.

"It's also my business too," he said. "I don't take kindly to the idea of my guests being shadowed. I presume you are in love with her?"

"Perhaps. Are you?"

"Not in the way you think. At least I have sense enough to know where she belongs."

"She certainly doesn't belong to that drunken thief."

"Those whom God has joined — "

"Don't drivel," snapped Neville. "That's one thing I simply can't stand. I've seen enough of Algood to know that he is a cowardly rat and — "

The door opened and into the room came Isobel, followed by Algood. Neville's heart seemed to be pounding against his ribs, for she was now quite different from when he had seen her such a short time ago. All the colour had left her cheeks, and there was something about her eyelids which convinced him she had been weeping. For a moment her eyes rested on him, and then she turned to Cardinal.

"What is it?" she asked heavily.

"This man broke into the house a short while ago. He says he is a friend of yours, and his excuse is that he believed you were a prisoner here."

"I did not say that," protested Neville.

"Well, it comes to the same thing. He saw your husband coming here and arrived at the conclusion that you were in some danger. I merely wanted to convince him that that is quite untrue. He intimated that I was a liar. So perhaps you will put him right about that."

Isobel turned to Neville. For a moment or two she seemed to be quite at a loss for words, and Algood in the background was obviously enjoying the situation.

"You shouldn't have come here, Neville," said Isobel. "What Cardinal told you is true."

"You mean it is true that you and that — that crook are going to live together again?"

"I won't stand for this," roared Algood. "Who's he to call me names? What's the right name for a man who runs after another man's wife and tries to take advantage of her?"

Neville's fists became clenched. Algood had come back without the sword, and it seemed an appropriate moment to drive his fist into that hateful face, but Cardinal intervened in time.

"Insults will get us nowhere," he said. "Isobel — you haven't answered him."

"It's true," said Isobel slowly. "We are going to try to live together peacefully in future. But it's only fair to say that my husband was unjust. You — and your sister — have been very kind to me, and I shall always remain grateful, but — but this must be good-bye."

"You really mean that?"

"Yes."

She lowered her head as if she were ashamed to look at him, and Neville winced.

"So now you know," said Algood. "It must have been you who nearly ran me over. Only missed me by a few inches."

"What a pity," said Neville acidly. "I should have put you in jail when I had the opportunity."

"In future you steer a wide path," retorted Algood. "Any trouble from you and I'll mess up that face of yours."

"Oh, give over," pleaded Cardinal. "Isobel, I don't think you had better stay any longer. All this is a miserable business. Go now, my dear. You too, Algood."

Algood took Isobel by the arm. For a moment she seemed to be transfixed, but a tug from Algood set her moving towards the door. As she reached it she averted her head a little, and Neville saw what he took to be a tear in her eye. Then the door closed on them.

"Well, I hope you're satisfied," said Cardinal.

Neville was trying to think coolly — a thing scarcely possible while Isobel had been present. Something was wrong. The whole set-up was fantastic. Why was Isobel behaving in this extraordinary fashion? For hours he had been in her company — had raised her from brooding sadness to elation. True there had been reservations, but at no time had he cause to believe that she regretted for a moment the flight from her villainous husband.

"Not very satisfied," he said.

"You are a very hard man to convince. What do you find amiss?"

"Certain little things, but I'd prefer not to discuss them. I'm sorry if I've kept you out of bed. Now, I'll go."

He turned on his heel, with the object of getting back to the car as quickly as possible, but he now faced a wall mirror, and in the mirror he could see the man in the chair. He had a pistol in his hand.

"Yes, you had better change your mind, Mr. Brandon," said Cardinal crisply.

Neville turned round slowly. One of his several mental questions was being answered. It was — why had Cardinal appeared to be so disinterested in the contents of the cellar?

"I find good cause to believe that your second story is no truer than your first," said Cardinal. "Your gallant and romantic concern for the woman you profess to love was nicely done, but it doesn't deceive me. I am convinced you came here to burgle the place, and kept your ingenious excuse ready for such an emergency as this. Don't move, because if you do I shall be compelled to shoot in self-defence."

He propelled the chair with one hand to a bell-push and jabbed a finger on it.

"What is this, exactly?" asked Neville.

"You will soon know."

Neville hadn't long to wait. The door burst open and through it came the lean-faced dapper secretary. He took a look at Neville's face.

"That's the fellow," he said. "I caught a glimpse of him in the flash of the pistol. Why, he's the man who — !"

"Exactly! The poor fellow whose car had broken down. He came to spy out the land, and to-night he returned to take toll of us. I want you to ring up the police and ask them to send someone here at once. Tell them what has happened. But search him first. He may carry a firearm."

"If I did, I shouldn't be here now, but on my way to the police station," said Neville.

"Search him!" snapped Cardinal. "Brandon, if you start anything I shan't hesitate to shoot."

"Put up your hands," said Tony.

"I'll see you damned first."

Cardinal wheeled his chair to a flank. "Never mind about his hands. Go over his pockets. If he moves, I'll deal with him."

Neville gave him a glance and believed him. There was something very convincing in the cold metallic voice, and the pistol was held in a hand that seemed as steady as a rock. Tony slapped all his pockets, and was satisfied.

"Nothing there," he said at last, "except this knife."

He placed Neville's useful pocket-knife on the table.

"All right. Take this gun — "

"I've already got one."

"Good! Put him somewhere safe until we can get the police here. Tom had better go with you."

Tony pushed the barrel of his own weapon into Neville's back and followed him closely to the door. They passed through it, and Neville saw the man who had previously carried the shotgun.

"What's happening?" he asked Tony.

"We're to lock him up until the

police can get here."

"Don't make me laugh," said Neville. "The police are the last people in the world you want to see. All the same, you will see them, because I had sense enough to tell my people where I was going. People who have cellars full of drink and cigarettes, and — "

"I advise you to keep your mouth shut," snapped Tony. "Get moving."

"Where are we going to dump him?" asked Tom.

"The west wing — basement. You go ahead."

The procession moved down the narrow passage, and passed the door through which Neville had recently burst. They entered a part of the house which appeared to be deserted. The floors were bare, and the old wallpaper was cascading off the walls. Then they came to a door and Tony passed a key to Tom. To Neville's surprise they entered a finely-furnished reception-room. This had all the appearance of having been lived in recently, and at the far end was another staircase.

"Hurry!" said Tony.

But Neville had quite different intentions, for there were certain things about that room which interested him. One of them was the large and excellent Oriental carpet, with a 'Tree of Life' pattern. Another was a piece of furniture against the wall, with inlay depicting two dragons. Also there was a very fine Queen Anne settee in beautiful petit-point needlework — a forest scene with hounds and stag. Then suddenly he knew where he had seen these things before. It was not in some dream, but in the inventory of the furniture at Barrowtor. He remembered that Isobel had pencilled in the details of the needlework, and also the two dragons. Here — incredible as it seemed — was some of the furniture from Barrowtor.

"Ah!" he said.

"What did you say?" rasped Tony.

"Oh, nothing. I was only thinking. Have you ever heard of a man called Kubla Khan?"

He could not see Tony's face, but the ugly visage of Tom came round, revealing enormous surprise, and then Tony pushed the pistol into his back.

"Get going," he said. "You're not doing yourself any good, Mr. Brandon."

They passed by the stairs, above which were two oil-paintings which Neville was sure were from Barrowtor, and finally came to the door of the basement. Tom opened it with a huge key and switched on a light. It revealed stone steps leading to what appeared to be another extensive, but empty, basement.

"Down you go," said Tony.

"For how long?"

"Until the police arrive."

Neville gave one look at the pistol and decided it would be folly to attempt to do anything. As he went down the stairs he heard the heavy door close with a reverberating noise, and he began to wonder how long must pass before he saw the light of day.

16

WHEN the secretary and Tom got back to the room where they had left the cripple, a miracle seemed to have taken place there, for Captain Cardinal was no longer in his wheel-chair, but walking up and down with all the ease and energy of a perfectly fit man. He had removed his dark glasses, revealing a pair of coal-black eyes, which flashed like diamonds.

"What did you do with him?" he asked.

"West-wing basement," replied Tony. "He'd have to be a wizard to get out of that. What's it all mean?"

"It means we're in a mess. If he came through the basement he must have seen everything. He's no fool."

"You're right," blurted Tom. "Just now he said something that proves it.

He asked us if we had heard of a man called Kubla Khan, and he said it in a way that didn't call for any answer. He also said his people knew where he was, and that we'd soon have the police here."

"Shut up!" snarled Cardinal. "I can't think while you burble on. The situation calls for clear minds and swift action. From what Algood said, it's clear he has a car close at hand. I've sent Harry — Ah, here he is."

The fourth man entered hurriedly. He was a murderous-looking creature, with no sign at all of any culture.

"I've found it," he said. "Not far down the road — parked just off the side. A drop-head coupé — a beauty. Must be worth a couple of thousand quid. My opinion is — "

"I'm not asking you for an opinion," interrupted Cardinal. "And I can't wait for the boss. Every minute is precious. Brandon may be lying, but even if he isn't, the police are not likely to take any action until morning, so we've got at least ten hours to straighten things out. Tony, get some drinks. All right, boys, pull up your chairs and we'll get to business."

Tony brought some bottles and glasses from the cupboard under the sideboard, and the chairs were drawn up close to the large circular table. The glasses were filled, and now all eyes were on Cardinal, who had lighted a huge cigar, and was rolling it round his mouth while his brows were furrowed in thought.

"The stuff will have to be shifted," he said.

"Where to?" asked Tony.

"That's what we've got to decide. What sort of a night is it outside?"

"Clear," replied Harry, "but I reckon there'll be a mist before morning."

"That may suit us, provided it doesn't come too soon. How do we stand for transport?"

"Only the van and the Packard," said Tony. "But the van is full of brandy."

"Where's the old van?"

"Beecher has it at Plymouth — on the other job. It would take two hours to get it here."

"How many van-loads are there down below?"

"Eight at least. That would mean four loads for the two vans. But where can we dump it?"

"With Beecher. He'll have to make room for it until we can make other arrangements."

"But there won't be time," protested Tony. "And I'm absolutely certain that Beecher can't take all that stuff. Apart from which, I wouldn't trust him — not in a big affair like this. Then there's that swine — Algood. Is he to be trusted? If we start moving stuff in the middle of the night — "

"You needn't worry about Mr. Algood. S-sh!"

He waved Tony into silence as there came a rap on the door, and Isobel entered. She stood just inside the door staring at the festive gathering.

"Has — has he gone?" she asked.

"Brandon? Yes. I don't think he'll worry you any more. Where's your husband?"

"I don't know. I think he's in his bedroom drinking."

"I shouldn't be surprised. Why do you look so frightened?"

"There's no key to my door, and no bolt on the inside."

Cardinal looked at Tony.

"Can you do something about that?" he asked.

"Yes. I think the key is hanging up in the kitchen. I'll come with you, Mrs. Algood, and get it."

Isobel said nothing, but followed Tony through the door. Cardinal stared after them.

"Scared stiff," he said. "I don't wonder, either. A dirty little rat that. Thinks he's so smart too. Easy on that whisky, Tom. There's a lot of work to be done before we're through."

"You're telling me," grumbled Tom. "Reckon Tony was right about Beecher.

The boss warned us against him, and if he finds we've — "

"I'm dealing with this. He'll approve of what I do."

He picked up the knife which had been taken from Neville and tossed it in his hand for a moment or two. Then Tony came back and sat down.

"She's right about Algood," he said. "I got a glimpse of him in the next bedroom. Who gave him the bottle of whisky?"

"He must have helped himself — the low swine. Tony, you're probably right about Beecher. I've got a better plan — one that can be done without creating so much disturbance, and which won't call for Beecher's help. At a pinch all that stuff can be got into the west-wing basement, and the van can be moved."

"But Brandon is in the west-wing basement," objected Tony.

"We can shift him. There's nothing to suggest that there is a second basement if we cover up the entrance."

"How?"

"Lord, haven't you any imagination? There are a dozen ways. If the police do come butting in, they need find nothing here which isn't quite respectable. But that van will have to be unpacked, and the stuff placed with the rest of it. The van can be garaged somewhere, but the number plates must be made right. That's a job for you, Tom — after we've done the removing."

"What about Brandon's car?" asked Harry.

"I'm coming to that. One thing at a time, and the first thing is to get Brandon somewhere else, and start shifting the stuff. Finish up your drinks, and we'll make a start."

None of Cardinal's accomplices seemed to relish the heavy task which faced them, but they had sense enough to know that the programme was essential to their well-being.

"We'll be lucky if we get to bed before about two o'clock," grumbled Harry.

"You'll be lucky if you get to bed at all," retorted Cardinal. "This is the first bad spot we've been in, but if you do exactly as you're told we'll get out of it very nicely. Very nicely indeed. As for Mr. blasted Algood — But I'm wasting time. Get to it, boys."

17

TERESA had kept lunch back a little, hoping that Neville would return in time to share the meal with her, but finally she was compelled to eat alone. She was feeling a little depressed at Wallace's departure, but against this was the pleasant prospect of the future.

Some hours later she was in the garden, cutting some flowers for the vases, when she saw a telegraph boy cycling up the drive. She went to meet him.

"Miss Brandon?" he asked.

"That's me."

The boy handed her the telegram, and she slit open the buff envelope and read the enclosure. It said:

'Unexpected good news. Am coming back by road. Hope arrive about tennish. John.'

"No reply," she said.

The boy cycled off, and Teresa sat on the nearest seat to recover from her pleasant surprise. But what did it mean? What was the nature of the unexpected good news that was bringing John back post-haste? But of course that was in itself the good news. How had it come about? Could it mean that his unit was on its way home, and that John had received instructions to report on its arrival? She gave up guessing and tried her best to control her excitement.

As the afternoon and evening passed, she began to wonder what was keeping Neville, but it never occurred to her that anything could be wrong. She forwent the evening meal, feeling sure that Wallace would not stop on the road for the purpose of eating, and that it would be nice to have some supper with him. By that time Neville was sure to be back, and would get the surprise of his life. So she opened some tins and prepared the late meal, making a trifle to go with it.

At half-past ten she heard the noise of a car, and there was so much of it that she knew it was Wallace and not Neville, for Neville could speed up the drive with scarcely a whisper of sound. She ran to the front door and saw Wallace's old car come to a standstill. The next moment she was enfolded in Wallace's arms.

"Control yourself," she gasped. "What has happened?"

"It was a secret, but a real muck-up. You see, when I realised that my leave was coming to an end I wrote the skipper — my C.O. — and told him I had become engaged. At the same time I pointed out that I had missed a leave last year, and that if there was any chance of taking that back leave with my now prospective wife he had only to say so. I didn't tell you because I thought it was unwise to raise wild hopes. Well, when I got to the flat I found a note there advising me that a telegram was waiting for me at the post-office as delivery could not be made in view of the flat being locked up. By some mistake the telegram had been sent to the flat instead of this address which I gave in my letter. Well, I got the telegram. It gave me seven days extra leave."

"Oh, John — that's wonderful!"

"I'll say it is. I was bang out of petrol and desperate, so I went round to the garage which looks after my car and told a pathetic story. Used all my leave petrol — lovely girl waiting for me hundreds of miles away. No convenient train. Well, it worked, and here I am. Gosh, you look marvellous!"

"I must have changed a lot in twelve hours. But bring the bags in. Have you eaten since you left London?"

"Not a bean."

"Good! I've got a meal all ready."

Wallace took the two suitcases from the car, and dumped them in the hall.

"Where's Neville?" he asked.

"That's another story," replied Teresa.

"I've been worrying about him all the evening. The moment you left this morning he reverted to your experience of last night at that lonely house. He wanted to find out if you had really won that bet."

"Oh, about Isobel?"

"Yes. He looked up a map and found that the house was called Overlands. He said he wanted to have a look at it in day-light. It was no use trying to stop him."

"And has he been away all this time?"

"Yes. But go and tidy up now. Plenty of time to talk later, and Neville may be back before there is any need to start conjectures. It's only a cold meal, but I'm sure you won't mind."

"Who would — with you?"

"Oh, run along."

Wallace took the suitcases upstairs, and was absent for about a quarter of an hour.

"Here we are," he said. "I say — what a spread. I feel almost like

387

the prodigal son. Jolly good of the C.O. to make this possible. He's really the most decent old boy. But it's queer about Neville, isn't it?"

"Yes. If he had a breakdown he could easily have telephoned me from some place. I don't think it can be that. The most likely explanation is that you really saw Isobel last night."

"I'm absolutely certain I did. You mean that in that event he might have met her and been invited to a meal by her hostess?"

"Something like that. Poor Neville has got her completely under his skin, and I rather wish he hadn't."

"Why?"

"She's not so forthcoming as a girl should be — always keeping something back. First it was the husband — "

"You can scarcely blame her for not mentioning him," said Wallace. "I can't get over the cheek of the fellow — coming here and pinching our belongings."

"And now there's this strange business.

It's not remarkable that she should know the people who live at Overlands, since she has lived all her life in the neighbourhood, but she appears to have left London suddenly, as if — Oh, I don't know."

"We should know soon. I say, what about ringing up the house?"

"How can we? I don't know the name of the people who live there."

"But the telephone supervisor might."

"I don't think they would help — not without the name of the subscriber. But even if they did, what on earth could we say?"

"Have you got a directory — I mean a residential one?"

"Yes — ten years old."

"Where is it?"

"I'll find it later. Let's have this meal in peace. Neville may barge in at any moment."

But Neville did nothing of the sort, and when they had finished the meal Teresa found the old tattered directory. It took some time to find what she wanted, but at last she was successful.

"Here it is," she said. "Edgar Dykes — Bart. Overlands House — Higher Raccombe. That's the place."

"A baronet," said Wallace. "Sounds highly respectable."

"It doesn't follow that he lives there now. Ten years and a war make a lot of difference. But of course there's the telephone directory. That at least is up to date."

The telephone directory gave many Dykes, but none of them lived anywhere near Higher Raccombe.

"No use," said Wallace. "You know — I feel we should do something. It's close upon midnight."

"But what can we do?"

"We could run up there in the car — if I had any petrol, but I had only just enough to get me here."

"I've got a few coupons left, but there's not a chance of getting petrol at this time of night. And you must be dead beat, too. I think the only thing to do is wait — and hope that he'll return soon."

They sat up another hour, during which time Teresa told Wallace about the Inspector's visit. Towards the end Wallace actually caught himself nodding.

"I'm — sorry," he gasped.

"It's not to be wondered at, darling. You must have motored nearly four hundred miles since this morning. Bed's the place for you. Neville is capable of looking after himself. If he doesn't show up, we'll start a hue and cry in the morning."

"Perhaps you're right," agreed Wallace. "Yes, I certainly am tired. It's lovely to be back here. Good night, darling."

Half an hour later the house was dark and silent. But Teresa lay awake for a long time with her ears alert for any sound from outside, and at last she fell asleep. It seemed that no time at all had passed before she woke up and found the sun trying to steal into the room. It was broad daylight outside, and the clock showed the time to be nearly eight. Then she realised that the telephone was ringing downstairs, and she slipped on a dressing-gown and hurried down. To her surprise, it was Inspector Carson speaking.

"Oh, Miss Brandon?" he asked. "Is your brother in?"

"I — I really don't know," she stammered. "He hadn't come home last night when I went to bed. I'll go and see if he is in his room. Hold on a moment."

She rushed upstairs with her heart beating furiously. A knock on Neville's door brought no response. She opened the door and looked inside. The bed had not been slept in the previous night. A feeling of dreadful foreboding swept over her. The Inspector's voice had sounded a little strange. Was it bad news? She found herself at the telephone again — speechless.

"Miss Brandon?" asked Carson. "Are you there?"

"Y-yes," she stammered. "My brother

hasn't come back. Is anything the matter? Please — please tell me."

"Was he out in his car yesterday evening?"

"Yes."

"What is the make of car?"

"It's a Sunbeam-Talbot drophead."

"I'm afraid there is bad news. I propose to come out and see you at once. I'm now at Ashburton — following an early report."

"But my brother? Please tell me what is wrong?"

"It is feared that your brother met his death in an accident late last night. I'm dreadfully sorry to have to tell you this. I'll leave at once."

She hung up the receiver, and staggered to the couch. Her brain seemed to have stopped working — her body cold and numb. She wanted to run upstairs and get Wallace, but was unable to move. Then suddenly Wallace came to view — half-dressed.

"I heard the phone," he said. "Good Lord! What's wrong?"

In a moment he was beside her, and his close presence made all the difference.

"It's Neville," she said. "He's met with a fatal accident — in the car. That was Inspector Carson — speaking from Ashburton where he was called this morning."

Wallace's mouth twitched. In the past he had been used to losing comrades. But that was in battle when the scales were always weighed against living. This was different.

"Steady," he whispered, taking her two hands in his. "Where did it happen?"

"I don't know — yet. Carson is coming here at once."

"Thank God I'm here," he murmured. "Yes, cry if you feel like it. It's better that way."

Teresa did so for a minute or two, but then she dried her eyes and contrived to smile at him.

"That's better," he said. "Now you go and dress, while I get the breakfast."

"But I don't want — "

"Oh yes you do. We've got to face this out, darling, and starving ourselves is no help. All I need is a collar and tie. Carson should be here in half an hour."

She nodded, gave him a kiss, and went upstairs. He was about to set the breakfast-table when the daily help arrived, full of beans and with no excuses for her absence the previous day.

"Oh, sir," she said. "I thought you had gone back to Germany."

"I didn't have to go after all. Get the breakfast as quickly as you can. We have had some bad news. Mr. Brandon has been involved in a car accident, and the police are coming here to take some evidence."

"Oh golly!" said the girl. "I hope he isn't hurt much."

"I'm afraid he is."

"Oh, what a shame. I'll bet it wasn't his fault. The way some people drive is shocking. Why, only yesterday I had a narrow escape from being mangled — "

Wallace crept away, finished his dressing and was down again in a short time. Teresa appeared soon afterwards. Her cheeks were pallid and her eyes a little swollen, but she was now complete mistress of herself, and glad to find the irresponsible maid back again.

"I'm so sorry, Miss, to hear about the bad news," said the girl.

"Thank you."

"And I'm sorry I couldn't come yesterday. My rheumatics came on again."

Teresa nodded but could not help thinking that the rheumatics had vanished with quite remarkable speed. She and Wallace then ate a somewhat tasteless meal, and had scarcely finished it when the big police car arrived. Carson and his sergeant were shown into the lounge, and Teresa and Wallace joined him after a minute or two.

"This is Major Wallace," said Teresa. "I don't think you have met him before.

He has been staying with us."

Carson nodded soberly, and his Sergeant produced a notebook and pencil.

"I'm very sorry to have to give you this bad news," said Carson. "A report came in this morning to the effect that a burnt-out car was found soon after daybreak at the bottom of Pitts Hill, which is about four miles from Ashburton. There was a body in the car. The numberplates were of the aluminium type, and gave the number D.V. 2206. I believe that is the number of your brother's car?"

"Yes," replied Teresa.

"Wheel marks on the side of the road at the sharp bend show that the car went over at that point. There is a precipitous fall of about two hundred feet, and there is nothing left of the car but the metal parts. I have never seen a more complete burn-out. It is established that there was ground mist at that point during the night, and it seems that that was the cause of the accident. It probably hit the bend and the driver was over the side before he could do anything. In the circumstances, identification of the body is impossible, but I have some items which were found on the site."

He opened a small case and took out a large knife, a silver ring, and a bunch of keys. All were severely burnt.

"Do you recognise these?" he asked.

"Yes," replied Teresa. "They all belonged to my brother."

"I thought that would be the case. At what time did your brother leave home yesterday?"

"I think it was about half-past ten in the morning."

"Do you know where he intended going?"

"Yes. It was a house at Higher Raccombe called Overlands."

"A friend's house?"

"No. It was the sequel to an incident which occurred the night before last, while Major Wallace was with us. It's rather a long story."

"I should like to have the full details."

Teresa hesitated for a moment, and the Sergeant was waiting, pencil in hand. Then she related exactly what had happened, while Carson listened attentively and the Sergeant wrote.

"That's all," she said finally.

Carson thought for a few moments, while he took a few paces.

"Certainly a curious coincidence," he said. "Major Wallace, do you still think it was Miss Larkin whom you saw in that house?"

"Yes," replied Wallace. "I'm positive."

"Do you think she may have seen you, but preferred not to give any sign of it?"

"I wouldn't like to venture an opinion. She was side face to me, but she might have seen me."

"I presume you and she were on friendly terms?"

"Oh yes."

"Then why didn't you draw her attention?"

"I was so completely taken by surprise, and she was gone before I could recover my wits."

"While you were there, did you get the name of the owner of the house?"

"No. But we looked up an old directory. It gave the owner as Sir Edgar Dykes."

"Oh yes. I think I remember. He was killed in the war. I have an idea the house was sold a year or two ago. Well, I shall have to call there, as they may have valuable evidence to offer. There are just one or two points I want to clear up. Miss Brandon, I got the impression that your brother was rather fond of Miss Larkin. Have you anything to say about that?"

"Yes. My brother was in love with her."

"Was there an understanding between them?"

"I don't know. It is only recently that he discovered that she is a married woman, living apart from her husband."

"Did he know the husband?"

"He met him once — in London."

"What is his name?"

"Algood."

"Did Algood know that your brother was in love with his wife?"

"I think so. Oh, but does all that matter now?"

"It may have some bearing on what has happened."

"You — you mean that for the purpose of the inquest it is necessary to find out whether my brother may have had cause to — to take his own life?"

"Yes. But please don't misunderstand me. All the evidence so far indicates accident. But I won't bother you any more just now. I may look in on my way back from Overlands."

Wallace accompanied the Inspector and the Sergeant to the door. He wanted to ask Carson a question which was better asked out of Teresa's hearing.

"What about identification of the body?" he asked.

Carson shook his head sadly.

"In the circumstances it would be useless, and I'm glad for Miss Brandon's sake. You see, the body was completely incinerated. It was not thrown clear of the car and the heat was tremendous. But he received mortal injuries in the fall, and could not have suffered for any length of time."

Wallace felt almost sick as he visualised the ghastly scene. He went back to Teresa, and found her sitting still in a chair. It looked for a moment as if she were going to collapse, but suddenly she stood up and took his arm.

"It must have been God who sent you to me at this moment," she said with deep emotion. "I need you so much. Take me for a walk, darling — anywhere. Don't worry. I'm not going to crack up. Neville would like to know that you and I at least are happy."

18

INSPECTOR CARSON'S mind was busy as the car sped over the lovely countryside towards Overlands. This peculiar case had so many loose ends that he doubted his ability to make any sense out of it, but the more he thought about it the more he became convinced that the elusive character known as Kubla Khan was the mainspring. It was he who had engineered the robbery at Barrowtor, and it was he who had written that anonymous letter which had shown Suzy Cameron to be a masquerading adventuress, working with Gus Tamling and the Tollers. But the fingerprints on the implement which had killed the lodge-keeper at Barrowtor were certainly not Kubla's. But why had the fellow gone out of his way to show up the gang? Had they, like so many others, been in his employ and fallen foul of him? Had he some interest in the large sum of money at stake? By what means could he possibly reap profit from what he had done?

"There's the girl," he said to the Sergeant. "She looked nice enough to me, but I must say her actions have been a little strange. She never told me that her real name was Algood, and she acted as if she didn't care a great deal about what happened to her father's estate, which her brother gave away to a chance acquaintance — to give the lady a name she scarcely deserves. But she vanished from London suddenly, and now we hear that Major Wallace saw her in the house we are visiting. Brandon, puzzled and probably jealous of what she might be doing there, takes out his car to do a bit of snooping, and comes to a sorry end. The point which the coroner will interest himself in is, did he discover something which was very unpleasant to him and take the swift way out of all the trouble?"

The Sergeant shook his head.

"He didn't look the sort of chap who might do a desperate thing like that," he said. "I liked the way he behaved."

"The point is, he loved that girl, and there were obstacles. One was the husband, but there might have been others. Curious the way they met too. She said she was coming to the house to see her father — not knowing he was dead. We've only her word for that. Well, I hope she is at the house, because I should like to ask her some questions."

At last they reached Overlands, and the Sergeant brought the car to a standstill outside the imposing entrance. Carson rang the bell, and after a few moments the door was opened by Tony, looking as neat and spotless as ever.

"We are police officers," said Carson, handing Tony his card. "And I am seeking evidence respecting a car accident which took place some time last night — some miles from here. Who occupies this house?"

"Captain Cardinal, sir."

"Is the Captain at home?"

"Yes, Inspector," said Tony, gazing at the card. "If you will come inside I will take in your card."

The two visitors entered the hall, and Tony went off with the card. He passed into a room on the left, and came back with the card on a salver. Then he vanished through another door, and was absent for only a second or two.

"This way, gentlemen," he said.

They entered the lounge where Cardinal was seated in his wheel-chair. He smiled at them and wished them good morning.

"Sorry to trouble you," said Carson. "There has been an accident over at Pitts Hill. A young man named Neville Brandon crashed his car into a chasm and was burned to death. Did he by any chance call here yesterday?"

"Not to my knowledge. I personally

had no callers. But I'll find out. Excuse me!"

He rang the bell and Tony entered the room.

"Were there any callers yesterday, Tony?" he asked.

"Only two tradesmen, sir."

"Not by any chance a gentleman in a car?"

"No one else at all, sir. I am quite certain of that."

"All right. Thank you."

Cardinal turned to Carson.

"I'm sorry to hear about the accident," he said. "Were you under the impression that the ill-fated man called here?"

"Yes. I am given to understand that it was his intention."

"But I didn't expect any caller. What name did you say?"

"Brandon — Neville Brandon."

"No. I fear your information is wrong. If not, then the young man failed to carry out his intention."

"That of course is likely."

"What I don't understand is why he

should want to see me, as I know no one of that name. Was he trying to sell me something?"

"Oh no. I gathered from his sister that he was under the impression that a friend of his was staying here."

"But I have had no visitors for months. I bought this place in the hope that I would be free of visitors — at least until I am able to meet them on different terms."

He gave a glance at his wrapped-up legs.

"The war?" asked Carson sympathetically.

"Yes. I had lung trouble too, and fresh air was recommended."

"You should get enough of it here."

"I do — in winter. But I'm interested in my intended visitor. Have you any idea whom he expected to find here?"

"Yes. It was a woman named Mrs. Algood."

Cardinal shook his head.

"I should like to know what put that idea into his head."

"I can enlighten you on that. It appears that he and his sister and a friend lost their way the night before last, and the friend saw this house and came here to ask the way. While he was waiting in the hall this friend saw the woman in question pass across the half-landing and vanish into a room. He swears that it was Mrs. Algood. He told Brandon later, and Brandon, disbelieving him, made a small bet that he was wrong. Brandon's intended call here to-day was to settle that bet."

"But to the best of my knowledge no one called here the night before last. Just a moment."

He rang the bell again and Tony entered.

"Tony, did anyone call here the night before last and ask the way to any place?"

"Yes, sir," replied Tony. "Walter answered the door. You had retired for the night. Walter came to me and asked me if I knew the road to

Shaldon. I told him and he went back to the hall."

"I see. But no one told me."

"The matter seemed too trivial, sir."

"Has Walter come back yet?"

"No, sir. I am expecting him at any moment."

Cardinal turned to Carson.

"Walter is the butler. He went on holiday yesterday morning. I'm sorry I didn't know about the man calling, but the rest of the story is fantastic. Tony, the young man who called is under the impression that he saw a lady in the house. What do you say to that?"

Tony opened his eyes in astonishment.

"A lady, sir!" he ejaculated. "But that is impossible. Now you mention it, sir, Walter told me that the enquirer acted as if he had dined rather too well. I took that to mean that he had had more than a few drinks."

"If he saw a lady here he must have, unless you are concealing some damsel about the premises, Tony."

"Opportunity is rather lacking, sir,

even if I felt that way," replied Tony.

"Yes, I agree." Cardinal turned to Carson. "Since I am suspected of harbouring females I suggest you look round the place, Inspector," he said. "You will find it a ghastly sort of mausoleum, most of it full of cobwebs and bad smells. I wish I could come with you, but there are far too many steps over which I have some difficulty. Do let's get this matter cleared up."

"I scarcely think that is necessary."

"I should feel much better about it if you would. It's a comic sort of house, and you might even enjoy it."

"Well, if it would make you feel happier — "

"It would."

For the next twenty minutes Carson and the Sergeant were escorted by Tony into innumerable rooms, and into the large empty basement. Carson noticed the exit from the basement.

"Where does that go?" he asked.

"Into the garage. It is a covered

way, used in very bad weather. Like to go up?"

"Yes — we may as well."

They passed along the passage, and finally reached the large garage. Now only the Packard stood there.

"The Captain's car," said Tony. "I usually drive him. But he doesn't use it much. Oh, there's the tower. I shall have to get the key for that. There are a couple of rooms at the top, full of old junk. It's a bit of a climb — seventy steps."

"Don't bother," said Carson. "I have seen enough, and haven't a great deal of time. It rather looks as if that young man saw a ghost."

"Spirits, Inspector," said Tony with a sly smile.

"Yes. Is Captain Cardinal getting better?"

"Oh yes, but it's a slow business."

"What Regiment was he in?"

"No regiment. He was in the Navy."

"I'd better see him before we leave."

By this time Cardinal was out on the

terrace, with the morning newspaper, doing the daily crossword.

"Finished?" he asked as Carson approached him.

"Yes. I'm sorry to have bothered you, but you can understand that I want to trace the movements of Mr. Brandon, as far as possible, from the time he left home until he met with his accident."

"Naturally. Well, it's a very sad business. Accident, of course?"

"I think there is no doubt about that."

Half an hour later Carson was back at Fouracres. He passed Wallace and Teresa in the drive, coming back from their walk. By the time he had got out of the car at the house the walkers were present.

"What luck?" asked Wallace.

"None. I saw the man who owns the house. He is a Captain Horace Cardinal, late of the Royal Navy, and crippled in the war. Very charming type of man. He swears that Brandon never called there, and denies that there was any woman in the house the night before last. He brought a servant to corroborate."

"A very old man?"

"No. The old man whom you saw was on holiday, but it was the young man who gave him the details you needed."

"So it is suggested I am a liar?"

"Not quite. It is suggested that you had had a drink too many."

"Damned impudence!" said Wallace. "Inspector, do you believe that story?"

"What story?"

"Their version."

"I don't know what to believe. Anyway, it doesn't appear to be a matter of the first importance. There may have been a woman there whom, for some reason, they do not wish to have questioned, but it doesn't necessarily follow it was Mrs. Algood. You might possibly have been mistaken about that."

"I'm sure I wasn't. Neville rang

414

up her address and found she wasn't there."

"That would seem to back up your assertion, but of course it isn't conclusive. I propose to make some enquiries about Cardinal, and also about Mrs. Algood. I'll let you know if anything comes of it. Now I must get back to headquarters."

When he had gone Wallace gave full vent to his feelings. As a man who prided himself on his abstemiousness, he resented deeply the suggestion that he had been drunk on that memorable occasion.

"You should know," he said to Teresa. "Was I canned?"

"You were a little merry — no more."

"Teresa, don't you believe that I saw Isobel in that house?"

"I don't know, darling. It's all so — so bewildering."

"Good heavens! You too!"

"Now I've hurt your feelings."

"You couldn't. Perhaps it's childish

of me to be so touchy. Let's go and see if lunch is ready."

Teresa smiled at him and took his arm. A little later they were sitting down at table, and Wallace was glad to notice that Teresa was making a fair meal. Afterwards he persuaded her to lie down for a bit. She argued, but finally consented, for she had had but a poor night's sleep. To her surprise she woke up to find that she had slept for nearly three hours. But she felt better for it — more able to face the painful facts.

"You should have woken me," she said, when she came downstairs.

"Not if you had slept all the evening."

"I feel I'm not much of a hostess. But I feel much — much better now. John, when is the inquest to be held?"

"Carson didn't say. Teresa, I've been doing some thinking, and I'm now certain that there is much more in this case than meets the eye. Nothing in the world will persuade me that I did not see Isobel in that house, and if that is true, one is bound to ask why the people who live there lied. People don't lie like that without a very good reason."

"That's true. But the Inspector searched the premises."

"Yes, but if the occupants had cause to believe that the police might call — "

"But why should they?"

"If Neville did call there, they might have to consider the possibility that his visit was known to other persons."

"That's true. But if Neville called there you — you aren't suggesting that what happened — to him — was not an accident?"

"It might not be. It could have been arranged to look like an accident."

"But the Inspector must have considered that possibility. There seemed to be no doubt in his mind."

"His mind is a little difficult to read. But at least he didn't know Neville as we did. Neville knew that hill — every inch of it. I don't believe that even in a fog he would have driven over the edge. The brakes on the car were first class. And another point — quite important. The thing must have happened very late at night, for there was no sign of any fog early in the evening. Now why should Neville come home that way from Overlands — presuming he spent his time prowling round the place? It is miles further than the direct route."

"Yes, it is," said Teresa thoughtfully. "But if it wasn't an accident, then the people who engineered it would scarcely have chosen a place right off his direct route."

"Not if they could help it, but that hill is just the right place to stage a fake accident. There's no other hill so far as I know which has such a dangerous bend and such a terrific chasm on the driving side. Is there?"

Teresa was bound to agree, but the possibility of such cold-blooded murder was hard to accept. It was the sort of thing one read of but never came in contact with. Yet there was much in

Wallace's argument which was true. Neville had always been a skilled and most careful driver. She knew he had been up and down that hill dozens of times. Yes, it was certainly strange — and vastly disturbing.

"Why — why should anyone want to kill Neville?" she asked.

"I don't know. But I believe there is a reason. It could have something to do with that will, or the murder of Barding at Barrowtor."

"But your whole argument is based upon the assumption that Isobel was actually in that house. Do you — can you bring yourself to believe that Isobel had anything to do — "

"Why did they lie about her? And wasn't it Isobel whom Neville went to see?"

"John, you are almost making me believe that what you are saying is true."

"I know it's all horrible to you, as it is to me. Teresa, I want to go up there."

"To — Overlands?"

"Yes."

"But what good can it do? Can you do more than the police have done?"

"Who knows? After all, the police are at a disadvantage. What could Carson do but go to the front door and ring the bell? The police are more hidebound by the law than we are. I want to see that old man who let me in, and ask why he lied about my condition? I want to tell him, and his employer, that I know Isobel was there. But before I do that I want to snoop round the place — "

"John, it's madness. The Inspector said he intended making enquiries about Captain Cardinal."

"Yes, and how long will that take? It will mean looking up records — being pushed from one War department to another. It might take days. Don't put me off, darling. Lend me all the petrol coupons which you have left."

Teresa reflected for a few moments.

"Only on one condition," she said.

"What is the condition?"

"That I come too."

"Oh no. That would never do."

"Why not?"

"Because — well, there might be danger."

"That's what I thought, and that's why two are better than one. I can stand by — in the car."

"You could, but — "

"There's another reason. Neville was all I had left — excepting you. If — if he was murdered I should like to contribute something towards bringing his murderer to justice. I'll find the petrol coupons, John."

Now that her mind was made up, Wallace knew that nothing short of a steam engine would move her. She vanished for a few minutes, and then returned with her handbag and a scarf tied round her hair.

"Only three units left," she said. "But I think I can wring the heart of the garage proprietor."

"I shouldn't wonder," he replied.

"This time we'll leave no vacuum

behind us. We'll cover all our movements."

"How do you mean?"

She went to the door and called the daily help.

"Listen, Betty," she said. "Major Wallace and I are going on a trip. I suppose you can't stay on until about ten o'clock?"

"Sorry, Miss. I've promised to go with my sister to the cinema in the town."

"At what time will you leave the cinema?"

"About ten o'clock."

"That will do nicely. You have to pass this house to get to your home. I want you to call here. If we are not back I want you to ring up this number and ask for Inspector Carson." She wrote the name and the telephone number of the County Police. "I want you to tell him that we have gone to Overlands — I'll write that down — and that he is needed up there. Is that quite clear?"

"Yes, Miss. But suppose I can't get him on the telephone?"

"Then tell the officer who speaks to you to get the message to Inspector Carson wherever he is. I'll leave this card on the table so that you won't lose it. You'll find the key in the usual place if we are not back. Will you do that?"

"Yes, Miss, of course."

"Good! Now repeat it all to me."

Betty did so, haltingly, but correctly.

A few minutes later Teresa and Wallace were in Wallace's battered vehicle. They stopped at the garage, and Teresa, after a private talk with the proprietor, appeared to get amazing measure for her three units.

"You'll find this is a change after the Sunbeam," said Wallace. "To think of that lovely bus burnt to a cinder."

Teresa closed her eyes momentarily and Wallace cursed himself for his tactless remark. But a moment later he felt Teresa's hand pressing his arm slightly and he knew he was forgiven.

Soon they were in the flowery lanes making towards their objective, with the fussy car rattling and squeaking in about fifty different places. They went the way Neville had gone, and ultimately reached the village of Presting. Here Wallace had to pull up behind a large delivery van, in front of the little general shop. A man was busy pasting a handwritten poster on a board. As he moved into the shop Wallace saw what was written on the poster:

'FATAL CAR ACCIDENT AT PITTS HILL.'

"The Exeter evening newspaper has arrived," he said.

Teresa now saw the poster, and turned her head away. But a moment later she looked at Wallace.

"Get one," she said. "I've got to get used to this."

Wallace left the engine running while he went into the shop. The man who had put up the notice was talking to the postman, who had a copy of the newspaper in his hands.

"I'll bet it was the young fellow who called here," said the newsagent. "It says there that it was a Sunbeam drophead coupé, and that was the car he had. I saw it when he pulled up, and thought how I'd like to own a bus like that. He came in and bought some cigarettes. Asked me about Overlands, and said he knew someone who had been employed there. Paper, sir?" he asked Wallace.

"Please," said Wallace.

"Well, I'll be getting along," said the postman, and left the shop.

Wallace tendered half a crown to delay matters, and then scanned the large headlines, and the photograph of the site of the disaster which showed the wreckage — still smoking.

"Bad business that," said the newsagent. "I was telling postie that I'm certain the young fellow called here yesterday morning. Nice chap he seemed to be too."

"But did he actually say he was going to call at the house you mentioned?"

"He did so. I warned him about the savage dogs they keep up there. Can't blame 'em, because it's miles from anywhere. But he just laughed and said he liked dogs. To think of him ending up like that. Shows you never know what lies waiting for ye."

"Have you told the police that?" asked Wallace.

"What good would that do?"

"The police would probably like to check up the young man's movements. Facts like that are useful at an inquest."

"Maybe you'm right," said the man, lapsing into his native dialect. "I never thought of that."

"I suppose he really meant to call at Overlands?"

"That's what he said. Yes, I'll ring up the police and tell 'em just what happened. Thankee, mister."

Wallace went back to the car looking very tense.

"Why so long?" asked Teresa.

"An extraordinary thing happened. Neville called at that shop on his way to Overlands. The man who runs the shop remembers the car, and Neville asked him about Overlands. He said he was going there, as he knew someone who used to be employed there. That of course was a rather necessary fiction, but it all goes to back up my belief that Captain Cardinal lied to Carson. Up to within a few miles of Overlands Neville still intended to call there. Why should he change his mind at the last moment? There's another thing — the man mentioned savage dogs kept by Cardinal. It all goes to build up a rather grim picture of the place."

Teresa nodded and watched Wallace thrust the newspaper into the cubbyhole of the dashboard. She had no desire to read immediately what the news-reporters had to say about the tragedy at Pitts Hill. That was better done in private.

"Keep your eyes open for the house,"

said Wallace. "We must be getting close to it now."

A few minutes later the lodge came to view, and the wrought-iron gates which led to the drive. The gates were now closed. Wallace slowed down the car at the notice board marked 'Private'.

"Can't see the house at all," he said. "But that must be the lodge and the drive. I ought to be able to scramble over that wall. Let's take the car a bit closer."

He turned it into the private road, and then left the road until the car was nicely shielded by the many pine trees. Here he stopped it.

"What are you going to do?" asked Teresa.

"Find a way into the grounds. They appear to be well-wooded and offer plenty of cover."

"What about the dogs?"

"I'll have to risk them."

"Do you want me to stay here?"

"Yes. I expect I shall be back in a

few minutes. Give me a quarter of an hour, and then drive out on to the main road and wait another quarter of an hour. If I'm not back then get on the telephone to Carson, and tell him I'm being held, for that is what it will signify."

"John, dear, do you think we are acting sensibly?"

"What is sensible action in a case like this? I am about to commit trespass, and if they are law-abiding people all they can do is show me the gate — if they find me. Let's stick to the plan."

"All right," said Teresa, and looked at her wrist-watch. "But for goodness' sake take care."

"I will."

Wallace left the car and walked through the pines to the high wall. Moving to the left he soon found a breach in it, through which he could see part of the upper garden and the large house. He climbed up and for a few moments stood on the broken masonry. Nowhere was there anyone in sight, and the only sound which came to him was the sighing of the wind through the trees. He lowered himself to the ground on the other side, and advanced through thick undergrowth until he reached a spot from which the whole of the house could be seen, high up on a wide terrace. There was now a danger of being seen from one of the many windows, so he moved further to the left and used every bit of cover to bring him round to the eastern side of the building. Soon he was on a beaten track and the going was much easier. An old rustic building came to view. He stopped and peered through the dirty windows. It was a summer house, full of clutter which looked as if it had not been disturbed for years. He went on and soon the land began to rise. The path twisted through great clumps of rhododendrons which blocked out his view for a while, but then they thinned out and he emerged in a small group of umbrella pines on a hillock. He was now on a level with the upper terrace and able to see the house from a different angle. The tower in the centre seemed to be older than most of the building, and he thought there must be a very fine view from the balcony which surrounded it, for it seemed high enough to overlook all the surrounding timber. Then his wandering gaze went to the sunken Dutch Garden which lay midway between him and the house. On a seat facing the central pool was a solitary figure. He caught his breath as he realised it was a woman. She had her back to him, and was sitting perfectly still, as if in meditation. To approach her directly was out of the question, so again he went round to the left and finally found himself within fifty yards of her. But still he could not see her face. Picking up a large stone he pitched it away to his right. Its heavy fall had the desired effect. Her face came slightly round, and he drew in his breath hard, for he saw Isobel's unmistakable profile — just as he had seen it on the half-landing two nights previously. The next moment the profile was hidden from him, but the owner sat on — motionless as before.

He moved down from his higher position, and soon the yew hedge which surrounded the garden hid Isobel from view. Walking on tiptoe, he found the entrance to the garden, and stood for a few moments peering round the green edge. It was Isobel, hands clenched on her knees, staring down into the water. Then he noticed that in one hand was a clenched handkerchief. Her face looked pallid and the wind was playing havoc with her uncovered hair.

"Isobel!" he called softly.

He saw her start violently, and then her head came round and she saw him. The lips moved as if she were whispering his name, and he moved towards her. She stood up and gripped the back of the seat with her unoccupied hand. Within a yard of her he stopped.

"John!" she gasped. "What — what

are you doing here?"

"Looking for you — perhaps."

"But — but — " she stammered.

"Isobel — I've got to speak to you."

"But how did you know — ?"

"That's part of my story. I must talk to you."

"No — not now. I've got to get back to the house. I'm only a guest here, and I slipped out for a few moments. How did you get here?"

"Over the wall."

"You shouldn't. Why — why did you do that?"

"In the hope that I might see you privately. Outside is Teresa. She too wants to see you."

"Later — yes, but not now."

"Why are you afraid?"

"I'm not afraid. Why do you say that?"

"Because it is obvious. I think it is in your interest to come with me."

"What do you mean by that?"

"The police are enquiring after you."

"Why?"

"Don't you know why the police might desire to question you?"

"No. Tell me, please."

"Not here. Somebody might come and find us together. I don't want that to happen. Are you afraid to face Teresa?"

"Why should I be?"

"Then come with me. You can get over the wall quite easily. I promised to return to Teresa in a quarter of an hour, and it is nearly time I was back."

Isobel seemed racked with indecision, looking towards the house fearfully.

"I'll come," she said at last.

"Good."

Swiftly they made their way back by the route taken by Wallace, and soon reached the gap in the wall. Here Wallace helped her over and then followed her. A little later the car was seen. It was actually moving, but as it came round in a half circle Teresa saw the oncoming pair, and quickly brought the car to a halt.

As Isobel came closer, Teresa's face became very hard. She did no more than acknowledge Isobel's murmured greeting, and when Isobel and Wallace were seated in the back she stopped the engine.

"Now we can talk," said Wallace grimly. "Isobel, you know what has happened, don't you?"

Isobel now found two pairs of eyes focused on her face.

"I — I don't understand," she said. "Why do you stare at me like that? Neville must have told you I — I was staying here — with an old friend."

Wallace switched his gaze to Teresa's astonished face. But quickly astonishment changed to unmistakable doubting. Like himself, Teresa was wondering just how far she could trust this girl whose behaviour was so perplexing. And now it was Teresa who was asking questions, not in her usual calm, friendly way, but with a hard, penetrating incisiveness.

"When did you last see Neville?" she asked.

"Yesterday. I was with him nearly all day."

"You were with him?"

"Yes."

"When did you leave him?"

"In the evening. He drove me back here."

"What happened then?"

"I went into the house, and to bed."

"Weren't you at the house when the police called this morning?"

"No. I was out — walking."

"And your friend — Captain Cardinal — didn't he tell you that the police had called?"

"No. Why should the police call?"

Wallace was puzzled. It seemed to him that she was not acting a part, but telling the truth as she knew it.

"Perhaps you can explain why Captain Cardinal denied that there was any woman staying with him?" he asked.

"I — I can't, unless he considered it an unwarranted question. But why do you keep mentioning the police? Why were they asking after me?"

Wallace stared into her fine eyes, but found them quite steady.

"Don't you know what happened to Neville?" he asked.

"No. Oh, is something wrong? I promised to telephone him to-day, but — but I haven't done so. What is all this about? What has happened?"

Wallace leaned over the back of the seat and took the newspaper from the cubby-hole. Without a word he unfolded it and handed it to Isobel. She stared at the large headlines, and then shifted her gaze to the letterpress. Suddenly she gave a pitiful little cry, and dropped the newspaper. The next moment she was sobbing into her hands as if her heart would break. Teresa looked at Wallace, and Wallace shook his head sorrowfully. It was some minutes before Isobel could speak.

"I didn't know," she said. "It — it must have happened on his way home."

"But your friend, Cardinal, knew. Why didn't he tell you?" asked Wallace.

This question appeared to cause her some embarrassment.

"He — he didn't know — about me and Neville," she said.

"Didn't he know you had been out with Neville?"

"No. Neville met me along the road, and I telephoned to Cardinal to tell him that I had met a friend, and would not be back until the evening. He didn't know who the friend was."

"So you believe it was an accident?" asked Teresa.

"What else could it be? Oh, is that why the police wanted to see me? Do they think it might not have been an accident?"

"They have to make sure," said Wallace.

"But — but is there any evidence which would suggest anything else?"

"We don't know," replied Wallace. "The police don't talk much about such things. But it's strange that people in that house have lied so outrageously. Both Cardinal and the servants have denied that you were in the house, although I saw you with my own eyes — two nights ago."

Isobel stared at him, astonished.

"You saw me?" she asked.

"Yes. We were all on our way back from an hotel where we had had a celebration, and we lost our way. I saw the house and went to ask the way to Shaldon. I was sitting in the hall when I saw you on the half-landing. You were going to a door on the right, and I don't think you saw me. I told Neville and Teresa. Neville came here yesterday to find out if I was telling the truth. But if you were with him all day, he must have told you."

"Y-yes. I think he did."

Again Teresa looked puzzled. How could one trust Isobel in the face of her inconsistent answers? What was she holding back, and what were her reasons? Wallace too was exhibiting the same brooding suspicion.

"If the crash was no accident," he said, "we want to find the person responsible. You can understand that, can't you?"

"You ask me that question," she said resentfully. "Don't you realise that I loved Neville? There were obstacles in the way, but I loved him. I — I suppose there is no doubt at all that it was Neville — in the car?"

"Who else could it be? It was his car."

"But he might have been held up and attacked on his way home. Some murderous tramp might have stopped him with the sole object of stealing the car."

"That's incredible."

"So is the accident. Has he been identified?"

"It's not possible. There was a tremendous fire. But his keys, his ring, and his knife were found amid the debris."

"A knife?"

"Yes. A double-bladed Swiss knife with his initials on it."

"Yes — I remember it," she said

slowly. "But if he was waylaid and knocked unconscious, the thief might have stolen those things and perhaps his note-case. There's a way to prove if — if it was really Neville."

"What way?" asked Wallace.

"The small piece of shrapnel which was left in his leg — just below the hip. Neville showed me the X-ray photograph when — when I was at Fouracres."

Teresa gave a little gasp, and Wallace stared at her, for he himself knew nothing about this war memento.

"It's true," she said. "I never thought of that."

Isobel turned to her with a show of sympathy.

"Your loss is at least as great as mine," she said. "Perhaps I shouldn't have raised what may prove to be false hopes. But it's more likely that someone who didn't know the car nor the dangerous hill should meet with such an end. Neville knew them both. If there's anything I can do — "

"There is," said Teresa tensely. "You can come with us now and tell the police everything. John has been made out to be a liar, and I think that should be put right without delay."

"But I can't come now."

"Why not?"

"I — I can't explain."

"You mean you don't want to explain," said Wallace sternly.

"I mean I can't. There's something I'm not sure about, and I want to be certain — before I see the police. You must trust me."

"But for all we know the inquest may be held to-morrow."

"To-morrow everything may be different. Please let me go."

Wallace looked at Teresa, to find out her reactions to this queer conversation, and after a few moments Teresa nodded her head. Isobel gave a little sigh and got out of the car. Without a word, she hurried towards the gap in the wall.

19

CAPTAIN CARDINAL was reclining in a deep chair in the lounge, with a long drink by his side, and a cigar between his lips. The dark glasses which he wore on occasion were beside him, and away in the corner was his wheel-chair. He was sunk deep in reflection, and one was at loss to know whether his thoughts were pleasant or otherwise, for at intervals his expression changed from anxiety to contentment. Outside, the declining sun was throwing long shadows over the garden, and painting the edges of the scattered clouds. A rap on the door brought Tony into the room. The sleek secretary carried a folded newspaper in his hand, and without a word he passed it to Cardinal. For a minute or two the reclining man read what was printed under the heavy headlines, and finally he grunted and laid the newspaper on the table.

"Nice meaty account," he said. "Sort of thing these scribblers love to write about. That was a good job done."

Tony helped himself to a drink.

"Touch and go, if you ask me," he said. "What's K. going to say about this?"

"I don't care a damn what he says. Have you seen him this evening?"

"Yes. He seemed about the same. He was alone."

"Alone? Where's the girl?"

"I don't know."

"Then find out. I don't want her roaming about the place. I told you to keep your eye on her."

The door opened and Tom came in. Cardinal's gaze went to him.

"Well?" he asked. "What's the position?"

"It's okay. I've got the other vans. We can make a start as soon as it's dark. I'll feel happier when the job's done."

"What the devil are you waiting for, Tony?" asked Cardinal. "Go and find the girl. Tell her she's to stay in."

Tony went out, and Tom looked longingly at the bottle of whisky.

"Not now," grunted Cardinal. "I want clear heads. Is everyone here now?"

"Yes."

"Good. Are the gates locked?"

"Yes."

"Then you can let the dogs loose. They'll warn us if anyone is snooping around. I don't want a repetition of what happened before. See to it now."

When Tom opened the door he found Isobel just outside. She was breathless from hurrying, and Cardinal looked at her suspiciously.

"Come in, Isobel," he said. "All right, Tom. Do what I told you. Shut that door."

Isobel came down the room, and as she drew near the side-table Cardinal picked up the newspaper and thrust it behind the cushion of the chair in which he was lounging.

"You look all hot and bothered," he said. "Where have you been?"

"In the garden."

"I thought I told you to stay in your room."

"You did, but I needed some fresh air."

"Why are you staring at me like that?"

"I've got to talk to you."

"Go ahead then. What is biting you?"

"Why didn't you tell me the police had called this morning?"

"Who told you that?"

"I happen to know."

"Clever of you. Perhaps you know why they called?"

"I do."

"Then you'll understand why I preferred to keep it from you. I presume you have seen the evening newspaper?"

"Yes."

"Where? Have you been into the village?"

"No."

"Then who showed it to you?"

"That's my business."

Cardinal laughed and shook his head.

"You're an astonishing girl," he said. "I quite thought the bad news would produce a fit. But I was wrong. Where are all the tears I thought you would shed at the loss of your lover?"

"You — you beast!" said Isobel.

"At least do me credit for my good intentions. It was a shocking accident — "

"It was no accident."

"Indeed. How do you arrive at that astonishing conclusion?"

"A knife was found near the wreckage. A Swiss knife. It says so in that newspaper account."

"What of it?"

"When I came here last night — the last time — you told me that he had gone home."

"So he had. At least that is what I concluded."

"And you never saw him again?"

"No."

"Then how came it that his knife — that Swiss knife — was lying on that table?"

"Nonsense! It couldn't have been."

"I saw it, but did not think anything of it at the time. Now I know that you must have seen him again, and that you must have put that knife in his pocket — "

"My dear girl, your logic is appalling. What did I stand to gain by putting that knife in his pocket?"

"I don't know, but there must have been a reason. Why did he go home that way — so late at night? I should have thought — "

"What?" he asked after a long pause.

"Nothing."

"Is another possibility entering your bright mind? Shall I tell you just what happened to that Swiss knife — after you saw it on that table? Do you want the plain, ugly truth?"

"What do you mean?"

"Your precious husband took it, just before I kicked him out. If I hadn't done that he might have claimed certain marital rights. The fool really thought he had got you back again by his dirty piece of blackmail."

"But that was after Neville — Brandon — had left."

"Yes. But Brandon hadn't actually started for home. Perhaps he couldn't start the car. Perhaps he was still hanging around. But there was a nice expensive car — a dark night and no witnesses. It may be that it was Algood who went to his death in that car — after he had taken his revenge, and disposed of the man he hated. If that is so, it would be a rather nice act on the part of Providence, for they both knew far too much."

Isobel was breathing heavily. Here was a ready explanation of the disappearance of the Swiss knife from the table, but the explanation was far from perfect, and it did not invalidate the other possibility which had been knocking at her brain ever since she had learnt of the disaster. And now suddenly she saw through the whole thing.

"Can you tell me why — if Algood killed Neville — and then rode off in his car, he took with him Brandon's keys and a silver ring which he wore on his finger? Can you?"

"He was a thief and would take anything. He probably took money as well — "

"You liar!" said Isobel. "I can tell you what happened. When I came here and you told me that Brandon had gone, you lied. You found his car out there and you saw a way to silence my — Algood for ever. You wouldn't have kicked him out, knowing what he knew. You must have killed him first and then put his body into the car. You killed Algood and made it look as if it was Brandon — who had met with an accident. He was too dangerous. Algood might not be missed, but Brandon would. It was clever — fiendishly clever. That's the truth, isn't it?"

Cardinal reached out and poured himself a strong drink.

"As usual you are wrong, my dear," he said. "Suppose I admit it might have been Algood in the car, it doesn't follow that I killed him. He was making himself an infernal nuisance, you know, and there are quite a number of persons in this house, none of whom have cause to love him. Don't you realise that a slimy but dangerous animal has been removed from your path?"

"It was murder."

"Oh no. He got a bad blow accidentally. I simply made the best use of the situation."

Isobel was staring at him, amazed at his unruffled equanimity.

"Where — where is Brandon?" she asked.

"Gone."

"Gone where? You wouldn't let him go."

"Why not?"

"Because you want him officially dead."

"For a time perhaps. We have to leave here — without much loss of time. The place has served its purpose. By morning this place will be a pile of ashes, and the danger will be removed for ever."

"What have you done with Brandon?"

"Forget him. He has been a blasted nuisance. You and I and Kubla can restart operations elsewhere, or we could retire for good in some quiet spot."

"Get away from me," said Isobel. "You fill me with loathing. If you have harmed Neville, you'll pay for it. I'll tell the police everything. I'll keep back nothing."

"You will. But why should we quarrel? We're all in the same boat, and if one of us rocks it too much, it may sink. I'll do a deal with you about Brandon."

"Who are you to do deals? Since when have you been master here?"

"Since Kubla was unlucky enough to get that bullet in his ribs. He can't be in circulation for a long time, and someone has to steer the ship. It's rather fortunate that I hold a navigator's certificate. That's not intended to be a joke either."

"I imagine not," said Isobel.

"Then sit down and let's talk."

"About what?"

"The future. You must be interested in the future."

Isobel hesitated, and then sat down. Cardinal nodded his head appreciatively, reached out for a glass and poured out some whisky and soda.

"Drink," he said. "It will do you good. Oh, come on."

Isobel took the glass and drank a little of the contents.

"That's better," said Cardinal. "You're a good-looking, smart girl, Isobel, and I hope I can convince you that my plans offer you something better than you have been used to since you left home. I've been busy during the past twenty-four hours. I've sold out."

"You mean — the stock?"

"Yes. Cash on the nail and delivery to-night. Everything's laid on and this is going to be the pay-off. I've a safe place to go to, and in ten days you and I and Kubla could be in a plane on our way to South Africa, where there's sunshine and food galore. You're a free woman now. Nothing to prevent you from marrying again — "

"Marrying!"

"Me."

"You — you must be mad."

"Why mad?" he asked in a burst of quick anger. "We know too much about each other to be separated. I've got enough money to make us independent for life. I know you were keen on Brandon, but what has he got to offer you? It was he who got us into this mess. You've no future with Brandon. I wouldn't stand for that."

"You haven't told me where he is."

"What's the matter. I tell you he's alive. It rests with you whether he stays alive. I want to know whether you are with me or against me. What's it to be?"

Isobel drank again from the glass, not because she wanted the very strong drink, but because she wanted time to think.

"You lied about Algood," she said. "Why shouldn't you be lying about Brandon? You may have killed him already."

"I could have done that had I wanted to, but he is not the danger Algood was. Once we are clear of this place there is little to fear from him."

"But I must know he is alive."

"And if he is?"

"I might — But take me to him first."

"It is some way from here. I will take you to him early tomorrow morning — when we have done the removal."

"And — Kubla?"

"He can be moved in the back of the Packard. It is not a very long journey to our temporary refuge."

Isobel was silent for a few moments, while Cardinal watched her face. He fingered his heavy beard and smiled.

"You'll find I'm quite a handsome fellow with this face fungus removed," he said. "Am I to take you to Brandon in the morning?"

"Yes."

"Then be ready at six o'clock."

Isobel stood up and walked slowly to the door.

"Good night, my dear," he called.

"Good night."

The door closed, and after a few moments Cardinal rose and hurried along the hall to the telephone. There he disconnected the receiver and took it away with him, after laying a book across the receiver rest. Then he crept upstairs and listened outside the door of Isobel's room. A sound from within revealed that she was there. He turned the key carefully and then slipped it in his pocket.

20

ON reaching home, Teresa found the note on the table, and as this had now no useful purpose to serve, she consigned it to the stove. Then she went to Neville's bedroom, and after searching through some drawers she found the large X-ray photograph. It revealed a portion of Neville's anatomy, with a small piece of metal lying snugly in a fleshy part. She took it down to Wallace.

"There it is," she said.

Wallace nodded his head, and then looked at her.

"It's a chance," he said. "But I'm almost afraid to risk it. We have to realise, darling, that Isobel's ingenious solution may be completely wrong."

"I know."

"But if it is — "

"I've accepted the worst — the most

probable. While there is the slightest bit of doubting, my mind will not be at rest. Ring up the Inspector."

"All right. He may not be at headquarters, but, in view of all the work in hand, we may be lucky."

"I'll get some food ready."

Wallace was glad to have her out of hearing, for the conversation with Carson — if it took place — would not be such as to do her any good to hear. He enquired for the number, and got it without delay. On asking if Inspector Carson was available, he got no definite answer, but was asked who he was and what was the nature of his business.

"It concerns the accident at Pitts Hill," he said, "and is very urgent and personal."

He was told to hang on, and after a very long wait he was glad to hear the voice of Carson.

"I'm glad you rang up, Major Wallace," he said. "I was going to ring you to check up Mr. Brandon's height. My Sergeant's notes give it as five feet eleven inches, but there seemed to be some discrepancy with the measurements of the remains. Not very much, but more than one would expect in the circumstances. Is five feet eleven inches correct?"

"Yes," replied Wallace. "But what I have to say should help to establish identity. Miss Brandon was too upset to tell you at the time, and I didn't know. Brandon was shot up in the war, and a small piece of shrapnel was left deep in his left buttock. I've found an X-ray photograph which shows the metal very distinctly."

"Splendid," said Carson. "As you say, that should settle the matter beyond a doubt. It was more convenient for me to remove the remains here, and now I can get an X-ray photograph done without delay. But I should advise you not to encourage any wild hopes on the part of Miss Brandon. The poor girl has quite enough to bear without a last-minute bitter disappointment."

"She understands," said Wallace. "Will you ring me back — later?"

"Yes. Within an hour I hope."

During the meal which followed Wallace encouraged Teresa to talk about dairy farming, and Teresa was glad to do so. By the time they had finished and were drinking coffee, the telephone was still silent. Then came Betty — straight from the cinema.

"Oh, so you are back, Miss," she said. "There's no need now — "

"No — thank you very much, Betty. Did you enjoy the picture?"

"It was lovely — but very sad at the end. I cried and cried — so did everyone else. If you don't want me any more, Miss, I'll go, because my sister is waiting outside."

"That's all, Betty. Good night!"

The next half-hour was full of suspense, which neither of them attempted to hide. Then the telephone bell rang, but it was a wrong number, and Wallace came back to Teresa.

"I can't make up my mind about Isobel," he said. "Her exact relations with Cardinal. Can you?"

"Perhaps there's nothing in it. I'm trying my best to believe that she is the nice girl I took her to be when I first saw her."

"That's the generous attitude. But some of her remarks were a bit conflicting. Ah, that must be Carson."

Teresa clenched her hands as Wallace went across to the telephone. He picked up the receiver, and to her surprise she heard him say: "Oh, it's you, Mr. Winslow. I'm Major Wallace — Neville's friend . . . Yes, terrible. She's here . . . Yes, of course . . . " At last Wallace put back the receiver and came to Teresa.

"Winslow," he said. "He's only just heard the bad news. Wants me to express his deepest sympathy to you. I — I thought you would rather not speak to him."

A few minutes passed and again the telephone bell rang. This time it was

Carson. Teresa knew that the moment Wallace put the receiver to his ear. A word and then a silence.

"Wait!" said Wallace. He turned his head to Teresa. "The X-ray shows no embedded shrapnel," he said.

"John!"

"Just a moment, darling."

He turned his attention to Carson.

"Listen, Inspector," he said. "If that corpse is not Brandon — and it can't be — it may mean that Brandon is alive. If he is, I believe he is somewhere in that house — Overlands. Things are getting a bit clearer. We have seen Isobel Larkin. She is still in the house, so Cardinal lied to you. She behaved strangely — refused to come with us to give evidence. I think there isn't a moment to spare. Will you act on this? You will. But how soon? Good. But I'm going up there at once. This discovery makes all the difference. I'll wait for you outside. I know — I know, but I can't sit here doing nothing. For Neville it may well be a matter of life and death. I'll see you outside the house."

Teresa had risen from her seat. Now her eyes were bright, as fresh hope surged in her breast.

"John, this is a miracle."

"No miracle, darling. There's danger. What became of that pistol which Neville brought back with him?"

"It's in the drawer under his dressing-table."

Wallace left the room and bounded up the stairs. He found the pistol, and also the loose magazine which was nearly full of cartridges. In a few moments he was downstairs again. Teresa was tying a scarf round her head.

"No, dear — not this time," he said.

"Please don't argue, John."

"But there really may be trouble."

"If there is, four eyes are better than two. Besides, I heard you tell Carson you would meet him outside."

"He can't get there until half an

hour after we arrive. Besides, he won't welcome you — nor me, for that matter. He regards this as pure police business."

"Well, I don't," said Teresa. "Did you find the pistol?"

"Yes."

"Then let's go."

"You've really made up your mind?"

"Definitely."

"All right. How much petrol did that chap put in the car?"

"Six gallons. At least that's what I paid for."

"Good! That gives us a bit in hand."

It was now quite dark, with a clear sky and a rising moon. From the higher land Teresa looked across to the ocean.

"Lovely," she said. "If only our personal affairs were half as hopeful as that."

Wallace was silent as he drove the car swiftly over the undulating road.

"John, dear, I'm talking."

"Sorry," he said. "I was deep in

464

thought. Queer finding that body in the car — and the things belonging to Neville. Isobel's murderous tramp doesn't fit into the picture. It was intended that we should believe it was Neville, and that's where I stick."

"I'm not quite stuck," said Teresa. "Isobel comes into the picture more than ever. I'm sure she had reason to think it wasn't Neville. She said she had to go back to the house — to make sure about something before she would go to the police. She must have been referring to her mysterious friend — Cardinal. It must have been Cardinal who took those things from Neville and planted them on the unknown corpse. That suggests that Neville is — "

Wallace looked at her appealingly and stopped her.

"Yes, I know," she said. "But I can't help thinking that if Cardinal wanted to kill Neville he would have done to him what he did to the unknown man. Is that illogical?"

"No — merely unwise. I'd give

something to know just what Isobel is doing at this moment — also exactly what her relations to Cardinal are."

"There is something much more apposite — what Neville discovered to cause Cardinal to act as he appears to have acted. Carson said he searched the premises and was satisfied. I don't think he could have searched very thoroughly."

Wallace made no comment for they were now in a very narrow winding lane which called for the greatest care. What he dreaded was a puncture in one of his very inferior tyres, or some engine trouble which would cause prolonged delay, but the valiant old car snorted and creaked and still went on.

"We're doing well," he said. "Must be getting near that village where I bought the newspaper."

A few minutes later they entered the hamlet. It was in complete darkness, and the only sign of life was a huge black cat engaged in some nocturnal romance. On the further side of the village Wallace met the first road vehicle which he had seen since they left home. It was a large van — so wide that Wallace had almost to put his wheels into a ditch to avoid a crash.

"You damned fool!" he shouted as the lumbering van passed him at reckless speed.

"Your language!" said Teresa.

"Sorry, but he very nearly wrecked me. The idiot, to drive at that speed in a narrow lane."

Ten minutes later they reached the junction with the private road which led to Overlands. Wallace could see the lodge and the iron gates in the moonlight. The gates were now wide open.

"We'll park the car where we left it earlier," he said, and drove over the verge to the shelter of the pine trees.

Having reached the most favourable spot, he stopped the car and switched off the engine and the lights.

"Now a smoke," he said. "We've earned it."

Teresa accepted a cigarette, and they sat and smoked for a minute or two. Then from the direction of the gates there came a light which drew their attention.

"It's a van — just coming out of the drive," said Teresa. "It's stopping. Good job the headlights aren't facing in this direction. John, do you think that other van came from the drive?"

"That's certainly what I was wondering," murmured Wallace. He let down the window further, and put his head out. "Someone is talking to the driver. This — this may be important."

"You mean a moonlight flit?"

"Well, they say the rats scuttle when the ship is in danger. This is a bit of a dilemma. I promised to meet Carson here, or — "

"I can go," said Teresa sharply. "We can't afford to miss this chance. It — it might be Neville — anything, John, the van's moving. The gates are being closed again."

"You're right. Let's see which way the van turns. Yes, there it goes, after the other one."

Teresa put her finger on the self-starter and the engine fired.

"What are you doing?" asked Wallace.

"I'm going to follow them — at least for a while. Get out quick — if you must stay here."

"But I can't — "

"I'll be all right. I can tuck myself in behind the van, with only the side lights on. The moon is helpful. I'll come back when I've trailed them some distance. They may not be going very far. Please, John."

"All right, but for heaven's sake take care. If they stop, go right ahead at once, and they're not likely to suspect you. By jove, I'd like to know what is in that van."

He leapt out of the car, gave Teresa a quick kiss, and watched the car move up the private road until it swung into the main thoroughfare. A few moments later and it was out of sight. It was then that he began to wonder whether he had done right in letting Teresa take that course alone.

21

NEVILLE lay on his side in complete darkness, wracked with burning thirst and a splitting headache. His hands were bound behind his back, his ankles lashed together, and every bone in his body was aching. Where he was and how long he had been there were mysteries he had not yet solved. But he had good reason to know that the place was small and airless, and that the floor was uncommonly hard. His last memory was the invasion of the cellar where he had been put, and where at least his limbs had been free. Shortly afterwards, Cardinal and two men had returned, bound him against furious resistance, and then deliberately drugged him by holding a suffocating pad over his nose and mouth. After that was the black-out and wild dreams.

Not a single sound had come to him since, nor a ray of light. Not a spot of food nor a drink to ease his torment. It seemed to him that he had been taken from the cellar and left where he now was to die. It was not like him to give up hope easily, but the present circumstances were such as to put a slow and increasing damper on his spirit. Most foolishly he had stepped clean into the spider's lair.

His thoughts turned to Isobel, who had deceived him so completely. Surely she could not be completely ignorant of what had happened to him. Surely she must have known that after his discovery of the booty in the larger cellar Cardinal would never permit him to go free. After her professed detestations of her villainous husband she had chosen to go off with him. But as he raged inwardly against her for her perfidy, there came little doubts. Was it possible she did not know just what sort of a man her friend Cardinal was? Was it possible that she had never seen that vast horde of obviously stolen goods, and realised their significance? No, it was more likely that pressure had been brought upon her to choose between the gang and him, and that she had chosen the line of least resistance.

Lying there through the long hours, he had made one discovery that puzzled him. It was the absence of the silver ring which he had worn on his little finger — his 'lucky' ring as he had dubbed it. He was certain this had not come off during the brief struggle before he was bound and rendered unconscious. But why had it been taken from him? It's value was only a few shillings. There must be a reason. But what was it? There was congealed blood on his wrists, caused by frantic but useless efforts to free himself from the tight bonds, and now he lacked the strength to renew his efforts. All he could do was change his position from time to time to ease the myriad pains in his joints.

At first he had believed that his

plight would not be of long duration, for Teresa would be sure to do something. She knew where he was going and would obviously inform the police when he failed to return. Why had nothing happened? It must mean that the police had been hoodwinked — that he himself was miles away from Overlands, and that the chances of his being located were rapidly diminishing. What he wanted most was a drink. Beside that need the pangs of hunger were as nothing.

By rolling about the floor he was able to get some idea of the dimensions of his prison. At the most it could not be more than ten feet square, and it seemed to contain nothing but himself, for his kicking feet encountered no other objects. It was like being in a tomb, and he began to regard it as such. As with a man facing death, he let his tired mind rove over the past — his early life at Fouracres with his father and mother, and Teresa — the lovely days spent by the Devon sea and on the moors. How jolly life had seemed then. With the coming of the war he had known other joys — and also deep sorrow, and some delusion. But through all the horror and fighting he had managed to keep some of his ideals, exemplified as they were by many fine friendships, forged in dangerous quests. There was John Wallace — one of the best. How glad he was that Wallace and Teresa had decided to join forces. At least there was a bright future for Teresa. She would probably find her little farm, and raise a family of boys and girls as well as cows. That was all in the future, but at that moment Teresa must be nearly out of her mind. Why had things to be like this? Why had Larkin laid upon him a duty which in its fulfilment had brought him to this pass? Why had he been idiot enough to accept that responsibility, for it was that acceptance which had got him into this sorry mess. And where did all the strange events join up and become co-ordinated? How many hours, or days, must pass before the end came? And what would it be like when it came?

His tired mind was going round and round in endless circles, when he was aware of a definite sound. It grew louder and louder, and then he realised that its origin was not in his brain, but outside. It was someone approaching the door. Hope, almost dead, rose in his heart. Was it the police — at last? A key grated in the lock and a ray of blinding light entered the small chamber. It came from a torch held in the hand of a man with a beard. He knew that beard — the rather deep-set dark eyes, and the thin straight nose. It was Captain Cardinal, and in one hand he carried a large china jug.

"Thought I'd have a look at you," he said. "I note your surprise to find me so active, and without my glasses. But that little pretence would appear to be superfluous now."

Neville's lips moved but his voice refused to function.

"Here, have a drink," said Cardinal.

"My — my hands — " croaked Neville.

"I'll help you. You may be a little too useful with your hands free. Here!"

Neville sat up and Cardinal placed the jug to his lips. Neville sipped a little, and then took a deeper gulp. Cardinal placed the jug on the floor.

"What a fool you were when you broke into the house," he said. "I've nothing against you but that. Of course the police came, but it wasn't difficult to satisfy them."

Neville glared at him, and now found his voice again.

"They're bound to find me ultimately," he said weakly. "I think it's better they should find me alive than dead — don't you?"

"On the contrary, I think it is much better that they should find you dead — as they have done."

"What — what do you mean?"

Cardinal produced the newspaper from his pocket and held it before Neville's eyes while he directed the ray of the torch on the bold headlines.

"Read!" he said. "I think they are not likely to worry much longer about you. Do you?"

Neville had read enough.

"You — you swine!" he said. "My sister will have read that."

"Naturally. But aren't you glad it really wasn't you?"

"Why have you done this?"

"To stop the hunt — and perhaps for another reason."

"I don't quite get it. If you want me out of the way, why haven't you shot me? Perhaps you haven't the guts to do that in cold blood."

"I shouldn't bank on that if I were you. Desperate needs call for desperate remedies. You'll appreciate that I can't let you go free without taking what one might call extra business risks. You should never have come here, Brandon. That was an act of supreme folly on your part. You are dangerous to me and I hope you won't pretend that you don't know why."

"Why be so long-winded? I know you for what you are — a liar, a racketeer, and quite possibly a murderer. At Overlands I saw furniture which came from Barrowtor where an old man was battered to death, and since the police know that the man behind that was Kubla Khan — emperor of the black market — I am pretty certain that your second name is Kubla."

Cardinal laughed easily.

"You are even more encyclopaedic than I imagined," he said. "But you are wrong on several points. Possibly I may introduce you to Kubla Khan — or I may not. A lot depends upon the next few hours, and upon a certain person of your acquaintance."

"Do you mean — Isobel?"

"Ah, that tickles you, doesn't it? But I haven't come to tease you. The fact is, I don't want you on my conscience, and for a consideration I might agree to set you free."

"I can't imagine the consideration. But in any case you are wasting your time."

"All the same, you shall hear the terms. All I want from you is your signature on certain documents — "

He stopped as he caught the expression of deep contempt in Neville's eyes.

"So you've made up your mind to be awkward, eh?"

"I'll do no deal with you on any terms whatsoever."

"I had an idea you would be heroic. But at least I thought you had some regard for the fair Isobel."

"You can leave her out of it."

"That's precisely what I can't do. She is in this up to her eye-brows, as your own sense should have told you by this time. Perhaps the girl had no chance. Perhaps pressure was brought to bear upon her. Perhaps she regrets — certain things. But this I assure you — you can't touch me without touching her. So don't be in such a hurry to do that heroic stuff — apart from the fact that it is going to hurt you quite a lot. Think it over, Brandon — and think it over quickly, because I have very little time left. Now you can have another drink. It may help you to think more clearly."

Neville saw no good reason to refuse the drink, but Cardinal's offer astonished him. This eagerness to spare his life — on terms — could scarcely be due to humanitarian motives. It meant that someone was pleading for him — someone who carried a certain weight. He decided to hedge a little — and to play for a little time.

"What sort of documents have you in mind?" he asked.

"Nothing very incriminating — so long as you kept your mouth shut."

"Is this Isobel's idea?" he asked.

"Partly. She wants security too."

"I thought she had gone off with her husband."

"She had her own reasons for saying

that. Come, be sensible. You're young and there are plenty more fish in the sea."

"Suppose I refuse?"

"In that case this place will be a heap of ashes before morning. Not a nice outlook, I fancy."

"How do I know you'll keep your word?"

"You'll have to trust me."

Neville gave a short laugh.

"I've no further time to waste," snapped Cardinal. "What's it to be?"

"I'm not buying a pig in a poke. I should like to see what sort of documents you want me to sign. They might involve me in murder."

"Oh no. Nothing like that."

"Then show me the actual documents. Have you got them?"

"No. But I can draw them up in a quarter of an hour."

"All right. I'll give you my answer when I see just what I have to sign."

"Good! I'll be back."

"Leave me the torch," pleaded

Neville. "I'm sick of the darkness."

Cardinal hesitated, and then nodded. He left the torch standing in the now empty jug, and then passed through the doorway, and locked the door behind him. Immediately Neville brought his mind to bear on the immediate problem. He had no intention of signing anything, but it had occured to him that he could not be expected to sign without a free hand. But what were the limits of what a man could do with one hand only? The empty jug held out a hope — a very slim hope. His brain was working much better now, for the slaking of his thirst had removed his worst discomfort. It was easy enough to break the jug, by backing up against it and smashing it on the stone floor, but would it provide him with the kind of weapon he desired? He made up his mind to put it to the test. Backing on the jug he found he had enough movement of his hands to seize the handle. He removed the torch first, and then gave the jug a bang on the floor. It broke at once into five pieces, but when he examined them he found that none of them would suit his purpose. The largest piece was that to which the handle was attached. He hit the floor with this, and surveyed the result. To his great joy a long piece had flaked off. It was about six inches in length, tapering to a fine point. He gripped the broad end and was satisfied. The next task was to get this improvised dagger into his coat pocket, and this called for the most painful movements of arm and body, but try as he might he could not accomplish this. Finally he decided to sit on it.

Thinking that the other broken pieces of the jug would arouse Cardinal's suspicions, he pushed them with his feet into a corner and then arranged the torch so that its light was towards him. If Cardinal missed the jug the whole thing might fail. But would he?

Breathing hard from his exertions, he took up a position to cover his improvised weapon, and now he waited for the great moment. Minutes passed, and his breathing became normal. He wondered whether he had set himself an impossible task, but at least it was a bid for freedom. Much would depend upon Cardinal's exact movements, and whether there was help immediately available to him. Why didn't he come?

At the sound of footsteps approaching the door his heart seemed to bound. There came the old sound of the creaking lock, and the door opened. Cardinal was alone, carrying a writing-pad and a fountain-pen.

"Here they are," he said, and did not even look towards the spot where the jug had been standing.

Tucked into the corner of the pad were two written documents. Both were receipts for large sums of money for 'services rendered' and both were dated back a week or two. To each of them was attached a receipt stamp.

"Services rendered can mean anything," he said airily.

"Anything from forgery to murder.

All right. I've very little choice in the matter. But I can't sign — like this."

"We'll soon attend to that."

He put down the pad and the pen, and produced a pocket-knife with which to cut free Neville's right hand. Suddenly, before he could use the blade, he stiffened, and Neville knew why, for from somewhere in the distance came the savage barking of dogs, mingled with horrible snarling.

"You'll have to wait," said Cardinal. "There's something wrong. I must — "

He stopped and gave a little gasp as there came the loud report of a firearm. Then, without another word, he ran to the door, slammed it behind him and turned the key. Neville cursed the interruption, but was intrigued by its significance. It meant that he was still in Overlands — that the hideous noises came from the same brutes who had almost got Algood. But who had fired the shot? Was it possible that help had come at last? There was more barking, and then a second report — apparently at longer range. This was followed by dead silence. Then he thought he heard shouts. It was all weird and mysterious — hopeful, yet ominous.

Then he heard a strange noise in the direction of the door. It sounded like someone hissing at the keyhole. He bumped his way across to the door, and now he knew he was not mistaken. He heard his own name mentioned, and the voice was undoubtedly feminine.

"Neville — are you there? Neville!"

"Yes," he said.

"It's Isobel. I've got some duplicate keys. One of them may fit."

"Then try — for heaven's sake."

He got out of the way and heard her trying feverishly to open the door. Then suddenly he heard a welcome click and Isobel came to view. She was grimed with dirt and there was a crimson smear on her left cheek. Her eyes were wild and her hands shaking.

"I — I've been locked in my room," she gasped. "Had to get out of the window and crawl over a lower roof. Oh, Neville, you poor dear! You must get away from here. Why — why didn't I bring a knife?"

She got to work on the knots in the rope, using her teeth at times, and in a few minutes his hands were free. The rope round the ankles gave her slightly less trouble.

"Can — can you stand up?" she asked.

Neville stretched his cramped arms, and moved his legs up and down.

"I think so," he muttered.

She gave him aid and he stood on his feet, but almost fell again.

"I'll be all right — in a few moments," he said. "Just cramp."

"You must leave here at once," she said. "You're in the old tower. Cardinal tried to make me believe that you were miles away. Try — try walking."

Neville took a few steps and winced.

"What's going on outside?" he asked.

"I don't know. The dogs were set free and they attacked someone. It may be the police, but I don't think so. I saw Cardinal leave here and it was that which gave me a clue. I've been looking for you for hours. Feeling — better?"

"Yes. Do we have to go through the house?"

"Yes. There's a secret door. The main door to this place is locked. Are you ready?"

"Yes."

"Quietly then. We have to descend a lot of steps. I think nearly everyone is in the garden. If you can get out on the garage side, you should be able to get away."

"And you?"

"I — I must stay."

"Why?"

"Oh, Neville, don't ask. There is so much that I can't explain. I — I tried to ring up the police a little while ago, but the line has been cut and the receiver removed."

They had reached the end of the short passage, and had started the descent of the stone stairs. They wound round the square tower, and after descending about twenty steps they came to a landing with a door on the left. From behind the door there came a sound like groaning.

"What was that?" asked Neville.

"Nothing — nothing."

"But I'm sure I heard — "

"You must hurry," she begged.

At that moment a door was heard to open below them, and the voice of a breathless man was heard.

"It's all right," he said. "They've got him. Just one man. He shot the two dogs, but got mauled a bit. They're bringing him along."

"Good. You had better stay here. Got a gun?"

"Yes."

"Then keep your ears open. Don't move until you hear from me. I've got to sort this out."

Isobel looked at Neville.

"We — we can't go on," she whispered. "I wish I knew what to do. I wish I knew."

Again came the groaning, and now Neville was sure of it. He moved closer to the door.

"Someone is in there — in pain," he said. "Great Scott! He called your name."

Isobel closed her eyes for a moment as if in agony, and when she opened them again Neville saw tears.

"Isobel — Isobel!"

It was the despairing cry of a dying man — echoing weirdly up and down the narrow staircase. Neville looked at the girl.

"Aren't you going in?" he asked.

"Oh, Neville, I didn't want — But now you had better know. Come — come with me."

She went to the door and opened it, and Neville passed by her and waited for her to switch on the light. When she did so he found himself in a large room, which was lighted in daytime by a high glass dome. It was well-furnished, and on one side was a bed in which lay a man. The face was almost covered by the bedclothes, leaving only a tangled mass of reddish hair visible. But the voice was still muttering Isobel's name.

"Who is he?" asked Neville.

"Do you remember — Kubla Khan?"

"The man who wrote the letter. The man who carried out the robbery at Barrowtor?"

"Yes. The leader of this gang of racketeers. I had to come to him because he was ill."

"So you are really mixed up in this thing, Isobel?"

"Go closer, Neville. Look at him."

He stepped closer to the bed, and moved the bedclothes a little. Then he gave a little cry of amazement, rubbed his eyes, and stared again.

22

IN the lounge in the lower part of the rambling house Captain Cardinal sat in his invalid chair, with the rug over his knees, and the dark glasses over his eyes. Soon there came the heavy sound of many footsteps down the hall, and the door opened. Held firmly by two men, Wallace entered the room. Part of his coat had been torn from him, and his left forearm was covered with blood. Two other men followed up, both carrying guns — one a twelve-bore and the other a sporting rifle.

"All right," said Cardinal. "Let go of him."

The two ruffians let go of Wallace's arms and stood back a little.

"Now," said Cardinal. "Who are you, and what do you mean by breaking into my property and shooting my watch-dogs?"

Wallace made no immediate reply. His glance had gone to the arms of the wheel-chair where Cardinal's two hands rested, and from there his gaze switched to the bearded face.

"Answer!" snapped Cardinal. "Who are you?"

"I think you know, Sergeant Ross. You always had a good memory," said Wallace.

"What do you mean? My name is Cardinal."

"Your name is Sergeant Ross, and you are a deserter from my own regiment. I remember that little scar on your right hand, and I remember too your voice, hair and ears. I always wondered why you had volunteered for a dangerous task, and now I know. You used that opportunity to desert the regiment. You abandoned Captain Larkin, and are responsible for the death of the other man who went with you, and later of Captain Larkin. There are deserters and deserters, and you are of the baser kind — the kind who betray their comrades in action. Take off those glasses and look me in the face — if you can."

"You're crazy," snarled Cardinal.

"Oh no. I have a good memory for voices, and I shall remember yours until my last day. You are the rottenest man that ever wore the King's uniform, and heaven knows how you got your stripes. You were transferred to us from another regiment, who were doubtless glad to be rid of you. You were no ornament to that regiment, and you disgraced mine. My friend Brandon came here, because I told him that I had seen poor Larkin's sister here. He didn't believe me, but now I know I'm right. What I don't know is why she came here — to the lair of a man who betrayed her brother, and who poses as a war-shattered Naval Captain."

"What you don't know would fill many books, Mr. blasted Adjutant," sneered Cardinal.

"I know enough almost to hang you. What have you done with Brandon?"

Cardinal reached out for the newspaper and flung it at Wallace.

"Read that," he said, "if you don't already know."

Wallace threw the newspaper back at him.

"That lie is already exploded," he said. "The corpse in the car was not Brandon."

"Who told you that?"

"The police."

"You liar! They couldn't establish that."

"They could. There was something important that you over-looked."

Cardinal made a noise like an infuriated animal, tore off his dark glasses and almost leapt out of the wheel chair.

"Now the leopard displays all his spots," sneered Wallace. "And what spots they are!"

Cardinal produced a pistol from his pocket, cocked it and raised it. He looked insane with rage, and was literally frothing at the mouth.

"You are close to death at this moment," he said thickly.

"I've been close to death many times, but never in a better cause than this. If I hadn't been most carefully brought up I should spit in your cowardly face."

"Stop, I tell you!" cried Cardinal, brandishing the pistol.

"So it hurts, eh. Perhaps there are ghosts around here. The ghost of Captain Larkin, and Corporal Wentworth, and of lots more who died that Sergeant Ross might live to run a bunch of gangsters and sycophants and still play the war hero."

Cardinal took a step forward and pushed the end of the pistol into Wallace's ribs. He was sent reeling backwards by a blow from Wallace's fist, and now Wallace waited for the bullet. But it never came.

"Take him away!" screamed Cardinal. "Shooting's too good for him. Truss him up and put him with his friend. Here's the key."

Wallace was roughly seized and bundled to the door, his arm dripping blood as he went. At the door he turned his head.

"You'll need to be mighty slick this time, Ross," he said, "for the police are all round this house, and the game is up."

One of the men shoved the barrel of a rifle into his back with painful result, and the door closed after them. Cardinal almost collapsed into a chair, breathing and snorting horribly. He rang the bell and the old man — Walter — entered.

"Go down the drive, Walter," he said. "See if there is anyone about. Then bring the Packard to the front door. Hurry! We may have to leave at any moment."

The old man looked frightened. He was of a different calibre from the rest of them. He stood there quaking until Cardinal roared at him, then he went scuttling to the door. Cardinal muttered under his breath and helped himself to half a tumbler of neat whisky. Then he produced a suitcase from a safe that was concealed behind a sideboard and opened it with a small key. It was full to the brim with bundles of notes of all denominations and was almost as much as he could lift. Yet he managed to cram into this receptacle a trinket box, the contents of which he did not trouble to examine. All he did was to shake it and grunt.

Walter returned after a few minutes and said that he couldn't see a sign of anyone, nor any parked car near the entrance. He had left the Packard outside the front door. Cardinal nodded and told him to go back to the kitchen and await instructions. Walter had scarcely left when the door opened and the man with the sporting rifle entered.

"We — we took that fellow up to the tower," he said. "Brandon's not there."

"What!"

"The place is empty. The rope is

lying on the floor, and some bits of a broken jug."

"Is the door smashed?"

"No."

"Then someone must have a key. Are there duplicates anywhere?"

"There were — in the kitchen. But they aren't there now."

"Damn it — someone has ratted."

"Couldn't it be — ?"

The old man feared to utter the name, but Cardinal knew what was in his mind.

"I locked her in her room," he muttered, "and I've still got the key. All right, I'll attend to this."

He hurried into the hall and up the broad staircase to the room which had been occupied by Isobel. On opening the door with the key, he found the room empty and the wind blowing the curtains into the room.

"The bitch!" he muttered.

Running down the stairs, he passed through the secondary hall, and then through the central lounge. From here there were several passages, and in the more important of these he pushed back a section of panelling and emerged into a recess in the lower part of the tower, where a man was sitting, playing with a pistol. He gave a start as Cardinal suddenly appeared.

"Oh, it's you, boss," he said.

"How did that man get out?" he rasped.

"Search me. I'll swear he never came down the stairs after you left me here."

"Did the girl go up?"

"No."

"Then she must have been up there all the time. Are the others still up there?"

"Yes."

"All right. You stay where you are."

He mounted the stairs two at a time until he came to the landing where the central room was situated. He crept to the door, and with great care tried the handle. The door resisted him, and he went up to the small chamber and entered it. Wallace was in process of being trussed up with the rope that had so recently been round Neville.

"Hurry up!" he said. "I want you all downstairs. We've got to work quickly."

"You certainly have," said Wallace. "But why waste your time?"

For this interruption he was rewarded with a fierce blow in the side, which knocked most of the breath out of him. Then his ankles were bound and he was pushed down on the hard floor. Cardinal stooped and picked up the long sharp piece of pottery, which was lying by itself. Its significance was not lost on him.

"That was intended for me," he muttered. "A nice pair of tricksters. But it was a sorry day when you barged into this place. All right, chaps — that will do. Now we'll deal with Mr. Brandon, who jumped out of the frying-pan into the fire."

Cardinal bolted the door and then led the way down the stairs until he reached the arched doorway.

"It's bolted on the inside," he said.

"Harry, get an axe."

But Harry and his companions had ideas of their own, and they invited Cardinal away from the door that they might express their views of the matter. Weasel-faced Tony was the spokesman.

"You said Kubla was done for," he said to Cardinal.

"So he is. But the girl is in there, and probably Brandon."

"So what?" asked Tony.

"Haven't you got any damned sense? I must get Kubla away."

"Why?"

"Because if he did fall into the hands of the police he might say a lot."

"Does he know where you've removed the stuff?"

"No."

"Then leave him alone. I don't like that fellow Wallace turning up as he did. He knows Brandon is here, and it's a pound to a penny he's told the police. Our best bet is to clear out and to make it snappy. What do you say, boys?"

His two companions were in full

agreement, and Cardinal found himself facing a serious revolt. They were all armed as he was, and so any show of force was out of the question. He tried persuasion, but it was useless. His power over them had never been so great as that of the dying ring-leader, and now it was negligible.

"All right," he said. "Let 'em rot."

They now went down the stairs at speed, and at the bottom were joined by the waiting man.

"Get to the car, all of you," said Cardinal. "But take a good look round first. I've got to get a bag. See you in a minute or two."

He hurried through the lounge and found the suitcase where he had hidden it. But he did not take it at once to the car — for reasons of his own. The reasons were pretty solid ones, which he had not cared to advertise too widely, and they concerned his partner in crime. He placed the suitcase in the inner lounge and then sought for an axe.

23

NEVILLE, in the large concealed chamber of the tower, had had the shock of his life. Despite the several days' growth of beard on the face of the sick man, he had recognised him at once, and in that instant most of the strange happenings of the immediate past were made clear to him. He swung round on Isobel.

"Your brother — Phil?"

Isobel's lips quivered, and she nodded her head.

"But — but I don't understand. He was officially reported killed. They had his identity disc — uniform — "

"It was all a trick. He told me so himself — when I came here."

Neville passed his hand across his brow, shaken by this revelation.

"Good Lord!" he muttered. "A deserter!"

"I know it's terrible," she sobbed. "Especially to you — who were his friend. But he wasn't the only deserter. Another man went with him — the man who started him as a racketeer. His name was Sergeant Ross."

"I didn't know Ross. But John Wallace once mentioned him. Oh, this is ghastly. I would never have believed it possible. But Ross — where is he?"

"He's downstairs."

"You mean — Cardinal?"

"Yes. He and Phil made their way to Paris in a stolen car which they sold, and after that the rest followed as a matter of course. The farmer who had sheltered them, and who later gave evidence of death, had been bribed to do that."

"But how did you find out that Phil was here?"

"That anonymous letter first aroused my suspicions. There was something familiar in the handwriting. The police were able to say that Kubla Khan had written it, and then I remembered

506

that Phil and I had both been keen on that poem. Phil used to say that one day he would plan a wonderful garden like Kubla Khan. But the final confirmation came when I received a telegram. He had found my address by some means. The telegram said 'Alive, but seriously ill. Please come at once. Phil.' It gave the address of this house. I caught the night train. That's why I wasn't able to see you the next morning."

"Go on," said Neville, quietly.

"I found him desperately ill from a bullet wound. He would not say how he got it. I wanted to call a doctor, but he forbade me. I begged him to make a full confession, and tried to persuade him that his sentence would be light. But it was no use. But he said he would get well, give up the racket, and go abroad with me. He seemed to rally for a little while, but to-day he had a bad haemorrhage. This evening I knew he was in a very bad way, and I made up my mind to call a doctor, but Cardinal — I mean Ross — had cut off the telephone. You see, Cardinal is planning to leave to-night. I believe all the booty from the cellar has been removed. Earlier I had seen Wallace and Teresa."

Neville gazed at her in bewilderment. "But Wallace is back in Germany."

"No. I saw them together — in Wallace's car. They showed me the newspaper containing the news of your death. They wanted me to go to the police and tell all I knew, but — but I wasn't sure that you were dead. You see, after you had left — or rather after Cardinal told me you had left — I saw your Swiss knife lying on the table in the lounge. Yet that knife was found near the corpse. Cardinal confessed that the body was that of — of Algood."

"Good God!"

"He swore that Algood was killed by accident, and it was then he thought of the idea of making it appear that you had died in a car crash."

"But why? He could have killed me had he wanted to, and it could have been me in the car. It doesn't make sense."

"Oh yes, it does. He dared not kill you while Philip is alive. That's one thing Philip would not stand for. So he just played for time."

"Yes, I'm beginning to see it all. I ought to sympathise with you, Isobel — and I do in some respects, but I can't weep tears for Algood. What was the pull he had on you, if he didn't know about Phil?"

"He did know, and through my carelessness. He broke into my flat after I had left and found that telegram."

"Ah, that explains a lot. I take it that Algood started a bit of blackmail?"

"Yes — my future good behaviour for his silence."

Neville thought for a moment.

"I haven't much to thank Captain Cardinal for," he said. "But he certainly was too smart for Algood. I should have thought that Algood would know how dangerous it was to take a ride on a tiger."

Isobel dabbed her wet eyes, and Neville went to her and took her hands.

"Forgive me if I doubted you at times," he said. "But had I known just how you were placed — "

"I dared not tell you, not only for Philip's sake, but because you believed in him. I loved you deeply, but it seemed to me better that we should part and never meet again. Oh, Neville, what a lot of trouble I've brought upon you."

"And what a lot of happiness."

"You can say that — "

She stopped as Neville placed a finger to his lips. From outside came the sound of feet, growing louder and louder. They passed the door and then faded away.

"They're going to that room," whispered Isobel. "They'll find you have gone and then come here."

"In that case I'll take a chance. The

man who was downstairs on guard may now have gone."

"He may, but let me look first. If he sees me it won't matter so much."

She unbolted the door and was about to step outside when there came the sound of a man running down the steps from above. Quickly she closed the door, and the footsteps went past it.

"It's no use," she said. "That's the alarm."

"But at least I can make a bid — "

"No, Neville," she begged.

"But here I am like a rat in a trap."

"They may not come. I think they are in a great hurry and may decide to go at once."

"That wasn't what you said just now."

"No, but I have just remembered the shots in the garden. Something was happening down there. If they should come here, you can hide."

"I can't see much in the way of hiding-places."

"There's the bed. You get — "

"No, please," he begged. "Crawling from under beds isn't quite in my line. It's the first place they would look — in fact the only place."

"Then stay, because I can't bear to be here alone."

"All right," he said reluctantly. "I'll take a chance."

Isobel crept towards the bed, and took a look at the still form. The eyes were closed, and the lips half-open, but she could see from the slight movement of the bedclothes that he was still breathing. Neville drew closer to her.

"Has he been like that long?" he whispered.

"All evening. What was that?"

Neville had heard the sound of footsteps again passing the door, but they vanished as before. Then, a little later, there were more footsteps, which appeared to stop near the door. This was followed by low murmuring. He crept very close to the door and listened. When silence came again he joined Isobel.

"They were talking out there, but I couldn't hear a word. I wonder what is in the wind? When I saw him he threatened to burn down the house before morning. But I rather doubt that intention."

"Why?"

"It would attract attention and bring the police or the fire brigade here sooner than he might wish. What he needs is time to get clean away."

"But all the booty has now been removed — I think."

"All very quiet now," said Neville, after a long pause. "He must have known we were here. Very queer."

"We must wait a bit before — before we do anything."

"Yes — a little longer, but it's hateful to think of that crook and his cronies beating the odds like this. Isobel?"

"Yes."

"Teresa must have been distressed

when you saw her?"

"She was — terribly. But I was able to plant a little seed of hope. I remembered that you showed me that X-ray photograph of the bullet in your leg — "

"Scarcely my leg."

"Well, near enough. Wallace seized on that at once. It may be that they telephoned the Inspector as soon as they got back. In that case Teresa may know by now that the corpse was not you."

Neville kissed her gently on the mouth.

"Bless you for that," he said. "I wonder Teresa didn't think of it herself. Now shall we go out and see if the coast is clear?"

"Yes, but let me go first."

They unbolted the door again, and Isobel listened for a few moments. Then she crept out and reached the top of the stairs, with Neville close behind her. She took but half a dozen steps, and then stopped, for from below came the unmistakable sound of ascending footsteps.

"Damn!" muttered Neville.

"Come on — please!" she said, dragging him by the arm.

Back in the room they bolted the door behind them, and then waited in aching suspense. The footsteps stopped outside the door, and the handle was tried. Then came a heavy double rap. They held their breath.

"Open!" said Cardinal's voice. "I know you're there."

Still they remained silent.

"You fools — you can't hoodwink me. Open, or I'll break the door down."

There was a pause and then suddenly one of the panels of the door was burst asunder, and the keen edge of a heavy axe was seen. Again and again the blows came until the hole in the panel was six inches square. Through the gap came an arm with a pistol at the end of it, and behind the arm a pair of flashing dark eyes.

"Stand back, Brandon," said Cardinal. "Or I'll let you have it."

Neville retreated a few yards, and Cardinal found the inside bolt and pulled it back. The next moment he was in the room, surveying them cynically.

"You seem to be so fond of each other's company that I am going to remove you to a place where you will have no audience at all. If you come quietly no harm will come to you."

"In that case why not beat it while the going's good?" asked Neville.

"I have something to say to Kubla."

"He's dying," said Isobel. "He cannot speak to you. I won't go and leave you alone with him. You hate him — "

Cardinal suddenly thrust out his unengaged hand and caught her by the arm, projecting her so violently towards the door that she fell with a crash to the floor. Neville drew in his breath, and crouched to spring, but Cardinal swerved his body just in time, and levelled the pistol.

"Join her," he said. "And quick about it, or take what I owe you for your damned inter — "

It was the last syllable he uttered in this life, for there rang out three shots in quick succession, and Cardinal staggered, fell, made a few spasmodic movements and then lay still. Neville's gaze went to the bed. The sick man was lying back on the pillow, but one hand was now over the coverlet, and the fingers of it were grasping a heavy automatic. On his face was a curious smile of great satisfaction.

"Philip!" cried Isobel, and staggered to the bed.

"I kept the gun — for such an occasion," whispered Larkin. "He meant to close my — lips — before he scuttled. He killed poor — poor Tom Barding. All needless. I wanted — furniture for — this house. It was mine. I didn't want Barding — hurt. Been conscious for a while now. Neville!"

Neville drew closer to him, and it

was clear that he was now on the point of death. His speech was so thin and blurred it was most difficult to know what he was saying.

"Sorry — Nev — wasn't always bad soldier. You — good example. I had — lapse. Drank — too much — Ross most persuas — persuas — "

"Oh, Phil dear!" sobbed Isobel.

"Always — bit rotter," mumbled the dying man. "You two — only ones believed in me. Something I had to do — can't remember. Something to be undone — something — something — "

"He means that will," whispered Neville. "Listen, Phil," he said. "You made a will in favour of a girl named Berenice Waters. Do you — "

"Berenice! That was it. Yes — yes. Must put that right. But you must hurry. Isobel — paper — pen — "

While Isobel searched for these items Neville leaned over the body of Cardinal. It was immediately clear that he was beyond human aid. Then from below came the unmistakable sound of a car. He went outside, and opened one of the narrow tower windows. It faced towards the main entrance, and he saw the car arrive. Four men stepped out of it, and to his great joy two of them wore helmets.

"The police!" he cried. "They may yet be in time to get the rest of the gang. I must go down."

"No — let me go," said Isobel. "You won't be able to find the way through to the house. Here's paper and a pen. Do — do what Phil wants."

She ran off and Neville went to the bed.

"What do you want me to write, old chap," he said.

"Last will and testament. Everything to my beloved sister Isobel. You — you know the wording."

Neville wrote the conventional wording, and lifted Larkin a bit higher on the pillow.

"Can you write?" he asked.

"I don't know."

"Don't sign yet. I expect Isobel will

come back with Inspector Carson. Are you in pain?"

"Not now. Nev, are you — in love with Isobel?"

"Yes."

"That's good. She has — husband — somewhere. Terrible chap — worse than me. You'll have to — "

A fearful bout of coughing choked his words, and Neville doubted if he would survive it, but he did so, and lay quiet for a bit. Then came Isobel and Inspector Carson. The latter stopped near the door and leaned over Cardinal.

"Yes — he's dead," he muttered. "Who shot him?"

"Kubla Khan," replied Neville. "Otherwise Philip Larkin — here."

Carson came to the bed and looked down at the pallid face. Then he rolled back the bedclothes and revealed blood-stained bandages round Larkin's body.

"Did Cardinal shoot him?" he asked.

"We don't know. He found his

sister's address and wired her to come to him. But there's an urgent matter — this will."

He showed the document to Carson, who read the few lines.

"Is he capable of writing?" he asked.

"I don't know. If I help him, will you be a witness?"

"Delighted."

A minute or two passed before Larkin could be roused to full consciousness. The will was then read to him, and he whispered that it was just as he wanted it. The pen was put into his right hand, but he spurned assistance, and managed to complete his signature.

"Thank God that's done," he muttered, and almost immediately lapsed into unconsciousness.

Carson and Neville then witnessed the simple document, which Neville then placed in an envelope and slipped it into his pocket. Within a minute there came a curious little rattle from the bed, and a sharp cry from Isobel as she ran forward. They left her there, and removed the body of Cardinal as they went out.

"What an ending!" said Carson. "Kubla Khan dead, and the will settled satisfactorily. But it still leaves me with the Barding case."

"No. Cardinal killed Barding — against the wishes of Larkin. It was Larkin who planned that robbery. He wanted the furniture to use here. Cardinal must have gone to Barrowtor to make sure the job was carried out, and Barding must have got in his way. Didn't you recognise some of the things in that room?"

"By jove, I didn't. But what became of Major Wallace? He promised to meet me outside the house, but there's no sign of him or his car."

Neville's mouth twitched. He recalled the shots in the garden, and now drew a grim significance from them.

"I didn't know that," he said. "Where are your men?"

"Searching the premises. There doesn't seem to be a soul anywhere. It looks very much as if the rest of the gang got safely away. Ah, here comes someone."

A plain-clothes man came up the stairs with a suitcase in his hands. He dumped it at Carson's feet.

"No one anywhere, sir," he said. "But we found that in a room below. It's very heavy and is locked."

"Break it open. That axe should help."

The blade of the large axe was placed under the catches and the suitcase was quickly opened.

"Phew!" ejaculated Carson. "What a haul! Cardinal must have intended to take that with him, before calamity overtook him. That chap was a clever scoundrel. Put me a bit off the scent, I must admit. True, I searched the rest of the house but not this tower. At that moment I imagined we had your corpse."

"I'll tell you about the corpse later," said Neville. "I'm worried about John Wallace."

Carson turned to his assistant and told him to go up to the top of the tower.

"You said you searched the house when you came here," said Neville. "Didn't you go into the large basement?"

"Yes. It was empty."

"But when I saw it, it was full of booty — great piles of it. It wasn't shifted until to-night. Oh, wait a moment. Did you only visit one basement?"

"Is there another?"

"Yes. I was a prisoner there at first, but they drugged me and moved me soon afterwards. Now I understand. They must have piled all the booty in the smaller basement, and covered up the entrance."

Carson's assistant came running down the steps.

"I've found Mr Wallace," he said. "He is locked in a room above. But there's no key there. He says he is all right."

Neville went into the room where he

had left Isobel. Her eyes were dry now, and she welcomed the good news.

"This is the duplicate key," she said. "Oh, let me come too."

Within a couple of minutes Wallace was outside his cell, blinking at the electric light. He looked a sorry sight with his torn coat and blood-stained sleeve, but he wrung their hands as if he would never stop.

"Where's Cardinal — I mean Ross?" he asked.

"So you know?" said Neville.

"Yes. I recognised the swine, despite his beard."

Neville told him what had happened in a few words, and Wallace gasped his amazement. Then he looked at Isobel.

"I'm sorry," he said. "But that was a solution I never dreamed of. Now I can appreciate your dreadful position. Forgive me."

"There's nothing to forgive," said Isobel. "Quite the other way round. But how did you get here?"

"In my car."

"But the Inspector said he couldn't find any car."

"You — you mean Teresa isn't back?"

"Teresa?" asked Neville. "Was she with you?"

"Yes."

Wallace explained what had happened, and saw Neville's face fall.

"I was crazy to let her go alone," said Wallace. "But she promised only to go a little way, with a view to finding out what their direction was. If anything happens — "

"She really hasn't had much time," put in Carson. "By jove, if she could trace that stuff to its destination — "

He stopped as he became aware that both Neville and Wallace failed to share his outlook. Neither of them cared two hoots about the booty, or the fate of the rest of the gang. It was fifty times more important that Teresa should be safe and sound.

"You'd better put out an S O S,"

said Wallace to Carson. "My car number is — "

"The telephone has been disconnected," interrupted Neville.

"That's true," said Isobel. "Cardinal cut off the receiver so that I couldn't use it."

"Well, it must be somewhere about," said Wallace. "Let's make a search."

The receiver was subsequently found in a drawer in the lounge. It was re-connected with the main instrument, and Carson then rang up his headquarters. While he was speaking, Wallace pricked up his ears. What he heard was music to him.

"My old bus!" he said. "It's coming up the drive. I'd know it in a thousand."

He ran to the front door and opened it, as his ancient contraption stopped outside, with its radiator throwing off clouds of steam. Teresa emerged, and stared at him.

"My goodness!" she ejaculated. "What have you been doing to yourself?"

Wallace seized her in his arms, and winced.

"Are you wounded?" she asked.

"No — just nipped by a mad dog — now dead. But tell me what happened?"

"I trailed them — all the way."

"You mean you know where they are hiding out?"

"Yes. It's a farm — not very far from here. Where is the Inspector?"

"Inside — dying to see you."

What Teresa told the Inspector brought a broad grin to his face. He telephoned for an ambulance and gave instructions for more men to meet him at a spot near the rendezvous of the gang, and then he and two of his three assistants sallied forth for the final phase.

24

THREE months later in a quiet Devon church there was a double wedding, and despite the comparative secrecy of the dual event, it was attended by swarms of spectators and legions of Press photographers. The wedding breakfast was held at Fouracres, but afterwards the two couples drove off in the fine car which had replaced Neville's burnt-out coupé. Of the two brides Isobel was perhaps the prettier, but certainly not the happier.

"But for all this austerity we might be bound for Italy, or Switzerland," said Neville. "But Barrowtor isn't a bad substitute."

"It's perfectly lovely," said Teresa. "You're going to like it, John. Neville and Isobel have worked like slaves up there. All the stolen furniture is back, and hordes of men have transformed the garden into what it was years ago. But even I have not seen the final touches. They have refused to have me up there. Aren't you excited, Isobel, to be sleeping there again?"

Isobel's blushing cheeks and bright eyes were sufficient reply. She had come through her painful ordeal with commendable courage, and she stole a glance at her husband, whose eyes were supposed to be on the winding road — but were not. Most of the time they were on the happy face of the girl beside him, and as they drew near Barrowtor he stopped the car in the middle of the very steep hill.

"Look," he said. "That's the spot where I first saw you — carrying that suitcase. We never guessed that before the leaves began to fall we should be coming here — on our honeymoon. What a dreadful day that was."

"Drive on," pleaded Teresa, "or the car will run backwards."

Neville laughed and got the car

into motion again. As Neville had said, the autumn leaves had not yet fallen, but they were browning on the hedgerows and trees, and contrasting marvellously with the rich green foliage of the conifers. Here and there were brave masses of late summer flowers, twinkling like stars, and over all the deathless spirit of the moorland.

"What a haul old Carson had that night," mused Wallace. "I shall never forget his expression the next day when he came to tell us that he had captured eight members of the gang and all that booty that was removed from Overlands. The credit was due to you, Teresa."

"Just a bit of luck," said Teresa. "It was certainly a nice bit of clearing-up. But one thing has never been cleared up, and that is what that scoundrel Tamling really did with his wife. Scotland Yard seems to be sure that he did away with her. If he did, he cut off his own nose in doing it."

"Your logic is faulty," said Neville.

"For the ending would have been the same anyway. But don't let's talk of that. It's all in the past and is better forgotten."

A few minutes later they entered the open gates of Barrowtor, and the car swept up the drive to the house. The lovely gardens came to view — utterly changed from when Neville had first seen them. The house too had been redecorated, and over all was the homeliest atmosphere.

"Lovely!" said Wallace.

"Wait till you see the twenty acres of accommodation land which I ploughed up," said Neville. "You see, Isobel and I have turned farmers now. We'll be your fiercest competitors when Teresa finds her ideal farm."

"We're going to produce milk and not mere vegetables," sniffed Teresa. "But John has another six months to do in the Army yet. You wait and see."

"There's a man up there walking about," said Wallace. "It looks like Carson."

"It is Carson," said Neville.

The Inspector came to the car as it stopped, and raised his hat to the two brides.

"Couldn't get to the wedding," he said. "So I thought I'd come here and pay my respects. Most unusual I know. No place for a married man with three children."

"Well, come inside and have a drink," said Neville.

"No. Thanks all the same. I had a bit of news about an hour ago and I thought you would be tickled to hear it."

"Not unpleasant I hope?" asked Neville.

"Not now. I heard from London that the real Mrs. Tamling turned up in person to claim her inheritance."

"What!" gasped Neville.

"No doubt this time. She was the real woman all right. It appears she ran off with another man — to some Greek island. Her attention was only drawn to that advertisement months after it appeared, and she caught the first available plane, and burst into Mr. Winslow's office. There she heard the doleful news. I gather that Mr. Winslow had a bit of trouble with her. She said he was a dirty cheat, whereupon he invited some members of his staff into the office, and dared her to repeat that accusation. She then changed her tune and asked him to make good all the expenses she had incurred. But of course she got nothing."

Neville shook his head.

"I can't help feeling sorry for her," he said.

"Oh, you needn't, Mr. Brandon," said Carson. "There's a name I could call her, but I won't. Well, I wish you all the happiness in the world. Now I'm taking half a day off to do a bit of fishing. I know a spot where there are trout as long as my arm."

"I bet you do," laughed Neville.

Carson went to his car, and by this time Isobel's two servants were standing at the entrance to the house.

"Here we go," said Neville. "John, let's carry our wives over the threshold in the good old-fashioned style."

And so Barrowtor became inhabited again.

THE END

A GENTEEL LITTLE MURDER
Philip Daniels

Gilbert had a long-cherished plan to murder his wife. When the polished Edward entered the scene Gilbert's attitude was suddenly changed.

DEATH AT THE WEDDING
Madelaine Duke

Dr. Norah North's search for a killer takes her from a wedding to a private hospital.

MURDER FIRST CLASS
Ron Ellis

Will Detective Chief Inspector Glass find the Post Office robbers before the Executioner gets to them?

A FOOT IN THE GRAVE
Bruce Marshall

About to be imprisoned and tortured in Buenos Aires, John Smith escapes, only to become involved in an aeroplane hijacking.

DEAD TROUBLE
Martin Carroll

Trespassing brought Jennifer Denning more than she bargained for. She was totally unprepared for the violence which was to lie in her path.

HOURS TO KILL
Ursula Curtiss

Margaret went to New Mexico to look after her sick sister's rented house and felt a sharp edge of fear when the absent landlady arrived.

THE DEATH OF ABBE DIDIER
Richard Grayson

Inspector Gautier of the Sûreté investigates three crimes which are strangely connected.

NIGHTMARE TIME
Hugh Pentecost

Have the missing major and his wife met with foul play somewhere in the Beaumont Hotel, or is their disappearance a carefully planned step in an act of treason?

BLOOD WILL OUT
Margaret Carr

Why was the manor house so oddly familiar to Elinor Howard? Who would have guessed that a Sunday School outing could lead to murder?